ALGONQUIN AUTHORS SALUTE THE
❦ 10TH ANNIVERSARY OF *PASSING THROUGH* ❦

"*Passing Through* was first published when Algonquin Books was operating out of a garage. It was their first novel. As I started reading it, I became very pleased and proud that my novel (then about to be published by Algonquin) would be in company with this one. I remember studying—and learning from—Leon Driskell's brilliant handling of point of view. But mainly I loved the people in the story and, as I recently reread the book, I was reminded of how tenaciously these characters and this story have stayed with me through the years while so many other novels have drifted away, out of memory, out of sight."—**Clyde Edgerton**

"Lord, what a fun and funny book! And moving as well. Leon Driskell's zany characters become folks you cherish as your own."—**Julia Alvarez**

"What a gem this book is!"—**Cindy Bonner**

"A wonderfully hilarious, rollicking ride with characters you'll long remember."—**Jill McCorkle**

"Leon Driskell can write like an angel—a wacky, comical angel who seems to know some dark, dark stuff that the rest of the angels didn't learn. Honestly, I can't remember when I've been so touched or when I've laughed out loud so many times during a book as I did when I was reading *Passing Through*."
—**Lewis Nordan**

❦ A Note from the Publisher ❦

Passing Through is Algonquin's first book. To be more precise, we should say that this latest of our Front Porch Paperbacks, a novel by Kentucky writer Leon Driskell, was the very first book to carry the imprint of Algonquin Books of Chapel Hill. We have been particularly fond of Mr. Driskell's book ever since it came off the presses for our Fall 1983 list—the first Algonquin list—a decade ago. It seemed especially appropriate that the first publication of the new paperback edition coincide with the occasion of Algonquin's tenth anniversary.

Passing Through is a first novel. In this, and in many other ways, it represents the kind of book Algonquin has always believed in. Mr. Driskell's story of a Kentucky family is quiet and straightforward and centered on strong characters. It begins in the long tradition of broadly comic Southern fiction, then gradually blossoms into a complex and moving story of love and sacrifice.

We were proud to lead off our first list with *Passing Through,* and we were determined to bring it to public attention—even though few people knew of Mr. Driskell's work, and even fewer knew of Algonquin Books, and even though our first hardcover printing was just 1,500 copies, simply because we couldn't afford to print more. When the printer was late in delivering those 1,500 books to the warehouse, our fledgling staff rallied for an emergency shipment of books to Louisville, Kentucky, so that copies would be in the stores by the time the book's first review ran in the Louisville *Courier-Journal.* Louis Rubin, Algonquin's founder, described that frenzied day in a letter to *Passing Through*'s editor:

I will not take the time to go into a long story about what happened with the Driskell and Royster book shipments, and how we got the *Courier-Journal* circulation area orders off overnight UPS two days before Sallie Bingham reviewed the book in the paper (today) . . . two weeks ahead of time, despite my, Driskell, and the local Louisville book dealer begging her to delay the book review. Suffice it to say that at one point I was, at the age of 58, literally crawling atop stacks of boxes of books, not pressed close together but loose and wobbling, to find the Driskell in order to lug them home where Diana and I stuffed and mailed or rather UPSed the orders. . . . Well, if I don't go either nuts or to the cardiac intensive care ward in a month's time, we will be Launched.

Even coming from an unknown author and a publishing company no one had ever heard of, *Passing Through* received strong reviews and substantial notice. That first small printing sold out, and we printed more. And in spite of its breathless beginning, the book has remained in print, and in our catalogue, ever since it first arrived late from the printer and was stacked in wobbling piles in a North Carolina warehouse. Meanwhile, in the ten years since those first heady days, Algonquin itself has been Launched. We have published close to 200 books and sent them forth in search of readers. We would still publish *Passing Through* if it came over the transom today. With this tenth-anniversary paperback edition, we're pleased to bring this novel to the larger audience it deserves—one we could not give it ten years ago, when it was our first.

Passing Through

LEON V. DRISKELL

ALGONQUIN BOOKS OF CHAPEL HILL

1993

Published by
Algonquin Books of Chapel Hill
Post Office Box 2225
Chapel Hill, North Carolina 27515-2225
a division of
Workman Publishing Company, Inc.
708 Broadway
New York, New York 10003
© 1983 by Leon V. Driskell
All rights reserved
Printed in the United States of America

Design by Joyce Kachergis.
Front cover photograph © 1993 by Erik Landsberg.

First Front Porch Paperback Edition, October 1993. Originally published
in hardcover by Algonquin Books of Chapel Hill in 1983.

"Dun-Roving" and "The Day That Elvis Presley Died" first appeared in
Carolina Quarterly (©1977 and ©1979 by *Carolina Quarterly*) and are
reprinted with permission of the editors. "Bright Star" and "A Fellow Making Himself Up" first appeared in *Wind Literary Journal* (©1981 and
©1982 by Wind Press) and are reprinted with permission of the editor.

Library of Congress Cataloging-in-Publication Data
PS3554.R497P3 1983
813/.54 19
Driskell, Leon V. 1932–
Passing through: a novel / Leon V. Driskell.
p.   cm.
ISBN 1-56512-056-6
Chapel Hill, NC: Algonquin Books of Chapel Hill, 1983.

10 9 8 7 6 5 4 3 2 1

To Sue and Mae
To Rebecca, Terry, Julia, Laura, and Michael
and
To the Memory of Noel True

Passing Through, Passing Through,
Glad that I ran into you.
Tell the people that you saw me,
Passing through.

—RICHARD BLAKESLEE (1948)

Contents

Passing Through

Dun-Roving

"Blackberries," read Augie. The sign was on his side of the road. Augie was almost nine but was just beginning to learn to read, for his mother Lurline had kept him out of school. She said he was delicate and had a heart condition, but now she was at the Women's Detention Center in Louisville for forging checks and Augie was learning to read. He wanted to write her a letter but was afraid she would figure out from that that he was going to school. Augie felt maybe he had let Lurline down.

"Blackberries," he repeated. "$2.50 a gal."

"Gallon, stupid," said Audrey. "Not *gal,* gallon." She said the words slow and distinct as if speaking to a deaf person.

"That's a lot," said uncle Rosco waking up from a catnap. "$2.50 a gallon's a lot. We used to pick all day for fifty cents when I was a kid."

Audrey groaned. She did not want to hear again how hard uncle Rosco had it when he was a kid. He made it sound like everybody born after 1965 had it made. Audrey wanted to be a movie star, or at least a TV personality, and she thought her family was likely to hold her back. She was careful of her speech and looked up words in the dictionary so she would know to tell the others when they said anything wrong. They did not even appreciate it.

"Shit," said uncle Lester. "I wouldn't give you a shit for all the blackberries in Owen County." Uncle Lester was not born in Owen County and he generally disparaged everybody and everything that was.

"Now, Lester," said Mama Pearl for maybe the twentieth time since they had left home.

"We're not IN Owen County," shrilled Audrey.

"We're in HENry County," said Augie, who had read that fact aloud along with all the advertisements and most of the names on mailboxes.

"Well," said uncle Lester, "I won't even tell you what I wouldn't give you for all the blackberries in Henry County."

"Now, Lester," warned Mama Pearl.

"What does it start with, uncle Lester?" pestered Andrey. She knew it must be something really bad if it was worse than what uncle Lester had already said. Augie whispered something to her.

"It doesn't either start with a *f*, does it uncle Lester?"

Uncle Lester who was fourteen but looked younger spread his lips and made a repulsive sound.

"Pffff-aaaht," he said. "Pfffff-aaaaaaht."

"Now, Lester," said Mama Pearl again.

Uncle Lester did not even smile, while Augie and Audrey howled. He pretended to be concentrating on the highway. He was driving as usual, though he shouldn't have been especially now that they were two counties away from home where nobody, not even the law, would say anything about his being too young to drive. Whenever anybody else drove, uncle Lester acted so ugly that nobody else could enjoy the trip. Besides, Mama Pearl said she felt safer when Lester drove, for, as she said, his legs were shorter than Rosco's and he could not bear down so hard on the gas pedal. It did no good for uncle Rosco to point out that he could not reach the brake pedal as well either.

Uncle Lester seemed eager to get out of Henry County, for he was driving considerably faster than his accustomed sixty miles an hour. He rarely drove slower than sixty, which was almost as fast as the car would go, and he got it up to sixty as quick as he could. Now, however, he seemed determined to make the car go seventy.

"Children, children," Mama Pearl said complacently; Audrey and Augie had stopped giggling and were trying to reproduce the sound uncle Lester had made.

"We're getting close to Shelbyville," said uncle Rosco, shifting himself so he could get a peek at the speedometer. "Mighty close," he added when he saw the needle inching up toward seventy. What he said was his way of letting uncle Lester know it was time for him to pull off the road and let uncle Rosco drive the rest of the way to aunt Muddie's house. Uncle Lester said nothing, and uncle Rosco knew this meant Lester had forgotten his promise to let Rosco take over driving outside of Shelbyville.

Uncle Rosco determined to come nearer to the point.

"There's lots of po-lice here," he said. "Always has been lots of them in Shelbyville, and they don't know you from Adam's off-ox."

Uncle Lester speeded up a little as if to show Rosco that no police would be likely to catch him. He and Audrey saw the unmarked patrol car at about the same time. Everyone

3

could tell the police car had stopped clocking them and was now chasing them.

"Now, Lester," said Mama Pearl, "don't slow down now."

"Yes'm," uncle Lester said. He scooted up in the driver's seat a little so he could watch Mama Pearl in the rear-view mirror. She slid over toward the window and yanked Augie into her lap. The surprised boy tried to get away. "You be still," she said, and pushed his head down on her shoulder.

With her free hand, Mama Pearl dabbed at her eyes. The patrol car began flashing its light and pulled into the left lane next to uncle Lester. The two cars moved along, side by side, and the policeman signalled that Lester had better pull off the road quick. By now, Mama Pearl was crying to beat the band, and though Augie was giggling, it looked like he was crying too.

Audrey was interested. She could not tell if Mama Pearl was pretending Augie was hurt and they were rushing him to the hospital, or if maybe she was pretending they were all on their way to a funeral. She decided not to ask just then, for questions might spoil the effect. She began crying herself and wringing her hands as she had learned to do to express anxiety. After all, she was supposed to be the family actress, though she did admit Mama Pearl looked pretty convincing. Her face was all wattled up, and she was dressed just exactly as if she was on her way to a funeral. The policeman would not know that Mama Pearl always dressed that way.

The policeman could not seem to figure out what was going on. He alternated between glaring at uncle Lester and nodding sympathetically at Mama Pearl. He drove alongside the car until he saw a semi barreling down the road toward him. All this time, nobody in the car looked at the po-

4

liceman. Audrey kept watch of him out of the corner of her eye.

Just in time, the police car got back into line. The truck driver was trying to look unconcerned and to slow down without appearing to do so. He had the look of a man who has had a great shock and will never be the same again. Seeing him, the policeman decided what to do and began to turn his car around. The family cheered when they realized the police car was going to chase the truck now. Uncle Lester's eyes glittered as if he had proved something important to everybody.

Audrey was sorry it was all over. She had been getting her story ready to tell the policeman. She was sure the rest of the family would let her talk for them. She was the only one named for an actress, though her name had been a mistake. Her mother Erline (Lurline's sister) had meant to name her Autry for Gene Autry, but the woman taking the information at the hospital had got it all wrong. "Audrey?" she said. "You're naming her for Audrey Hepburn." Erline had repeated as clear as anything, "Autry, like the movie star," and the woman said, "How lovely, I think she's wonderful too." And before Erline could tell her that Gene Autry was a he, not a she, the woman had written down Audrey.

It was a mistake, but later, Audrey didn't mind because her older sister Dale Evans Waters took sick and died. Mama Pearl said the Autrys were as bad luck as the Rogers—just look what happened to Trigger.

After the police car had stopped bothering him, uncle Lester slowed down some, but he still wasn't thinking about giving up the driver's seat until he had to. He didn't blink an eye when Mama Pearl said "Now Lester" for the twenty-third time. You could not tell what he was thinking, and, half the time, you could not tell if he was even thinking.

Uncle Rosco was fidgeting and Augie was half-strangled and trying to whisper to Audrey that Mama Pearl had smushed him right down between her ba-zooms—he could feel them plain as anything. Audrey told him to grow up, for she was thinking how she would have had the policeman lead them right to the Shelby County Hospital and how she would get out of the car and thank him for his help. She was also trying to figure out what she could have done to save the day when they got to the hospital and the policeman saw that Augie wasn't dead, or sick, or anything.

"Aunt Muddie's got blackberries," challenged Augie. He was remembering the sign he had read out loud and how uncle Rosco seemed to think $2.50 a gal. was a lot. He expected to be contradicted; he wouldn't have been surprised if somebody had told him there wasn't a blackberry in Shelby County, though he knew different. He remembered eating them at aunt Muddie's last time.

To Augie's surprise, nobody disagreed. Everybody but uncle Lester, who rarely even smiled, laughed. What he had said was so successful that he tried it again, and this time even uncle Lester smiled.

"Maybe we could pick some. Sell them," volunteered Augie. "For $2.50 a gal."

"Gallon, stupid," said Audrey.

"You two can work for me," said uncle Lester. "I'll make the sign while you pick."

Audrey and Augie began to argue about which of them would pick more berries and how they would divide the money. Uncle Lester resumed thinking about Lurline and

6

how it would maybe be better to leave her where she was, in the Women's Detention Center, instead of breaking her out as he and Augie had planned.

But how would he tell Augie he had changed his mind? They were supposed to get started with their plan the next week, right after they got home from aunt Muddie's. He had the letter to Lurline in his pocket. He and Augie had written it together to tell her when to expect them and to be ready to run for it. Uncle Lester had written it down with his left hand and had not signed it, but they thought Lurline would be able to read it and would figure out who it was from. He meant to mail it from Shelbyville, which he thought would throw the cops off the track in case they intercepted it.

Uncle Lester and Augie had agreed on every point but one about the rescue. Augie thought they might as well let all the prisoners out while they were getting Lurline, but uncle Lester thought the others should have to pay to get out.

"I'm not going to all this trouble for a bunch of common criminals," he told Augie, and Augie got mad and told him not to call *his* mother a common anything. And then, Mama Pearl made them stop whispering and turn out the light. Later, in the dark, uncle Lester tried to explain. He whispered that he did not mean to include Lurline among the criminals, for he knew as well as anybody that Lurline had paid the supreme sacrifice.

Audrey, who was not asleep as they thought, spoke up then to say that nobody alive had paid the supreme sacrifice; all Lurline had done was forge checks to raise money for the pacemaker she thought Augie needed.

"Dying," Audrey said. "That's what the supreme sacrifice means."

7

Uncle Lester told her he thought he ought to know a thing or two about the supreme sacrifice, for he was a teetotal orphan as a result of his own parents' supreme sacrifices. And they were dead, weren't they? What more did Audrey want?

Neither Audrey nor Augie knew what to say to that, for the circumstances of uncle Lester's parents' deaths were hazy in their minds, chiefly as a result of uncle Lester's changing the circumstances to suit himself. Sometimes he would worsen his plight as a teetotal orphan by claiming that his parents' bodies had never been reclaimed from the Kentucky River. Other times he boasted that he had seen both his parents laid out before he was even as old as Augie.

Uncle Lester wanted to be unique, and he would not agree that Audrey was even a partial orphan just because her parents were divorced. He did soften and consent that Augie was almost an orphan after Lurline went to prison, but normally he could not stand for anybody to say the word—except in books. He liked to read books about orphans, real and imaginary, so he could compare his lot with theirs. He like to never have forgiven Mama Pearl for admitting that both her parents were dead.

"You mean you're a teetotal orphan?" he asked. "How old were you when it happened?" He felt better when he learned she was at least fifty.

Nobody knew very much about Mama Pearl except that she was not really anybody's mama. Erline and Lurline said she was no kin to the Waters family and that Somebody better make sure that none of the family property fell into her hands, for half the dead in Cedar Creek Baptist Cemetery would get up and walk if *that* ever happened. The children did not much care how Mama Pearl was related to them; they were used to her. But they secretly hoped she would get the property.

Mama Pearl did not let Erline and Lurline's talk bother her much; she kept living with the Waters family and acting like kin because she said she didn't hardly remember anything else. She had been in Owen County that long. And, as she said, Erline and Lurline were no worse than most real daughters. Actually Mama Pearl was the second wife of an automobile mechanic who had come to Owen County back when practically nobody had an automobile. He had married LeMartine Waters for lack of anything else to do and continued to hang around even after LeMartine died in the 'flu epidemic. No one ever figured out why he stayed on unless it was for love. By the time he married Mama Pearl, everybody had a car, but he was sixty-five then, and retired. Mama Pearl was thirty. He used to say the world had passed him by, and Mama Pearl would say, "Well, Omer, I am still here."

Mama Pearl stayed with Omer in what they continued to call LeMartine's room, and finally he died just before his ninety-first birthday. She stayed after his funeral because, by then, everyone in the family was used to her, or dead. After Erline and Lurline and Lester's mama and daddy were killed, she took on the job of nursing Lester. Soon afterwards, uncle Rosco had come to live with them, and people who didn't know thought uncle Lester was Mama Pearl's and uncle Rosco's son. That was why Mama Pearl let Lester get by with so much.

Erline and Lurline had been glad enough for Mama Pearl to raise Lester, for they were busy spending up the insurance money they got after their parents drove off the side of the Gratz Bridge and into the Kentucky River. They divided the money even, three ways, and later did the same with the State money they got when the lawyer Mama Pearl had hired proved that the bridge was unsafe. They said Mama Pearl had hired a lawyer before the bodies were cold, but, at the time, the bodies were still in the river and it was January, so as Mama Pearl said, they had exaggerated as usual, which they denied. The lawyer proved his point by loading an A&P cart with bricks and rolling it into the side of the bridge. It went straight through. Erline and Lurline said they could have made a killing by taking their case to the highest courts.

"Shelbyville: 1 mi.," Augie read.

Audrey sighed. It did no good to correct Augie, and she thought she would just quit trying. Uncle Lester hunched forward and tightened his hand on the steering wheel. He couldn't decide whether to stop and mail his letter to Lurline or go straight on to aunt Muddie's. He wanted her to see him driving, and the more he thought about things, the more certain he was that springing Lurline from prison wouldn't help things much. What she needed was money. Lots of it.

"I wish aunt Muddie's name was Waters, like ours," he said. Mama Pearl and uncle Rosco said nothing. They were too worried Lester would get himself arrested as Lurline had done, and the family's name would be wholly ruined. But Audrey wanted to know why aunt Muddie should be named Waters.

"What's so great about the name of Waters?" she asked haughtily.

"So her name would be Muddie Waters," uncle Lester explained.

Audrey and Augie screamed with laughter; then they tried to outdo uncle Lester.

"Or Pool," said Augie.

"Lake," breathed Audrey. "Like Veronica Lake."

"Puddle?" tried Augie.

"Nobody's named Puddle, stupid," said Audrey.

"Her name's not any of those," said Mama Pearl factually. "It's Henderson—like your daddy's first name, Lester. He was named for her side of the family. And her name's not Muddie either; it's Maud, but Henderson couldn't say that when he was little. It came out 'Muddie,' so now everybody calls her that."

It was a long speech for Mama Pearl, and everybody but uncle Lester looked impressed.

"At least," she added, "everybody in the *family* calls her Muddie."

It was obvious she wished that Lurline could be out of jail to hear her say that.

"I knew all that," uncle Lester grumbled. "I knew it all so long I like to have forgot it."

Uncle Lester did not like people talking about his daddy's family. That was the worst thing about Lurline. Sometimes she would tell him he was lucky not to remember anything about mama and daddy, and the next minute, she would say "Poor little Lester—never knowing a mama's love and being raised by the likes of Mama Pearl."

Lurline did not think it was decent for uncle Rosco to live with Mama Pearl, and she would not call him by anything but his first name. She said she was going to do something with Lester's money before "that woman got her hands on it." Hers and Erline's money was all gone by the time they got married. Their husbands did not at first realize this fact, and both sisters found themselves alone when their husbands discovered there was no more money where the first had come from. When Audrey was born, Erline turned her over to Mama Pearl and opened up a beauty shop, though Mama Pearl said most of her customers seemed to be men. Lurline, a good mother from the start, spent her time worrying about Augie's heart and Lester's money. What time she had left, she worried about Mama Pearl's living in sin with uncle Rosco.

Writing a check signed with Lester's name got Lurline arrested, so he naturally felt responsible.

Lurline had been in trouble before, and that made it worse when she was caught forging Lester's name on a one-thousand dollar check. She was not supposed to take checks at Demopolis' Cafe where she sometimes waited tables on Saturday night, but she was so good-hearted that she hated to refuse. She ended up keeping them for herself, and learned to copy old man Demopolis's signature so well that she even got his own sister to cash one of them for her. So far as anybody could tell, she had never stolen cash. Mama Pearl said it was just like Lurline, for there was a world of difference between stealing and forging. Forgery had more class, almost as much as embezzling.

It seemed to uncle Lester that Lurline wanted to go to jail, for she had not been at all careful. She had signed his name on one of her own personalized checks with her name and address lined out. The check was for a thousand dollars, and the signature was perfect. She would have got the money if only uncle Lester had had a checking account. Lurline's defense was that she was saving up to get Augie's pacemaker. A doctor from Frankfort testified that Augie did not need a pacemaker though he might if he lived another seventy years, and Lurline's lawyer said that the facts made no difference at all: if Lurline *thought* Augie needed something, that was as good as his needing it. Mother love, the lawyer said, is a strange thing.

That got uncle Lester to thinking. If Mother Love made Lurline steal and keep Augie home and in the bed half the time, maybe it wasn't a very good thing. He tried to tell the lawyers and everybody he didn't care about the thousand dollars, but they told him that didn't make any difference. They said Lurline had to pay her debt to society, but so far as uncle Lester knew she didn't owe any money, and it all made him think less of the law and lawyers than he used to. He felt bad about everything that had happened, but he felt good that Augie no longer went around with his hand clapped up against his chest as if his heart wouldn't go unless he poked it all the time. Augie had forgotten to be sick without Lurline around to remind him.

Uncle Lester watched for road signs. He was looking for Kentucky 255, for that was where aunt Muddie lived. Highway 255 two miles the other side of Shelbyville. He slowed down when he saw the railroad sign, but Augie and Audrey still bounced a good deal when they hit the tracks. He stopped at a traffic light and the people at the corner stared at him peeping up behind the steering wheel.

"You'd think they never seen a 1937 Chevrolet before," uncle Lester said.

Mama Pearl was blinking at the stores and quick-food joints which lined the street. She wished she was at home, or at aunt Muddie's—preferably home.

"Well," Mama Pearl worried, "don't you think we better ask the way?"

13

"I think maybe I better drive," suggested uncle Rosco, "now we're in the city."

Audrey hooted. "You call this a city?"

"Not unless we stop and eat," said uncle Lester. "If we stop and have some Kentucky Fried Chicken," he bargained, "I'll let you drive when we're done."

"Well, Lester," said Mama Pearl, "The Lord knows we're not likely to get more than a mouthful at aunt Muddie's, so maybe we should eat before we get there." After a pause, she added "To build up our strength," as if she regarded the visit as a contest.

It had been one hour and forty minutes since they got in the car and over an hour since Audrey and Augie had finished the lunch Mama Pearl had packed. Everybody was starved. Audrey declared she would eat nothing but seafood, and Augie opted for a cheeseburger. Uncle Rosco looked around him vacantly and said he used to know a good plate-lunch place somewhere in Shelbyville, and the children hooted at the idea of driving so far just to eat a plate lunch.

Uncle Lester turned into a Jerry's Restaurant (Quik Food, Eat Here, Augie read), and guided the car to within inches of the plate-glass window. The people inside gawked at the car and then stood up quickly, for they could not see anybody driving it. Everyone stopped eating and stared at them when they came in, and uncle Lester led the way to a booth from which he could watch the car. Mama Pearl and Audrey sat on one side, uncle Rosco and Augie on the other. Uncle Lester pulled a chair up to the end.

After the waitress had come to the table three times and waited for them to study the menu, all of them finally decided what they wanted to eat. They ordered, and waited

14

impatiently. A family of bronzed vacationers, all wearing starched-looking white shorts, gazed at them curiously.

"I wonder are they white?" whispered uncle Rosco.

"Well," said Mama Pearl, "I guess it's a good restaurant, so they must be."

Audrey, whose ideas about good restaurants differed from Mama Pearl's, sniffed, and said there was no telling who you'd meet up with in a place like this, and Augie spilled his milkshake on the table. By the time the waitress came to sop it up, Mama Pearl had just about emptied the napkin dispenser on top of it. Only a little of it dripped into Augie's lap.

A rail-thin man wearing a neat brown suit came in and set a cigar box on the cashier's counter. He flashed his fingers rapidly at the woman on the stool behind the cash register. She accepted the card he handed her, glanced at it briefly, and nodded. Her expression suggested that she had never been surprised yet, and did not expect anything to happen worthy of her attention. The deaf-mute, on the other hand, looked ecstatic. Audrey would not have been surprised if he had kissed the cashier's hand.

The deaf-mute collected his box and began his rounds. He stopped at every table, grinned and flashed his fingers at the intimidated lunchers, then magnanimously produced one of his cards for every person at the table, even the children. He bestowed the cards as if they were priceless and fragile. Somebody, usually the man at the table, would put some change in the cigar box, and the deaf-mute would grin and bob. Flashing his fingers at everyone, he would sidle off to the next table.

"I wonder what does it say, the card?" whispered Augie.

Everybody but Mama Pearl and Audrey was whispering. Mama Pearl was too interested in what was going on to remember to whisper, and Audrey was too irked at having to eat in less than palatial surroundings.

"I bet it says 'Repent and Be Saved,'" said uncle Lester.

The little wiry man was nearing their table, and uncle Rosco was trying to get Mama Pearl to look at him. He had found two quarters in his pants pocket and wanted to know if Mama Pearl thought that was enough to give. He doubted it was, for he had seen the bronzed vacationer take something from his wallet, not from his pants pocket. The man in the brown suit had practically danced away, fingers flashing jubilantly.

Theirs was the next table. He eyed them briefly and headed into the next room.

Uncle Rosco clicked the two quarters in his pocket. Augie turned around and knelt on the booth to watch the deaf-mute make his rounds in the next room. Even Audrey could think of nothing better to say than "Thank Goodness, he's gone." She did not sound as if she meant it. Mama Pearl wondered out loud where he was from and why he didn't learn English if he had to live in Kentucky. Augie bet he was an Indian and was raising money for the reservation, but uncle Lester insisted he was a preacher. "Didn't you see that suit and tie?" he asked.

The family single-filed to the check-out counter, where the cashier accepted the ticket uncle Rosco presented her. She drummed the glass counter top with purple talons while uncle Rosco ceremoniously produced his wallet. Audrey and Augie stared at her hands, which were liver-spotted, and Mama Pearl studied her swirled, piled-up hair, which reminded her of cotton candy. Uncle Lester was staring in the other room watching the deaf-mute continue his solicitations. His eyes were dreamy and remote.

A beaky-nosed man, wearing khaki pants and a baby-blue shirt, sleeves rolled up to the elbows, blustered through the door behind the cashier.

"Everything okay, folks?" he asked. "Everything okay?"

He did not wait for them to answer, but fake-smiled at them and rumpled Augie's hair. Uncle Rosco answered him anyway, assuring him everything was fine. He made as if to loosen his belt to indicate how highly he regarded the food at Jerry's and how fine things were, but the manager was not paying attention. He was busy looking friendly. He dropped his hand casually onto the cashier's shoulder, and she shivered and shrugged as if she were a snake wriggling out of her skin. She looked up at the manager venomously, and only Audrey could tell what she mouthed silently to him.

Augie was raking his fingers savagely through his hair where the man had touched him, but stopped long enough to identify the man to Mama Pearl. "He owns all this," Augie told her. "He's worth plenty."

When the manager saw the deaf-mute, his face paled, then darkened. He muttered something to the cashier who looked nonchalant and touched her curls with her purple-nailed fingers. The manager headed toward the table where the deaf-mute flashed incomprehensible signs to the mesmerized diners. He nearly knocked Audrey down where she was standing reading the signs of the zodiac on the coin scale. She could not decide whether to put her penny in the scorpio or the sagittarius slot, for she had been born on the cusp.

Face set in a dreadful smile, the manager escorted the

17

deaf-mute to the door. The brown-suited man flashed hopeful fingers, and the manager reasoned with him in a low, poisonous voice. Neither knew what the other meant. Outside, the deaf-mute clutched his cigar box and pushed, tentatively, against the door. The manager barred his entry.

Turning from the door, the manager smiled expansively for his customers to see. His face expressed solicitude and concern. He went from table to table, starting with the one where the bronzed vacationers sat. "Everything okay, folks?" he asked.

Uncle Lester had followed the deaf-mute outside, hoping to speak to him. "Hey, mister," he called to the brown-suited man. "Reverend?" The man did not slow down. A Chrysler nosed out of its parking slot and crawled toward him. Lester watched as the preacher got in, fingers already flashing. The man driving the car paid no attention to the deaf-mute. He rooted through the contents of the cigar box, and did not seem pleased with what he found there. Then he saw uncle Lester.

"You looking for somebody, boy?" Uncle Lester shook his head dumbly. "Then get on back where you come from," the man said. The big car drove off.

When the others came out of the restaurant, uncle Lester was sitting in the back seat of the car.

"Nobody bothered the car," he volunteered. Augie got in and whispered to him while Mama Pearl was deciding where to sit.

"There's something in the bathroom," Augie whispered, "that makes your pee look blue." Audrey got in, and Augie turned to whisper to her as well.

"I know that, stupid," she said, "but *mine* looked lavender."

Mama Pearl finally decided to get in front with uncle Rosco.

"Well," she said, "that was nice." Discovering she was still holding her napkin, she wiped her mouth again and then put the napkin in her purse for later use.

"Grease cooking," Audrey said. "I can get grease cooking at home." That was something Lurline used to say about Demopolis's cafe.

"Now, Audrey," said Mama Pearl, "it beats what aunt Muddie will give us."

Miraculously, uncle Rosco drove straight to aunt Muddie's, but uncle Lester did not have time to get mad about that. For aunt Muddie was not at home. They could tell at once that aunt Muddie was not there. The grass, mostly weeds, was knee-high, and the house looked abandoned. They parked under the walnut tree, and sat looking at the empty house. Uncle Lester walked back to the road and checked the mail box; it was almost full. Aunt Muddie must have been gone several days. He sorted through the circulars and bills and found a postcard from Lurline. He read it.

Lurline wrote that she was as well as could be expected and that she thanked aunt Muddie for writing. Nobody else writes, she scribbled. She said that "that woman" would not allow her "precious child" to send her a single line. Uncle Lester guessed that Lurline had forgotten that Augie had never gone to school, and decided it would be safe for Augie to mail his letters to Lurline. Lurline wrote that she would be crazy for sure by now if it was not for the Thursday night guitar lessons she was taking, along with half the other women, from a radio and TV personality from Louisville. She had signed the postcard Loretta Lynn, and uncle Lester wondered where Lurline had found a copy of Loretta Lynn's signature and how long it would be before she got a chance to use it.

Back at the house, Mama Pearl was looking in all the windows and Augie and Audrey were chasing the chickens. Uncle Rosco came back from the barn and said somebody must be milking the cows and collecting the eggs, but Augie said he had found a nest of eggs down by the branch. The broody old hen wouldn't let him count the eggs, but he said there were so many they were rolling out from under her. Uncle Lester decided not to mention how much mail was in aunt Muddie's box.

Mama Pearl said Muddie's house was a mess as usual and that it was just like her to go off somewhere the once in a blue moon somebody came to see her. Uncle Rosco asked Mama Pearl did she write aunt Muddie to say they were coming, and Mama Pearl said maybe she did and maybe she didn't and that kind of thing didn't matter with kinfolks anyhow.

Uncle Lester said he bet aunt Muddie had gone off to see her *own* folks and didn't care whether she missed them or not, and uncle Rosco bet she had gone off to Louisville to see Lurline. Then Augie began to cry and say he wanted to go see Lurline too.

"Now, Augie," Mama Pearl said, "Louisville's too far—fifty miles and more and us without a place to stay."

Uncle Rosco hitched up his pants and said that if he pushed it he could get them home by dark, and nobody thought to remind him that it had taken them less than three hours to get to aunt Muddie's and it didn't get dark in summertime until almost nine o'clock. Dispirited, they sat in the hot car. Uncle Lester said he would get them home in no time, but he knew he didn't have a chance of driving again so soon. He could not decide whether to mail the letter to Lurline as he had planned, and that made him more irritable than usual.

"I wish we hadn't come," said Audrey. "I don't like aunt Muddie much anyhow."

They drove back to Shelbyville. "That's where we ate," said Augie sadly. It seemed ages ago they had stopped to eat, and now they had to go back home.

"There's the preacher's car," said uncle Lester. The Chrysler was parked at the Kentucky Fried Chicken place. Lester saw the driver. He was smoking a cigar and looking bored.

Uncle Rosco crossed the railroad tracks more gently than uncle Lester had, and Augie wanted him to turn around and cross them again—"the way uncle Lester would." That made uncle Lester feel better, but he continued to sulk, knowing that was the best way to get to drive. He wanted to drive back home by way of Pleasureville, for on the stretch between Pleasureville and Eminence, if you speeded up on hills, you would sink down into the hollows so fast it seemed you had left your body behind. That felt good. Everybody laughed when uncle Lester did that.

Audrey was practicing sign language. Eyes blared almost out of her head and her mouth pursed tightly, she flashed her fingers imperiously at Augie.

"Huh?" he said.

"Forget it, stupid," Audrey said, and leaned her head just far enough out the window to let the wind catch her hair. Maybe people on the road would think she was a movie star, a child prodigy, being kidnapped. Her eyes misted; maybe, they would know she was different and didn't belong in this dumb car at all.

Augie was reading the signs again. They were not very interesting. Somebody had laid creek rocks in their yard to form what looked like words, but the white-painted rocks passed before Augie could get past the first three letters— D-U-N.

"What word begins 'd-u-n'?" Augie asked.

"That's *done*," said Audrey. "The rest of it's *r-o-v-i-n*-g. Know what that means, stupid?"

Augie began to cry and remembered he wanted to see his mother.

"Now, Audrey," said Mama Pearl. "Now, Augie." She passed her crumpled napkin to Augie, who brightened up because he had spotted a police car hiding under the shade of an old barn at a crossroads. It was the turn to Pleasureville, but Augie did not have time to read the sign.

"Slow down, uncle Rosco," Augie squealed. "There's that same policeman."

Uncle Rosco, who rarely drove faster than forty-five, slowed down to forty. Uncle Lester groaned. "Jesus," he said, "Jesus H. Christ."

"Blow at him, uncle Rosco," suggested Augie. "Let's all wave."

Augie stuck the napkin into the wind and everybody but uncle Lester and uncle Rosco waved or nodded as they passed the police car. Mama Pearl looked exactly like an opera star taking a bow. The wind snatched Augie's napkin and tossed it into a weed-clogged ditch.

"Just look out now," said uncle Lester. "It's a fine of up to $500 for littering the road. Didn't you see that sign?"

"It's not fair," Augie complained. "I can't read that fast." He dropped to the floorboard. "I didn't do it," he said. "The wind did."

Uncle Lester poked him with a foot. "You can get up now," he said. "It's all right. He must not of seen. He's not going to chase us."

"Dun Roving," Audrey mused. "That means those folks back there aren't going anywhere anymore. Because there's no place to go but where you've already been."

Augie looked stricken. "There is too some place to go," he said. "We're going home now, and pretty soon uncle Lester and me are going to Louisville, aren't we, uncle Lester?"

"Now, Lester," said Mama Pearl, "you know you can't drive to Louisville. And, besides, you'd never find Lurline in a big place like that."

Uncle Lester said nothing, and Audrey began to chant: "No place to go, no place to go but where you've already been." Augie whimpered because he had run out of arguments. With the policeman safely behind him, uncle Rosco began to build up speed again. The speedometer needle wavered around forty-five again. A car which had appeared out of nowhere behind them sounded its horn.

Augie and Audrey knelt on the seat to look back at the car. Augie made faces, and Audrey looked indifferent. They recognized the bronzed vacationers, all three in the front seat and all wearing enormous sunglasses. Their car straddled the middle line, waiting a chance to pass.

Augie waved his arms at the car, and when Mama Pearl

turned around to tell him to behave, she knocked her hat over her eyes. "Now, Augie," Mama Pearl said, peering raffishly from under her hat. Augie subsided next to the window. "No Passing," he read; then, louder: "NO PASSING." "Shoot," he said a minute later. "Pass with Care."

The gigantic automobile behind them swung further into the left lane and began to accelerate. When it got even with her, Audrey could see the profiles of the vacationers, all looking straight ahead. The back side window was covered with stickers saying all the places they had been. "Stuck up things," muttered Audrey.

"Speed up, uncle Rosco," said uncle Lester quietly, and uncle Rosco, accustomed to doing as he was told, pushed his foot down. It made him nervous having a car driving so close beside him. He gripped the wheel hard and the speedometer needle passed fifty and kept going. Audrey could still see the vacationers' faces, all looking straight ahead.

Mama Pearl was having trouble straightening her hat when she saw another car coming toward them. She closed her eyes and finished pinning her hat on while she waited. What she heard was not the crash she expected, but the thump and wheeze of two cars straddling ditches on opposite sides of the road. The bronzed vacationer, already out of his car, stared after them in disbelief, his sunglasses dangling from his pointing, accusing hand. People were crawling out of both cars, and all of them stared and pointed down the road toward Pleasureville.

Uncle Rosco did not slow down, until finally uncle Lester told him to. The deroaded cars were out of sight and uncle Rosco had begun to tremble. He pulled the car off the road and sat with his head resting on the steering wheel. Nobody spoke for a long time. They were listening to uncle Rosco's heavy breathing. In the distance, Augie saw a handpainted sign; it looked familiar, but it was too far away for him to read.

No cars came from either direction. The sun seemed stuck in the sky, and the afternoon heat was intolerable in the still car. Uncle Rosco had not thought to cut off the engine.

"Well, Lester," said Mama Pearl, "do you feel rested enought to drive us home?"

"Yes'm," uncle Lester nodded and went around to the driver's side. Uncle Rosco slid over close to Mama Pearl.

The sign at the roadside stand said "Blackberries: $2.50 a gal.," but Augie did not read it aloud. He'd read it once.

Though he did not show it, uncle Lester was profoundly moved by what had happened. He had an idea. He thought maybe he would drive the car off the bridge at Gratz the way his daddy had done years before. That way, Lurline would not have to forge checks again, ever, and if maybe Augie lived, she could buy him a pacemaker whether he needed it or not. Erline wouldn't miss Audrey much, and maybe with all the insurance money, both she and Lurline could get them new husbands. All in all, it did not seem a half-bad idea.

Everybody was quiet and to cheer them up, uncle Lester speeded up at the tops of hills and enjoyed hearing Audrey and Augie shriek as they plummeted down. It seemed to Lester that one part of him had to hurry to catch up with the rest of him at the bottoms of the hills. Finally, Mama Pearl said, "Now, Lester, that's enough. I'm feeling sick almost." He slowed down, and Mama Pearl said she did not think her lunch had agreed with her.

"What'd you expect, eating at a place like that," said Audrey disdainfully.

Uncle Lester began wondering how he could get Mama Pearl out of the car before they got to the bridge at Gratz, but he could think of no good way. She refused ever to admit she needed to go to the bathroom and would not even go inside a bathroom at a filling station. Uncle Rosco would be no problem; he'd hop right out and go read what people had written on the bathroom walls.

Mama Pearl was a problem. Uncle Lester did not think it was fair for her to have to go off the bridge with the rest of them, for, as Lurline often pointed out, she was not, strictly speaking, a member of the family. For that matter, neither was uncle Rosco, but uncle Lester worried less about him than Mama Pearl.

They were getting close to the bridge and everybody but Lester seemed half asleep. He guessed he would drive off the left side. The same one his daddy had hit; that way, he would hit the water first. Mama Pearl and Augie might have a chance if they would get out of the car quick. He didn't know if Mama Pearl could swim, and he considered asking her.

Then, he saw Audrey's face floating in the rearview mirror; she was leaning on her arms and craning her neck so she could study her expression in the mirror. She saw him watching her.

"What do you think this means?" she asked, flashing her fingers rapidly. He watched her hands in the mirror. The bridge was in sight. He knew what her sign language meant, and wondered if she had copied what the preacher did back at Jerry's Restaurant.

"That's easy," he said dully. "It means there's no place to

go but where you've already been." Audrey hitched up a little higher to stare at him in the mirror. Frowning, she leaned over the seat to study his face better.

"Somebody told you," Audrey accused.

"Who could have?" uncle Lester asked.

He crossed the bridge and stopped at the Gulf station for gas, though they had used only a quarter-tank all day.

"Didn't expect you back today," said Harvey. "How's things at Shelbyville?"

"Aunt Muddie wasn't home," said uncle Lester, "so we come back to where we belong."

That'll Be the Day

Mama Pearl took the postcard out of the mailbox first, but waited to examine it last. It was on top of the other mail, for Leroy the mailman obviously regarded it as important. He had tooted his horn—two longs and a short—as he generally did when he thought the day's mail was worth having. Whatever the card said, Mama Pearl was certain Leroy and his wife Mae Evelyn had already talked it over.

Mama Pearl looked at the circulars addressed to Box Holder. She had never gone to the Dollar Days advertised at Owenton, but she guessed if they kept sending her ads long enough she would one day go. She looked briefly at the cover of the RURAL KENTUCKIAN, and wondered if the editor's wife was ever going to print her recipe for vinegar pie she had sent in. A woman in Owenton had requested a vinegar pie recipe, and Mama Pearl had a good mind to write to her direct so she could have the recipe. She did not open the Owen County Rural Electric Company bill, for she already knew how much it would be. It was always $3.42, and Mama Pearl thought they could just save their stamp.

She put the postcard on top of the other mail and walked back to the house. She was trying to tell what the postmark said, but it was blurred and hard to read. The date looked like June 10, just two days ago. It was from Texas, that she could tell, but she could not tell from where in Texas. At least not without her glasses.

The card was addressed to her and written in pencil in a hand remarkably like her own. She began to have the uncomfortable feeling she sometimes had when everybody but her was off somewhere and the telephone rang. Whoever the card was from did not know she was no longer Pearl Thirwell, but now went by Pearl T. White. It was addressed to Box 47, RFD 3, Owenton, Kentucky. It was the Lord's mercy the card ever got to her at all, and it wouldn't have if Mae Evelyn hadn't been postmistress forever and a day and knew everybody in Owen County. Mae Evelyn had finally stopped pretending to be a Republican when the Democrats lost, for she knew she would keep her job anyhow.

Mama Pearl was still studying the card when she got back to the house. It had no return address, just that blurry postmark.

"Who do we know in Texas?" she asked uncle Rosco, who was sitting at the kitchen table still stirring the cup of coffee she had poured him. It looked like he was trying to wear out the cup.

"Nobody, to my knowledge," he said. "Did somebody we don't know in Texas write us a letter?" Mama Pearl nodded.

"Then it could be just about anybody," said uncle Rosco. "Anybody in Texas could write us and we wouldn't know them." He laughed silently. "Why don't you read it and see?"

"Well," said Mama Pearl, "I mean to."

The kitchen was empty when Audrey let herself in the back door, being careful not to get her hands dirty on the screen door. She had spent the afternoon with her mother Erline at the beauty shop, and because there was nothing better to do, Erline had given her a manicure. Now that school was out, Audrey guessed Erline would be giving her lots of sets and shampoos and manicures. Since Erline had gone Catholic and put tracts and statues all over the shop, not much of anybody went there.

Erline did not live with Mama Pearl and uncle Rosco and the others. She said she deserved a life of her own, but, lately, she had begun to say that if business didn't pick up soon she would have to put herself at the mercy of "that woman." Erline and her sister Lurline always called Mama Pearl "that woman," though neither seemed to mind her raising their children. Audrey sometimes felt caught in the middle when Erline talked about Mama Pearl, for she and Augie had always lived with Mama Pearl. Now, Augie could not live with his mother, for Lurline was in custody.

For months Audrey had looked forward to school being out, so she could begin her self-improvement program. She had lists of things to do every day and what time to do them. She intended to be an actress, and thought she might as well memorize Shakespeare this summer, just in case. It would be good discipline, and her teacher said that discipline was the most important thing for an actress, even more important than good looks. Every day, Audrey spent more time in front of the mirror working on her posture and improving her facial expression, for nobody would listen to her say her lines. Not even Erline. Audrey sometimes wished she was somebody else.

The mail was on the table, and Audrey opened the RURAL KENTUCKIAN to read her name again in the list of 4-H Club awards. She had already seen the magazine at Erline's among the magazines she kept on a table in case she got a customer. Audrey read the list again with satisfaction; nobody's name appeared as often as hers, four times for awards and once as an officer (recording secretary). Pretty good for a twelve-year-old, she thought.

She read the postcard next, and, sniffing disdainfully, went into the living room to wait for uncle Lester to get home. She could hardly wait to tell him.

Audrey stationed herself on what she called the divan. She pretended not to know what Mama Pearl was talking about when she spoke of the settee. Uncle Lester would expect her to be on the divan, for she was there every day when he came home. Sometimes she pretended she was waiting for her brother, and sometimes that uncle Lester was her husband and she was waiting for him to come home from the Studio. (She was THE STAR, but not in the picture currently being shot.) Uncle Lester was not much taller than Audrey, though he was almost three years older and seemed to know everything. He was not like Augie, who blabbed all the time.

Audrey opened the front window drapes just enough to let a shaft of afternoon light fall on her, and just enough that she could see uncle Lester coming so she could get ready. She stared fixedly into the distance until her eyes began to mist, but they were dry again when uncle Lester came into view. He was walking slow, which must mean he had once more failed to get a job. Every day since school let out uncle Lester had dressed up in his best clothes and gone into Gratz, where he would stand on the front steps of the feedstore until the bank opened. Then he would go across the street and stand in front of the bank. He secretly hoped the bank would hire him first, but he said he was available to whoever made him the first offer.

"What happened to your hands?" uncle Lester asked. Audrey sighed. Unlike certain other members of the family, uncle Lester always noticed things right off, but his reactions did not always suit her.

"Just a manicure," she said faintly.

Uncle Lester leaned closer. "Did Erline do it to you?"

Audrey decided it would do no good to answer. Instead, drooping her head so her hair would fall slightly over her face, she said, "When will you be ready to start packing?"

"Me?" said uncle Lester. "I'm not going anywhere."

"Don't be too sure," Audrey warned, sneaking a sidelong look at him. She laughed hollowly. "I'm forgetting. You don't know. We got a card today."

Uncle Lester looked around the room fiercely. "I'm not going anywhere," he repeated. "Are you?"

Audrey ignored him. "Poor Mama Pearl," she said.

"Where is Mama Pearl?" uncle Lester demanded. "What's going on?"

"A card," Audrey repeated tragically, "from uncle Wiley, from off in Texas somewhere. He says he's coming home. For good." She let that sink in before continuing.

"He'll make Mama Pearl leave, and uncle Rosco too. You know she's not even a member of the family, or anything, and uncle Wiley will take the place away from her and then where will you and Augie and I be?" Audrey's tears now were real, and she could sense uncle Lester's panic.

"Or he'll be old and poor, and Mama Pearl will have to

wear herself out looking after him, and he'll die and we'll have to pay everything." She hadn't thought of this angle before and stopped to think about it. Then, satisfied with the effect she was having on uncle Lester, Audrey added in her normal voice, "The card's on the kitchen table, unless you want me to say it for you. I memorized it."

In a minute uncle Lester came back to the living room with the card, but Audrey was gone. He read the card aloud; then he put it back on the table.

When Mama Pearl came in from the garden, he was waiting.

"It don't say anything about taking the place away from us," he challenged.

"Who said it did?" Mama Pearl asked. "Wiley has been gone, and now he's coming back. That's all."

That night Erline dropped in, as she did once in a blue moon, and when she heard about the card, she said she knew it, she had sensed trouble. Everybody but Audrey was there, in the kitchen. Audrey liked to dress for dinner, and liked to take her time doing it.

"Well," said Mama Pearl, "I don't guess it's trouble just because uncle Wiley has decided to come home."

"He says 'for good,' Pearl," said Erline. To make sure, she leaned across the table to pull the card from under Augie's nose. He had not known how to read for long and was practicing on uncle Wiley's card. Erline pulled her mouth down in a little frown and read: "Dear Pearl. Am coming home. For good." She waited to see if Mama Pearl would turn around from the woodstove, where she was cooking supper. "For good means always, Pearl," she said spitefully.

Mama Pearl poured a splash of water into the big iron

33

skillet where the chicken had browned. She had the kettle down and popped the skillet lid on before the grease could spit on the stove. The pan growled and roared, obliging Erline to read louder. Augie went to the stove and passed his hands through the wisps of steam escaping when the lid rose gently as the chicken simmered.

"I have been gone almost forty years, but trust you are still there and as pretty as ever. Accept my belated expression of sympathy for your loss." Erline was bristling.

"Belated expression, my foot," she snapped. "He could have walked back ten times to tell you that, in the time it's been since uncle Omer died. Why, Omer has been dead so long I don't even hardly remember what he looked like." Erline was hitting what uncle Rosco called her overdrive, or passing gear.

"I didn't even remember he was in Texas, it has been so long," interrupted Mama Pearl. She sounded mildly surprised.

"Who?" asked Augie. "Uncle Omer?"

"No, silly, uncle Wiley," answered Erline. "Uncle Wiley—gone for forty years without so much as a howdy-doo, and now he thinks he can come barging in whenever he feels like it." She glared around the room. She still had her head tied up in a kerchief, which Mama Pearl secretly thought of as a head rag and did not regard as very good advertising for a beauty parlor.

Uncle Rosco looked down when Erline blared her eyes at him. He was still red from the part about Mama Pearl being as pretty as ever. He had never told her he thought she was pretty, and he wondered if this was the first time Wiley had done so. Uncle Rosco did not know Wiley, for he had not come to Gratz until after Mama Pearl's first husband had died, and uncle Wiley had left even before that.

"Can you beat that?" Erline demanded of uncle Rosco. He shook his head helplessly. "Tossing around compliments to a woman he hasn't seen in a century and who was married to his own uncle, and him too cheap even to send her a Sympathy Card when her husband died." She laughed unpleasantly. "Sounds like he's going to move in on you," she said, "in more ways than one."

Carefully, Mama Pearl dropped roasting ears into her biggest boiler. "Brother," she said, when she had finished. "Actually, brother-in-law, for Wiley was brother to LeMartine Waters, who was my first husband's first wife." She put the lid on the boiler and moved it slightly to one side of the stove so the corn would not boil too fast. She removed the top from the skillet and slid it over where the chicken could crisp.

Erline waved her hand impatiently. "Who cares about exact relationships?" she asked. "Though," she added illogically, "that is precisely the point."

Uncle Rosco looked up, confused but obviously impressed by Erline's neat turnabout.

"What," he asked, "is exactly the point?"

Augie asked when the chicken would be done and whether he had to stay and listen to all the dumb things Erline was talking about, and uncle Lester spoke up and told Augie he would smack him if he didn't hush. And Mama Pearl said "Now, Lester, now Augie" a few times. Then, she said Augie could go set the dining table for her, because it was not every night they had company for supper. "Erline," she said, "only comes once in a blue moon." Erline said that pretty soon Mama Pearl would have uncle Wiley for supper and every other meal every blessed day and that she hadn't meant to come right at supper time but that everything smelled so good she couldn't resist.

Augie turned up his nose at her, and as soon as he was half-way to the dining room, Erline said, "It's all right, Lester. I mean about Augie. Goodness knows, it's hard enough on him; I mean with his mother off at that awful place."

Augie stuck his head back in the kitchen and told Erline to go to hell, and then he started to cry. He went to the dining room and they heard him banging dishes around and sniffling.

"Oh my," simpered Erline. "Look what I have done, me and my big mouth."

She produced a package of Herbert Tareytons from her purse, and uncle Lester went to get the ashtray. When Mama Pearl saw the cigarettes, she sneezed, but Erline lit one anyhow.

By the time Mama Pearl was ready to put the fried chicken, boiled corn, beans, pickled beets, biscuits, and gravy on the table, Erline had begun to fan herself with the RURAL KENTUCKIAN. She was so hot her makeup was beginning to run, but she persisted in saying she would just as soon eat in the kitchen. "Goodness knows," she said, "I'm not company. Let's all be homefolks while we can."

Augie came back and asked if he should call Audrey, and he stuck his tongue out at Erline while Mama Pearl wasn't looking and Erline stuck hers out at him just as Mama Pearl turned around. "Now Erline, now Augie," she said automatically; uncle Lester scowled at a book he had propped up against the sugar bowl. He was looking something up in the World Book.

"I guess we better eat," said Mama Pearl, and picked up the chicken platter. Erline hopped to get the cut-glass pickle dish full of tiny baby beets, and got to it just before Augie. "Holier than thou," she mouthed at him; then, she sang out, "O, Pearl, let me help," as if she had just thought of a good idea.

They trooped to the dining room, everybody but uncle Rosco carrying a dish. He could not decide what to carry. Just as they were putting the dishes on the table, Audrey came in from the front hall. To make sure they noticed her, she had not dressed for dinner at all, but she had brushed her hair a new way so that it stood out from her head. Augie stared at her in admiration and could think of nothing to say to put her down.

"Poor baby," Erline said of Audrey to the room at large. "Mother wants you to eat a big supper. You're looking thin." Erline sat down and indicated the bowls of food, as if she had produced it all especially to fatten up her baby. Mama Pearl sat down, too, and frowned hard at uncle Rosco to remind him to say grace or to tell Augie to do so, but uncle Rosco thought she was telling him to go back to the kitchen and get something.

Mama Pearl had to call him back. "Isn't this enough to eat, Rosco? Do you want something else?"

He sat down, and felt the unaccustomed cloth napkin but decided not to comment on it. "If you'll just say the blessing, we can eat," hinted Mama Pearl. Augie already had a piece of chicken on his plate, but he bowed his head to see if he could watch Erline through his squinted eyes. He could, and intended to do so and find out what she did with her hands at the end of the blessing. Last time she had supper with them, he had seen just the tail end of it, and had thought she was swatting at a gnat or something on her face.

"Good Lord," muttered Audrey, casting her eyes upward. She did not think a blessing was likely to improve the quality of the meal. She tried to catch Erline's eyes, so she could give her the look Lurline always did, which meant "grease cooking." Erline's head was still bowed, and she was apparently eager for uncle Rosco to say the blessing quick so she could eat.

"But uncle Rosco," Audrey piped, "isn't it Augie's turn?"

"My turn to what," grumbled Augie, but uncle Rosco said yes it was and go ahead, Augie, so he did.

Eyes wide open and staring at Erline, Augie chanted: "God bless this FOOD to our USE and us to THY service," and then, before anybody could lift their heads, he raced on: "God bless mother and Mama Pearl and uncle Rosco and uncle Lester and Audrey, and—uncle Wiley." After a longish pause, he added "Amen."

Erline stared at Augie with slitted eyes that looked like icepicks. She was so shocked she forgot to cross herself until too late.

"Well, Lester," said Mama Pearl, "can you help yourself to chicken and pass it?"

"You left out Erline on purpose," said Audrey. Her voice combined accusation and admiration. Augie was eating his chicken leg and did not bother to answer, for he knew that if he did, Somebody would tell him not to talk with his mouth full.

Uncle Lester was busy filling his plate with food. Unlike Augie who would eat only one thing at a time, he wanted to see what he had and then eat it all. He took satisfaction in uncovering the design in the middle of the dinner plates. Audrey wrinkled her nose; she took baby portions of everything and always left part of that. Uncle Lester ran out of space on his plate before the beets got to him. He held the dish uncertainly.

"I wonder where in Texas it is," he said. When everyone looked at him, he began to spoon beets into his saucer. "I wonder where Tomball is, and how long it will take uncle Wiley to get here."

"Why, Lester," said Mama Pearl, "how did you know the name of the town? I had forgotten he was even in Texas, much less what town."

"I read it on the postmark," said uncle Lester. "It was clear as anything."

"I wouldn't want to be from there," said Augie.

"Don't talk with your mouth full," said Erline spearing a beet on her fork.

"Pass Augie the chicken," said Mama Pearl.

"The point is," resumed Erline in answer to uncle Rosco's question before supper, "that he thinks he owns this place now, and probably does." She clicked her heels smartly, as she passed from sink to refrigerator and back again.

"Much as Lurline and me love you, Pearl, and are grateful for all you have done over the years," she fake-smiled at Mama Pearl, "the fact remains that, strictly speaking, you are not a member of the family, and he is brother to LeMartine and to Papa." She smelled the coffee cream, made a face, and dumped it back into the gallon milk jar anyhow.

"We pay the taxes," said uncle Rosco.

Erline snorted. "Taxes," she said. "A few dollars a year. You know what this place is worth, close as it is to Frankfort?"

"Big deal," said Audrey. "They roll up the sidewalks in Frankfort even earlier than they do in Owenton, or Monterey."

Augie hooted. "They don't HAVE sidewalks in Monterey," he said.

Erline looked pained. "All that," she said, "is beside the point: the point is that property values have gone up, and here this perfect stranger—this MAN—intends to barge in on all of us, and take away our home."

"Wiley is not a stranger," Mama Pearl told Erline. Everybody looked at her until she explained. "I have not seen Wiley for years, but I knew him well before he went away. He used to come and sit with Omer and me, sometimes in this very room."

Erline shivered elaborately. "Somebody just walked on my grave," she explained.

"Mama Pearl can have my part," uncle Lester said unexpectedly. "I don't want it. If he says Mama Pearl is not part of the family, tell him I gave her my part."

"You can have my part too," said Augie.

Erline was about to pop her eyes out of her head trying to tell Audrey not to give away her part too, but Audrey wasn't paying attention.

"Maybe uncle Wiley has better things to think about than this dumb old farm," she volunteered.

"This dumb old farm," Erline snapped, "may be all that stands between you and the POOR farm, young lady."

"I'll have my career," Audrey said. "Perhaps as a place to retire—briefly—from the world, I'll come back—occasionally. But to live here, never."

"What all does that postcard say?" uncle Rosco asked.

"It says," recited Audrey, "'I am sick and tired of the panhandle, and am going to see the ocean before I die. I will let you hear from me regular. Yours, Wiley.' That's after the part you already know, uncle Rosco. Then, there is a postscript (P.S.) which says, 'These things used to cost 1¢—remember?—and now look. That man in the moon has run up the price of everything.'" Audrey had memorized the card while she was waiting for uncle Lester. It was easier than Shakespeare.

"It should be *regularly*, not *regular*," she said in her schoolteacher voice Augie hated, "and I don't know what the man in the moon has to do with the price of anything. Otherwise, it's well written."

"The man ON the moon," corrected uncle Lester. "He means Federal Spending, I guess, but I wonder does he really mean the ocean or just the Gulf?"

"What's the difference?" said Audrey. "Anything's better than a dirt farm in Kentucky. You can have my part too, Mama Pearl."

During the next week, Erline practically lived at Mama Pearl's, and when she was not there, she was calling up, all hours, to find out if Anything Had Happened. She had written Lurline a long letter with practically every word underlined and was anxiously awaiting her sister's response. She had even talked to uncle Lester about driving to Louisville to see Lurline. No one had gone to see Lurline since she had been put in the Women's Detention Center at Louisville, where to judge from her letters, she was having the time of her life.

On Monday, uncle Wiley's postcards started coming. Leroy the mailman blew his horn at least a dozen times. Erline sprinted down to get the mail and came back with her fist full of cards, picture postcards this time. Two were of the Astrodome in Houston, and one pictured Bay City, which uncle Wiley wrote was outside Houston and used to be a swell place to go weekends. It was pretty rough now, he explained, and not a place you would want to go on your honeymoon.

"Huh?" said Augie. "Who's going on a honeymoon, you and uncle Wiley?"

Mama Pearl did not answer.

"Nobody," said Audrey, "says 'swell place' anymore. He's got to be kidding."

Erline read all the cards out loud, as if they were addressed to her. Then, she pulled a long face and said she could hear the doors of her family home closing on her.

"Where will I go?" she asked, trying hard to squeeze out a tear, "if I have to close my shop, because this county is too narrow-minded to accept a Catholic?"

"Why, Erline," Mama Pearl soothed, "there's always room here. Lurline's room is empty, and there's the lumber room if worst comes to worst, and uncle Wiley will be in the spare room but Lester and Augie don't mind sharing a room, and Audrey's in there with them half the time, so I don't see what you're worried about."

"Oh, Pearl," Erline sobbed, "you're too good for this earth.

Don't you see what that awful man will do?—None of us can stay here, once he gets back."

The next day, Mama Pearl got three cards from Corpus Christi, which Augie said meant "God's Body." Audrey contradicted him and said it meant "the body of Christ."

"What's the difference?" Augie asked, and Audrey said that if he didn't know, she wouldn't tell him.

That week, they got cards from Port Aransas, Padre Island, and Harlingen, all in Texas. The card from Padre Island said uncle Wiley had met some nice hippies who were camping in the dunes and his ideas about hippies were changing; they had asked him to eat fried fish with them and had liked the hush puppies he made to go with the ocean cat.

The next week, they got cards from Brownsville, Texas, and from Matamoros, Mexico. The message on the card from Matamoros was short: "This is a hot town," uncle Wiley wrote, "in more ways than one."

Nobody wanted to miss uncle Wiley's postcards. Leroy the mailman had taken to blowing his horn as soon as he got in sight of their mailbox. He would wait for somebody to come get the cards.

"Six of them today," he would say. "He don't seem to be hurrying to get here."

Uncle Lester was fairly let down when he finally got a job. Nobody seemed interested, and it was at the feed store and not at the bank. He would be working at home the end of every month, for part of his job was to type up the bills and mail them out.

"Everywhere else, but Gratz, Kentucky," he said, "computers do that."

Then, Erline went to Gethsemane on a Retreat. She appeared without her head rag, and said she would be gone for three days. When she came back, she said she had met a man and that her soul was refreshed. Augie asked what she had done at the retreat and what was she running from, and Erline told Mama Pearl she would have to leave or she might forget herself and slap Augie's face.

Then it was Dog Days, and everybody was feeling low but Erline who said that life was wonderful, and she didn't even worry about uncle Wiley now that Francis had entered her life. She said she didn't care if he *was* an ex-priest or *why* he left the order; she said God moved in mysterious ways.

The postcards kept coming, and the phone calls began.

Uncle Wiley had tired of Mexico and was on his way home. He called, the first time, from Kingsville, Texas, and all the family gathered in the hall to listen to Mama Pearl talk to him.

"Well, Wiley," she said, "I am fine. I live here with Audrey and Augie, who are Lurline and Erline's children. No, I do not need anything. Erline is here this very minute, but Lurline is—away." She did not mention uncle Rosco, but, then, uncle Wiley seemed to talk a great deal and she said she did not have a chance to do more than answer his questions. "He never asked about Rosco," she explained.

He called again from Beaumont, and, in the meantime, Mama Pearl had received cards from Inez, Edna, and Louise, Texas, followed by Daisetta, Texas. One came a day or so later from Sugarland, but uncle Lester said he could not have been there unless he backtracked from Daisetta. Uncle Lester was following uncle Wiley's progress in his atlas. He had told Mama Pearl that Tomball was not in the Panhandle, and Mama Pearl said uncle Wiley had never said he was from Tomball. He simply mailed that first card from there. Then, a picture postcard came from Tomball, and uncle Lester said he had backtracked again, or the mails had been held up. It was the only place he sent two cards from.

Nobody heard Mama Pearl's conversation when uncle Wiley called from Beaumont, for he called nearly every day, and each time he was closer to Kentucky.

"None of the calls have been collect, so he must not be broke," relented Erline.

About that time, Mama Pearl began to worry. Everybody could tell, even Augie. She was always losing her glasses, and she would say things that didn't make any sense to anybody but herself, and would get angry if anyone asked what she was talking about. Sometimes, she seemed to be carrying on conversations with people who had been dead for many years.

Privately, uncle Rosco admitted he was worried. Pearl was nervous as a cat. She would sit straight up in bed, two or three times a night, and say "who's that?" Then, Rosco would lie there and worry about who it could have been until, finally, he would walk through the house looking. Once, she had cried out in her sleep, "We can't stay here, we can't." Uncle Rosco and Erline agreed she was worried about uncle Wiley and what he might do.

Uncle Lester learned from Ace Bourne that Mama Pearl had asked him to drive her out to the end of the Sawdridge Creek Road, to where she had grown up. Ace was county magistrate and had nothing to do but drive around. She had heard that her family's old house was abandoned, but when they got there, she learned a professor from Louisville had

45

bought it and was living there summers and weekends. Uncle Lester did not tell anyone, but he did hang around Monterey until he met the professor. He didn't think much of him and hoped he would go back to Louisville soon.

Late one afternoon, Mama Pearl produced a bunch of faded envelopes from her darning basket, and handed them to uncle Lester. "I found these," she said. "Letters from Wiley must have come in them, for they are written in his hand. See if you can read the postmark," she asked.

"Muleshoe, Texas," said uncle Lester promptly. "That's up the Panhandle, almost into New Mexico."

"How did you know that, Lester?" asked Erline grudgingly.

Audrey took one of the envelopes from the pile in front of Lester and read it for herself. Muleshoe. She winced. Why couldn't anybody in this family be from someplace that *was* someplace. "My uncle Wiley is coming home from Muleshoe, Texas, by way of Tomball," she imagined herself saying. People would die laughing. Nobody in the Waters family, to her knowledge, had ever lived places like Versailles and Paris, which were in Kentucky and handy but sounded foreign.

"Muleshoe is even worse than Gratz," she told everybody. "I'd just die if I had to be from there." Audrey intended to list her own place of birth as Sweet Owen, which was close enough to Gratz to be almost the truth. She had never been to Sweet Owen, and would probably have hated it if she had.

Erline was looking inside all the envelopes. "Where are the letters, Pearl?" she demanded. "I don't see why you would keep a bunch of old envelopes and throw the letters away."

"Well, I guess I did," said Mama Pearl, and gathered the

envelopes to put them back in her basket. She weighted them down with a china darning egg. Augie wanted to play with the darning egg, and Mama Pearl let him hold it a few minutes. Then, she made Erline put on one of her big floppy garden hats and go with her to pick some greens and tomatoes for lunch.

"I wonder why Mama Pearl wants Erline outdoors?" Audrey asked uncle Lester as soon as everybody was gone.

"So she won't snoop in the basket and find her letters," said Augie from where he was rolling the china egg.

"How do you know there are any letters?" said uncle Lester.

"I found them, but couldn't read them. They're written funny," said Augie.

"You shouldn't go through Mama Pearl's things," said Audrey reaching for the sewing basket. "Why don't you help uncle Lester get the stovewood in for Mama Pearl," she suggested.

"You never do anything to help," accused Augie.

"I'll let you use the ax," said uncle Lester, and they went outside.

Audrey found the letters at once, and she also found another china egg. She laid the letters on the table and examined the egg; it was smoky colored with a ripple of brown-yellow. The other was pure white.

Then she turned to the letters.

When Audrey heard Mama Pearl and Erline coming back from the garden, she had almost finished reading all of uncle Wiley's letters. They were written in pencil on lined paper, and were mostly dated 1922, though there was one—an important one—dated 1935. Augie was right; they were hard to read, for uncle Wiley's handwriting was old-fashioned and fancy, with curlicues and funny slants.

Audrey put the letters back where she found them, and then picked up Augie's china egg where he had left it on the floor. She dropped one egg down in the basket, and weighted the empty envelopes with the other.

She was studying uncle Lester's ledger book, from which he had to send out bills for the feedstore, when Mama Pearl came in. Audrey had promised to help him by reading out the names and amounts while he typed them on uncle Rosco's big Underwood typewriter.

She could hear Augie shrieking with laughter and the sound Erline made when she pretended to have fun. She was showing the boys she had not forgotten how to chop wood. Since she had met Francis, Erline was not half bad. Even Augie admitted that much. The chickens set up a squawk, and it sounded like uncle Lester, who rarely even smiled, was laughing too.

Mama Pearl looked out the window where she was washing the greens under dippers full of springwater.

"Audrey, go tell Erline not to kill my chickens with flying kindling," she said. "We are having ham for supper."

Audrey started for the door without even grumbling.

"Audrey." She turned and looked at Mama Pearl.

"Did you find what you were looking for?"

Involuntarily, Audrey looked at the sewing basket. The brown china egg glowed in the late afternoon light.

When she came back with the others, Mama Pearl and the sewing basket were gone.

Audrey had told the others nothing about the letters. Not even uncle Lester. They stood awkwardly in the kitchen.

Erline's hair, which she had lately styled and streaked, tumbled about her shoulders, and the exertion outdoors had made a little patch of color show through her makeup. Finally, uncle Lester decided he should make the fire and Erline said she would find a skillet to fry the ham. Augie went off to set the table, and Audrey finished washing the greens.

They talked in church-whispers about Mama Pearl. They knew they would hear her coming downstairs, for all the steps creaked.

"She needs new glasses, if you ask me," said Erline, returning to her old self. "Thank the Lord, you're cleaning the greens, Audrey. Goodness knows how many worms we'd eat otherwise."

"Ugghh," said Audrey. "I don't like greens anyhow."

Uncle Lester asked could they get Mama Pearl to go to the optometrist, and Erline said all she needed was a good eye-doctor and there was even one of those in Owenton. Audrey pulled a long face and said what she thought was that Mama Pearl was unhappy, and Erline asked what on earth for.

"I don't know," lied Audrey, "but I saw her crying the other day."

"Who?" asked Augie. "Who was crying?" He came back into the kitchen carrying a platter for the meat. He looked as if he might cry too.

"When, Audrey?" asked uncle Lester.

"Let's see," mused Audrey, enjoying all the attention. "Was it the day you got your job, or the day after?" Erline gestured her impatience.

"Who cares?" she demanded. "What do you think made Pearl cry?"

49

"I don't know," faltered Audrey. "But . . . maybe, it was that postcard from uncle Wiley."

"WHAT postcard? We've only got twenty-five or thirty cards from him," Erline exploded. "Which one?"

"The one when uncle Lester said he must have been back-tracking," Audrey said.

"The second one from Tomball," volunteered uncle Lester. "That came the day after I got my job."

"Well, that beats all," declared Erline. "That'll be the day when I see Pearl White crying."

Audrey was shrieking because she had found a worm on the greens and Erline was slashing away at the fat on the ham when Mama Pearl came in and said that she saw they had everything under control without her.

Augie came back from the dining room and said he would not eat if Audrey and Erline cooked supper, and Erline washed her hands and went to sit down.

"Well," said Mama Pearl, "where's my apron? I'll just make some biscuits to have with that red-eye gravy." That night, in between making out bills, uncle Lester and Audrey talked about the letters. Audrey had memorized parts of them. She recited them with great expression, but only after making uncle Lester promise not to tell Augie.

"I promise not to tell Augie, if you promise not to tell Erline," he countered.

"The earliest letters are mostly about Muleshoe and what he was doing there," said Audrey, "and they begin 'Dear Omer & Pearl,' but the later ones—the December, January, and February ones—say 'Dear Pearl,' or 'Dearest Pearl.'" Audrey shivered expressively, and gave herself a little hug.

"The best one goes like this: 'I am doing well for myself out here, but I will never be happy away from you. I thought I could, but know now that I can't. How long do you think this can go on? Me off here, and you with HIM.'"

Audrey paused for effect, and lowered her voice to a whisper: "Do you realize I have never even kissed you. Sometimes I dream I am kissing you." Audrey clenched her hands and twisted them. "Want me to go on?"

Uncle Lester shook his head. He was scowling at the typewriter keyboard, as if to memorize it. "Tell me some of the others," he said huskily.

Face set and prim, Audrey began: "Don't tell me not to write you letters *like that*. I tell you I'd be glad if Omer did open one and get himself an eyefull. He doesn't know how lucky he is. I just may come back there and get you."

Uncle Lester was nodding, as if in agreement. "I wonder," he said, "would she have gone?" After a minute, he nodded. "I guess she would."

They thought they heard somebody on the steps, and Audrey began to read names to uncle Lester and he made a great clatter on the typewriter. While he typed, she slipped into the living room to see if anybody was on the steps.

"The coast is clear," she said when she came back. "But let's do a few more envelopes, or Mama Pearl won't let us stay up late again."

Before they went upstairs, Audrey told him about the last letter, the one dated 1935. "Dear Pearl," it said, "It has been a long time, and I hope you do not blame me for not writing all these years. I thought maybe I could fall in love and get married, but it did not work. I have plenty of everything, though everybody talks about how hard the Depression is. I lay away a little all along, and can offer you a good life. I hear that Omer is likely not to make it through the winter (Leila Maud wrote me), and want you to know I am here. I do not wish any harm to Omer, but he has had a long life. Maybe yours is just beginning. Let me hear from you."

Uncle Lester and Audrey sat silently for a few minutes.

"She didn't write him," said uncle Lester flatly.

"Uncle Omer didn't die," said Audrey. "He lived to be ninety-one. By then, maybe she thought it was too late."

"Maybe it's not too late yet," said uncle Lester.

Audrey sighed. "It always is," she said.

All of a sudden, everything seemed to happen at once. Uncle Wiley's telephone calls stopped, and a postcard from Memphis said that he was tired and that Mama Pearl would get a call just before he came home for good. Then, Lurline called from the Women's Detention Center and said she might get out early if the Authorities were sure she would mend her ways. She said she was calling from the pizza place down the road, and that she could come and go now that she was a trusty. Mama Pearl said she could not hear for the noise in the background and that it sounded like a rough place, and Lurline said she'd been rougher places.

Augie did not want to talk to his mother, and Lurline said Mama Pearl had turned him against her. "Ashamed of the family jail-bird?" she asked. "Just remember," she said, "I am coming home and want my room back."

The next day Augie cut his foot with the ax, and uncle Rosco had to take him to the hospital for a tetanus shot, and while they were gone Erline came by, her head tied up in a kerchief, to say she had telephoned Francis and discovered he did not live with his mother but with a wife and four kids and that she had finally learned her lesson.

"Men are all alike," she told Mama Pearl. "I wouldn't even trust uncle Rosco." Then, turning to Audrey, she said, "Don't you trust them, either," and burst into tears. Mama Pearl had to put her to bed—in Lurline's room—and put cold cloths on her forehead until she fell asleep.

Audrey waited for Augie and uncle Rosco to get back, so she could tell Augie not to make any noise and wake up Erline. And that was how she managed to get the telephone call from Louisville.

The man calling had a deep voice and said his name was Charles B. Frady. He said he worked for Burns, Burns & Bridges in Louisville, and that he was calling for Mrs. Pearl Thirwell, and Audrey said could she take a message. After a minute she said she guessed she better call Mrs. Thirwell to the phone. Her eyes were big as dinner plates when she went upstairs to get Mama Pearl.

Audrey stood in the front door to watch for uncle Rosco and so she could hear what Mama Pearl said. She knew what Charles B. Frady was telling her, and she watched to make sure Mama Pearl would be okay.

Augie hopped into the living room, his face tear-streaked but beaming. He had a tremendous bandage on his foot, and uncle Rosco had bought him an ice cream cone.

"What are you doing in here?" Augie demanded. Nobody but Audrey ever sat in the living room, but now she and uncle Lester and Mama Pearl were all there.

"We had to wait," explained uncle Rosco. "That's why it took so long."

"What's going on?" said Augie, hobbling over to sit near Mama Pearl.

"Uncle Wiley," said Audrey, "is dead, and Mama Pearl is his beneficiary."

Uncle Rosco sat down heavily.

"They called from Louisville," explained Audrey. "Sleeping pills, but he left a letter to Mama Pearl and instructions for everybody. His lawyer is going to come here to see Mama Pearl."

"What's a beneficiary," demanded Augie looking at Mama Pearl with new interest.

"She gets his money," said uncle Lester.

"Maybe you'll be rich," Augie said to Mama Pearl.

"Well, Augie," she said, "I have never felt poor." Then to uncle Rosco: "He'll be coming soon, and we have things to do to get ready."

Uncle Rosco got up and looked around for something to do.

Mama Pearl had the Owen County phone book in her lap. She passed it to uncle Lester.

"If you'll look up Rev. Howell's number," she said, "I'll call him. I guess Wiley was still a Baptist and would want to be put in the Cedar Creek cemetery with everybody else."

Audrey watched Mama Pearl closely.

"I'll go see about Erline," said Mama Pearl, "and then I will call Mr. Howell." She let two tears run unhindered down her face.

"I never thought I'd see the day I couldn't read the phone book without my glasses," she told Lester.

Nobody, not even Augie, told her she had her glasses on.

A Fellow
Making Himself Up

What uncle Lester liked most about Rosco was that he had named himself, and Lester thought he had picked the perfect name. He did not look like a Ralph, or Robert, or Rupert, but exactly like a Rosco. Audrey said she did not think it was so great to be named Rosco, for she could not think of a single movie star, or even TV personality, with *that* name. Uncle Lester admitted that Rosco had not exactly named himself all the way, for he had started out with what his parents had decided to call him, which was R.P. White.

To Lester what uncle Rosco had done was better than any story in a book, even the ones about the frog who turned into a prince or the poor boy who became Lord Mayor of London. Lester made Rosco tell him all the details many times, and even when he was a baby, or practically one, he would make Rosco go back and tell it again if he left out any part of it.

Lester mostly called Rosco, Rosco—without any uncle before it—and you could tell he liked the sound of it. He had looked in the Owenton phone book to see if he could find any other Roscoes. It took him a whole afternoon to read all the first names. He found four of them, but he felt better when he called up and learned that one of them was deceased and another had moved off to Henry County.

How it happened that Rosco got the name R.P. White was that he was the eighth baby, and, by the time he came along, his parents had run out of names along with practically everything else. They had used up some perfectly good names on babies who had died, and Rosco said he guessed they felt funny about using the same names twice, especially since the dead children were buried a hundred yards from the front porch.

Their names and dates were painted on slate stones, and they were also listed in the family Bible, which uncle Rosco said he would give a pretty to have so he could show it to Lester.

Sallie Garland White/Jan 9 1902–Feb 2 1902
(At Rest Now)

Han. Leonidus White/June 11 1903–Oct 7 1903
(God's Own)

Eben. Ulysses White/Oct 30 1904
(Precious Moment)

Rosco knew what all was on the stones, and he said Han. stood for Hannibal which was too long to fit on the slate, and that Eben. stood for Ebenezer. Uncle Lester was glad that Rosco did not get either of those names, but he did not say so. He had seen an Ebenezer (and an Ichabod) on TV.

Rosco was stingy with nothing but words, and, with Lester, he was not even stingy with them. His hands hung a mile out of his sleeves, as Ichabod's did, but his shoulders were broad as a barn door, and Lester could not imagine him running from a headless horseman or anything else. Lester wasn't sure how he felt about the name Ulysses, for he knew that Ulysses was a hero and had traveled far as Rosco had, but he also knew that Ulysses was Greek—and the Greek who owned the cafe had been partly to blame for Lurline's going to the Women's Detention Center. Lester thought that since it was his name Lurline signed to a check he should have had some say about things, and not some Greek who wasn't even kin to Lurline.

Rosco said his Daddy had once worked at a textile mill in Walhalla, S.C., for a man named R.P. Swift, so when Rosco's Mama said *What can we name this one?* he came out with R.P.

"R.P.?" said Rosco's Mama. "What kind of name is that?"

They ended up writing it down in the family Bible anyhow—R.P. White, Dec. 6, 1917. That was how they named the children back then, at least in Walhalla. They wrote the name down in the Bible. None of them ever had a birth certificate, and uncle Rosco said that had caused him a world and all of trouble, though, as he said, you would think anybody with a grain of sense who saw him standing there would take it on faith that he had to have been born, even if he didn't have papers to show for it.

Until Rosco decided to name himself, lots of people said to him what his Mama had said to his Daddy.

"R.P.?" they would say. "What kind of name is that?"

His teachers would always tell him that he had to have more name than that. "You go home tonight," they told him, "and ask your Mama what those letters stand for so I can write it down." Uncle Rosco said he could never understand why certain people put so much stock in knowing things just so they could write them down.

One teacher told him that if he did not tell her his *real* name, she was going to call him Rastus—and how would he like answering to a nigger name? She called him that a time or two until he told her his Mama said that 'Rastus was short for Erastus and could not be what the *R.* stood for in his name—and besides, his Mama said *Erastus* was a lovely name. The teacher said she wondered who Mrs. White thought *she* was, but she stopped calling R.P. *Rastus* and took to calling him Robert, but he would answer to nothing but R.P.

Uncle Lester figured it was lucky that Rosco did not stay in school very long, for that teacher would have ended up naming him herself before he had a chance. Rosco said that he was never much for sitting indoors, and when his Daddy began to need him around the place, he just quit going to school though he did sometimes borrow books to read at night when the work was done.

By then, it was the Depression, though Rosco told Lester that the only difference he could see between the Depression and what come before was that the Federal Government began to notice that folks were poor. One of Rosco's brothers went off and joined the CCC. Rosco could not remember what the letters stood for, so Lester looked it up in the World Book and found out it was the Civilian Conservation Corps, and uncle Rosco said that was right. He said there was a CCC camp just below Franklin, N.C., and he had been there once. He said the boys there learned to plant trees and cut them down and how to build stone steps and walls on the National Park grounds. They had uniforms to wear and learned how to drive trucks and string electrical wires without hardly ever electrocuting themselves.

Another brother lied about his age so he could join the Navy and see the world, and what came of that was that he was at Pearl Harbor when the Japs made their sneak attack and he like to have been killed.

Rosco's sister, Rose Cameron White, took up with an older man and headed west not to be heard of for years. When Lester asked what happened to her, uncle Rosco shook his head. It seemed that Rose Cameron had prospered and now owned a large wheat ranch and had run through two more men. Another sister got herself married right off as soon as she was fifteen, though as Rosco's Daddy always said, she would have done better to head west too.

After a while Rosco's Mama died trying to have another baby. Rosco said she had already had eleven or twelve, he'd lost count, and was too old to have any more but didn't know what to do. His Daddy got married again soon so he would have somebody to look after the younger chaps.

"Chaps?" interrupted Lester.

"Chaps," uncle Rosco confirmed. "That's what Mama always called us children. Chaps, don't ask me why."

Rosco said he decided it was time for him to leave, and when Lester asked if his Daddy's new wife was a wicked stepmother, he said she was a good lady but that he did not feel at home with her. She was not much older than he was, and he felt funny every time he saw his Daddy hug and kiss her. He would think of his Mama and how old and tired seeming she had always been, and that made it hard for him to get used to a new, pretty Mama.

He did not get far the first time he ran away. Somebody in a buggy (he thought maybe it was the doctor) picked him up and brought him home before anybody even knew he was gone. They did not know he had run away until he told them, and he had time to help with the chores before he got his licking.

The next time he tried, he made it. He was fifteen and big for his age, and it was easy for him to find work even when all he got in exchange was his food and a pallet to sleep on. After a year or two, he took to sending an occasional postcard home, and once at Christmas he had sent a money order, but it was a long time before he saw any of his people again.

Mostly he bummed around, but he told Lester that he always kept himself neat and clean so nobody would think he was a hobo. He looked for work, and he sometimes settled in at a place for three or four months and then he would move on. He got all the way to California, and, though he liked the climate, he did not care for the people. None of the ones he met seemed to be where they ought to be, and most of them were trying to pretend they were not from where they came from. They were from all over, from North Dakota and Arkansas and Tennessee, but they all told him that California was God's country and they hoped they never had to go back to where they came from.

"Me," said Rosco, "I didn't think their Hoovervilles beat the mountain shacks I knew back home, and back there we at least didn't have guards walking around the fruit groves like they did in God's country. Every other person you'd meet would ask if you was an Oakie, and I said I didn't know that I was but I would answer to that name as soon as I would to 'cracker,' which is what they called people from Georgia."

Rosco was in Norfolk, Virginia, when the war broke out, so he just stayed there and worked in the shipyards. After a spell, he went from unskilled to skilled and joined the union and almost got himself married. If he had done that, he would never have come to Kentucky and met Mama Pearl, or any of them. He named himself there, in Norfolk, Virginia, at the place where his girlfriend worked.

The woman Rosco nearly married was named Irma and was a waitress at what Rosco called a greasy-spoon and pick-up joint. One night in 1942, Rosco was sitting at the counter in the eating half of the Gypsy Bar and Grill. "The *gyppy* bar and grill?" interrupted Lester.

"No," said uncle Rosco. "Though the words *gyp* and *gypsy* are probably kin, I have known a good many gypsies in my time and I have not found that they are any more likely to try and cheat you than other folks. Where Irma worked was called the Gypsy Bar and Grill because they had these round glass globes, like crystal balls, on the tables, and all the girls wore headrags and big loop earrings."

"Was Irma a gypsy?" uncle Lester wanted to know.

"I guess not," said Rosco. "I never noticed any of them was able to see much into the future, least of all Irma."

That night in 1942, uncle Rosco was feeling blue. The war was not looking good—Things Looked Bad for Democracy. He did not know if or when he would be drafted, and he did not know how he felt about killing people even if he did know that God was on our side. He was waiting for Irma to get off work at midnight, and he hoped they would have a few laughs together and he would start to feeling better.

Business slowed down in the cafe, and Irma began horsing around, first with one fellow and then another. Then she began razzing Rosco about his name.

She introduced him to a fellow she said was Angelo ("But don't let *that* fool you," she said winking at Angelo), and then she said, "Angelo, this here is R.P. White. Just don't ask me what that R.P. stands for, or I may tell you."

The men at the counter all laughed, and some of them started making up things that R.P. could stand for, and, though he tried, Rosco could not make himself laugh, and he said he felt his face going redder and redder. Pretty soon what they were saying got bad enough that it bothered even Irma, so she broke in and told them what she had read in the *Reader's Digest* while she waited to get her hair fixed.

"It was in this part they call 'Humor in Uniform,'" she told them. "This hick from somewhere down South got drafted, and the sergeant told him to write down his full name—"

"It's a wonder he could write," Angelo said.

"He could write," Irma said, "but he didn't know what to do, because all he had was initials before his last name, which was Jones."

"What's wrong with that?" Rosco wanted to know, but nobody paid him any attention.

"Sooo," Irma concluded. "He wrote down R (only), P (only) Jones, and the next morning at roll-call, they called him Ronly Ponly Jones."

Everybody but Rosco screamed with laughter, Irma louder than anyone else. Then somebody called Rosco Ronly Ponly and they all laughed some more.

Rosco stood up then, and looked hard at Irma until she stopped laughing.

"My name is not Ronly Ponly or any of those other things you have been saying," he told them. He was going to say his name was R.P. White and what is wrong with that? but one of the men said, "If your name is not Ronly Ponly, then what is it?"

"Rosco," he said with sudden inspiration. "Rosco P. White."

He walked out of the Gypsy Bar and Grill then, and he never saw Irma again.

The next morning he signed on with the merchant marines and spent the next two years at sea. When the man in charge at the merchant marines gave him a form to fill out and told him to print his name in full, Rosco thought again of Private Ronly Ponly Jones. He stared at the sheet of paper for a minute, and the man said, "Go ahead. Put your full name right there on the page. Last name first, no initials."

Uncle Rosco said that he printed WHITE, ROSCO—and since he had never thought about what the *P*. could stand for, he wrote down PAGE. He was so pleased with his new name that he had his social security card changed, and, after he got out of the merchant marines, he went looking for Irma. He said he wanted to let her know who he was.

The short-order cook at the Gypsy Bar and Grill said he thought Irma had married somebody named Angelo, but somebody else said they didn't think so. And somebody else said the man Irma was living with might or might not be her husband, but she knew for certain that he was no angel— and, from the looks of Irma, she had found that out, too. The short-order cook said he had never noticed that Irma was what you could call perfect.

Uncle Rosco said, "What's in a name anyhow?"

At this point in the story, Lester would always scowl and say under his breath, "Plenty. There's plenty in a name."

One day Lester said it out loud. "There's plenty in a name," he told Rosco.

"If you had stayed R (only), P (only) White, Irma would have called you *that* all your life, and you would probably still be hanging around waiting for her to get off work and you would never have come to Kentucky and fallen in love with Mama Pearl, and we would never have known you or anything and we would not be a family."

Uncle Rosco thought hard about what Lester had said.

"Well," he said finally, "I just made up those names as I went along, but for a fellow making himself up, I guess I didn't do half bad, did I?"

He looked down over the barn and out to where the tobacco was yellowing in the field.

"Not half bad," he answered himself. "Let's go split some wood, so maybe we can have hot biscuits for supper."

Passing Through

Mama Pearl was out in the wild garden picking polk and lamb's quarters. The wild garden was behind the regular garden, and Mama Pearl spent a great deal of time there trying to get rid of the weeds and encouraging the herbs and edible plants. She kept it neater than most people's kitchen gardens, and uncle Rosco regularly cut a five-foot swath around it with his Snapper Mower. He strewed wood ashes and bloodmeal around both gardens to discourage the rabbits.

"Well, Rosco," Mama Pearl would say, "the rabbits are welcome to anything in the wild garden they want. I just wish you could find a way to keep the snakes out."

"Shoo," uncle Rosco said, "a few old blacksnakes never hurt anything yet." He was chicken-hearted and could not stand the thought of cutting up a snake, or anything else, with his mower. He would push the mower up and down for the longest time in order to give the snakes time to skee-daddle.

Mama Pearl wore work gloves and a big floppy straw hat.

Her navy-blue dress came down near her shoe tops and buttoned at her chin, but she looked cool despite the blazing sun. Her basket was long and deep. In the bottom of it, she had put six onions, a dozen beets, tops and all, and a double handful of parsley.

She took off one glove so she could pinch the polk greens. The polk bushes had not spindled up and gone to seed; her constant pinching made them spread out and produce dozens of tender green shoots. She would drop the polk into boiling water and later drain that water off before laying the lamb's quarters on top of the polk to steam.

Slow steaming, bacon fat, and vinegar—that was what made Mama Pearl's greens special. Uncle Rosco said her greens were guaranteed to grow hair on anybody's chest, and Lurline said that was why she left them alone, that and not wanting to corrode her insides.

When Mama Pearl finished in the wild garden, she would return to the kitchen garden for the biggest of the beefsteak tomatoes to add to the dozens already ripening in the kitchen window. She would cover her basket with a burdock leaf, for she did not want the greens to wilt before she washed them in spring water and put them in a colander to drain. She was in no hurry, for she had nothing else to do. The house was clean, the dishes were washed, and the garden didn't need weeding. Uncle Rosco told everybody that he would have to cultivate weeds next year if he meant to keep Pearl busy. Her garden was as innocent of unwanted growth as her person of adornment.

She had pinched only three polk bushes, and already the beet tops had disappeared under emerald-colored shoots. Mama Pearl set her basket down at the edge of a patch of fresh young lamb's quarters. The plants were only three or four inches high. This would be slower work, and she would need both hands. She took off the other glove and dropped both gloves where she could kneel on them while she picked.

Something moved in the grass near her, and Mama Pearl leaned forward to see. She knew that a snake had made the sound, but she wanted to see what kind of snake. She wished she had brought a hoe with her instead of the short-handled trowel she used to dig burdock roots out of her rhubarb stand.

The snake lay still as if watching her. It blended in almost perfectly with the grass and weed stalks drying near the ground. It was clearly not a blacksnake.

Somebody—Lester, she thought—had told her that snakes cannot hear but that they can feel the vibrations of movement. Kneeling on the ground, she slid her basket from beside her to a position between her and the snake. It drew its head back warily, its body tense; then, with a marvelous fluid motion, it melted from her sight briefly before reappearing and zigzagging across the cleared space and into the high weeds beyond.

A copperhead. It was a copperhead and her with nothing but a short trowel. Mama Pearl knew copperheads; she had seen them both dead and alive, but she had thought they preferred rocky places like crumbling foundations of abandoned or burnt-out houses and graveyards.

Uncle Rosco would not believe her. He would say it was a rat snake. He tried to make out that every snake in the county wore itself out eating rats for the express purpose of saving the corn crop. Mama Pearl knew better.

She began pinching the tops of the curly lamb's quarters.

She examined each one before pinching it, and shook it to look for bugs and worms. She knew all the bugs and worms were down in her kitchen garden gnawing away at her lettuce and beans, but she looked anyhow. Her knees began to ache.

She wondered if it were true, as she had heard, that if you saw one snake, there was bound to be another nearby. The idea troubled her, and she pushed her basket back and forth in front of her to warn anything that might be hidden there. She recalled hearing that if you killed a blacksnake and left it in the field, its mate would come to it.

Mate. She trembled at the word, and the green and silver leaves wavered before her like a troubled sea. She could not say all she wanted to know, but something in her wanted to know, at last, what terrible attraction drew One to Another. She wanted to understand what it was that tried to draw the survivor closer and closer to the dead.

She rubbed her eyes, and the lamb's quarters came back into focus. Whatever it was, perhaps instinct, she knew that she shared it with all living things, even snakes. It makes them pair off, she thought, for better or worse. And us, too.

She herself had had three mates, some better, some worse. Two of them were dead. The first had not drawn her close in life or in death. The other, as long as he lived, had made her want to leave behind what was familiar, to go where he was. But she never had.

That was why she had never married Rosco after all these years. She had always thought, "What if Wiley comes back?" and that prevented her. People thought she and Rosco were married, and that seemed good enough. Now, she wondered, though sometimes she felt they were married more than if they had stood up in church together the way she and Omer had. She had not married Rosco because she knew Wiley was out there somewhere. Now he had come home.

She and Rosco had gone that morning to Cedar Creek Baptist Church and had transplanted flowers from the yard to his grave. Together, they had leveled out the mound of dirt the gravediggers left. Mama Pearl placed the flowers, while Rosco cleared away weeds and brambles from the graves near uncle Wiley's. A large stone covered Omer's grave, leaving no room to plant flowers.

The space beside Omer (1863-1955), was for her. She wondered where Rosco would go, for there was no space nearby. She wondered if he had thought about that too.

Before supper, when the sun had gone down, Rosco would drive her back to the cemetery. They had put the garden hose in the car, so they could water the geraniums, the coleus, phlox, and lobelia they had set out. Mama Pearl had taken a black-eyed susan and put it near the head of Wiley's grave, for he used to call her his black-eyed Susan. He was no more than a boy then, and she was already Omer's bride, already silent and efficient in his sickroom.

Then as now, the black-eyed susans grew like weeds around the backsteps and reseeded themselves plentifully each year. The one she put on Wiley's grave stooped and wilted.

"Think it'll make it?" uncle Rosco asked.

"Well, if it doesn't," Mama Pearl said, "we'll just pull it up and set out another."

Mama Pearl was covering her basket with the burdock leaf when she spied Lester striking off through the deepest weeds. She waved her gloves at him, for she wanted to tell him to be careful of snakes. He took a few steps toward her.

"Lester," she called, "where do you think you're going in the worst heat of the day?"

"Snake-hunting," he said.

Mama Pearl's free hand flew to her top button, and she said what she had called him to say.

"Look out for snakes," she told him.

"I mean to," said uncle Lester. He held up a forked stick for her to see. He swung it into a gigantic milkweed, and the top slumped over, mortally wounded.

Mama Pearl watched Lester stalking across the field and wondered why on earth anybody wanted to go looking for snakes. She wished it was not Sunday and Lester was safe at work at the feed store in Gratz. She hoped he would not catch any snakes and that if he did, he would not bring them home. She wondered if the mates of the ones he caught would follow him into her yard, possibly to be caught or killed.

"You never can tell," she decided.

Mama Pearl and uncle Lester were on the back porch. She was peeling peaches, and he was turning the crank on the ice cream freezer. He did not turn the crank the way Audrey and Augie did, in spurts, but slowly and steadily as if he was grinding up all his enemies and knew they could not escape.

Erline had eaten supper with them again that night, and after they had eaten and Mama Pearl set out her knife and pans to peel the peaches, Erline said, "Wouldn't old-fashioned homemade ice cream be good?" When uncle Lester went off to find the freezer and salt and Audrey began reading the recipe out loud so she could memorize it and Augie began to cry because he could not help, Erline sat down to wait for the ice cream.

Mama Pearl had peeled and sliced a peck of the ripest peaches to go in the ice cream, and now she was almost through with the first bushel. She intended to cover the thin slices with sugar and let them stand overnight under a cheesecloth cover so she could get an early start canning them the next morning.

She still had a bushel to go, and pointed out that fact frequently. It did not occur to anyone to offer to help.

Uncle Rosco was watching Audrey and Augie play Old Maids, and Erline kept busy smoking Herbert Tareyton cigarettes. She sat halfway between the kitchen table, where the children were playing, and the open back door. That way everybody could hear whatever she had to say. Uncle Lester and Mama Pearl showed up as dark blobs against the early night sky. Erline could see fireflies beginning to spook about in the locust trees.

Erline shivered expressively and waited for uncle Rosco to ask what was wrong. He did not ask, even when she repeated the shiver, for he was annoyed that Erline had refused to play when the children suggested that the four of them play Rook. Uncle Rosco was a whiz at Rook, but the only card game Erline would play was bridge, though she did not understand yet how to keep score.

Actually, Erline had hinted that she did not think any kind of card game was appropriate So Soon Afterwards, but Mama Pearl gave her a look which clearly meant that she had better tend her own knitting and Erline shut up, for she did not particularly wish to discuss the events of the past few days. At least not with the family, though she had plenty to say to other people.

Erline told everybody in town that she would never understand Mama Pearl and uncle Rosco. She implied, without quite saying it, that she had more than one cause to thank the Lord-Nellie they were neither one of them blood-kin to her. They were both going on after uncle Wiley's death exactly as if nothing whatsoever had happened.

There was Mama Pearl peeling peaches as if she had to do it and wasn't about the richest person in Owen County. And uncle Rosco wouldn't even stay in the room if anybody as much as mentioned uncle Wiley. You'd think the two of them had killed uncle Wiley, or something, the way they dodged when you asked them a simple question like what were they going to do now they were rich.

It looked to Erline as if they weren't going to do anything now that they hadn't done before. That very day at the post office she had told May Evelyn and her husband Leroy that she—Erline Waters Grissom—would know how to act if she got up one fine day and found herself beneficiary to a rich man's estate.

For starters, she told them, she would trade in that old Chevrolet of hers on a sportscar, and before the ashtrays were full, she would be off to Europe, where she would go to a bullfight and get herself an audience with the Pope. She had hinted to Mama Pearl that, even without a new car, she would be willing to go to Europe and that while she was there, she would ask the Pope to pray for uncle Wiley. Mama Pearl had acted as if uncle Wiley was too good to need the Pope's prayers.

Lester was grinding away and staring at a point somewhere near the top of the pear trees. He looked as if it was just a matter of time before all his enemies would be gone. Mama Pearl regularly emptied a two-quart saucepan into the biggest pot she owned, and leaned over to get another lapful of peaches. That, and what Erline said to nobody in particular, was all the sound in the house. Erline stood it as long as she could.

"I wonder," said Erline, "what it's like—after death?"

Uncle Rosco grunted as if to say he hadn't given it much thought, and Audrey said she was going to quit playing Old Maids if Augie didn't quit cheating. Mama Pearl dropped a peach stone into the second largest pot she owned, and leaned over to get more peaches.

"When I meet my Maker," said Erline, warming to the topic, "I hope I'll be carrying my beads and just come from Holy Communion." She paused dramatically.

"I sure Lord don't want any mortal sin weighing me down," she said after a few seconds. "If I'd taken my own life," she quavered, "I just don't think I could face the Lord."

"Well," said Mama Pearl, "if you were dead, I don't guess you could help who you had to meet. You'd just meet whoever there was to meet you."

"Whoever there was to meet you—" Erline echoed. "You sound as if you don't think every last living one of us will have to face up to God on that Awful Day." She searched the darkness of the locust thicket for some satisfactory answer to Mama Pearl's unorthodox views.

Augie, who had seemed too busy cheating to listen, piped up and said he didn't see why Erline had to be dressed up, with beads and all, just to die, and Erline said for him to shut up or she would send him to bed without any ice cream. He told her she could not make him do anything and that he minded Mama Pearl and his own Mama, not her.

That shocked Erline. She forgot what she had started to

say, and she rolled her eyes at Lester until he said "Shut up, Augie" and Augie shut up.

"I don't see what's so Awful about it," Mama Pearl objected. She had a way of not hearing what she did not want to hear, and she spoke as if nothing had been said since Erline said what she did. "We live and we die," Mama Pearl said, "and when we die, we get a little rest for a change."

She eyed the second bushel of peaches.

"It's getting late," she said, "and I could use some rest right now."

Uncle Lester said that the ice cream was about ready and why didn't Augie go and get some bowls so they could eat it as soon as the crank got too hard for him to turn. Augie said why didn't Audrey go get the bowls, and before they could get warmed up arguing about who would get the bowls, uncle Rosco went to see what he could find for them to eat ice cream in.

"Lord knows what he'll come back with," Mama Pearl confided to the darkness, but Erline had taken off running again.

"A little rest, Pearl," she said patiently, "is not the same thing as Eternal Rest." She let that sink in.

"I'd be sorry to admit I'm a Waters," she told them, "if I thought you'd go and do like uncle Wiley. . . ."

Erline shivered again and crossed herself.

"I hope," she said, "that kind of thing doesn't run in families—like red hair and freckles." She regarded Augie and Audrey darkly.

"To take the life given you," she breathed, "must be the worst thing you can do to God."

Mama Pearl put down her paring knife, which clattered

onto the floor. She pushed the second bushel of peaches a little away from her.

"You can't *do* anything to God," she said flatly. "He does to us, and we have to take it because it's Him doing it."

She did not seem to be through, but no more words came. After a minute, she leaned over to pull the peach basket back toward her and reached under the porch glider for her knife.

"Pearl White," Erline exploded. "How *can* you—and in front of the children? Don't you have any religion whatsoever?"

Augie, who was supposed to be shuffling the cards, flipped the entire deck at Audrey and shouted "Fifty-two card pick up!" Audrey mouthed at him that he was a son-of-a-bitching bastard, and uncle Rosco came back from the china cabinet with six teensy little Japanese flowered dishes and asked would these do. Mama Pearl told the darkness that it was about what she expected, and dropped another peach pit into the second-largest pot.

The sound set Erline's teeth on edge; it seemed to sum up Mama Pearl's absolute indifference to things that matter.

"Nobody around here," she announced, "seems to have a single solitary thought about Things Eternal."

Mama Pearl glinted her eyes and told Erline that *her* religion was deep down and that she didn't need to talk about it all the time like *some* people she could name. That reminded uncle Rosco of the old fiddler at camp meeting who told the fellow trying to tune his guitar that if he didn't stop picking at it, it would never get well.

Erline stood up so fast she turned her chair over backwards. Uncle Rosco naturally thought he had said something wrong and began explaining the point of his story and who the old fiddler was—a black man named Will Living who still lived down on the bank of the Kentucky River and was famous for his fish fries. But Erline was not even listening. She had lately turned Catholic and she thought she knew who Mama Pearl was talking about and why she had made that particular remark.

Erline told Mama Pearl that some things were so deep down they never showed at all and you might as well not have them. She asked Mama Pearl if she had ever read the story about hiding your talents under a bushel, and Mama Pearl said Erline could just leave bushels out of the conversation, for she did not think her peeling peaches on a Sunday night had anything to do with the subject.

Erline went too far in what she said next; she said that anybody looking for anything deep down in a woman the size of Mama Pearl might just as well give up and go and do something useful and easy, like maybe looking for a pea in a featherbed.

"Or a pin in a haystack," said Augie.

"Or a brain in your head," said Audrey.

"Now, Augie. Now, Audrey," said Mama Pearl.

Erline looked wildly around her for her pocketbook, but all she could find was her cigarettes and lighter. Things seemed to have gone too far for her to back down, so she stood there blaring her eyes half out of her head and wishing Mama Pearl would look at her.

Uncle Rosco, who did not like excitement, decided what Erline was looking for and padded into the dining room to get her pocketbook for her. When he held it out to her, she clapped one hand to her mouth and smothered a little scream.

With the other hand, she flipped on the back porch light. That made Mama Pearl look at her.

All the crickets outside fell silent. Mama Pearl was still peeling the peach she held in her hand. Uncle Lester cranked away, more slowly and thoughtfully than ever, but as if nothing out of the ordinary had happened. Audrey slipped past Erline to go stand near Mama Pearl. She wanted to see what Mama Pearl would do.

Mama Pearl finished peeling the peach, dropping one long, continuous spiral of peel into her second-largest pot; then, with a smart twist of her hand, she cut into it and separated it from the stone. Audrey leaned closer to see.

"Yuk," said Audrey, "a worm."

"The ice cream's ready," said uncle Lester.

"I'll get the spoons," volunteered Augie.

"Well," said Erline, fumbling for her keys, "I never."

"Me either," said uncle Rosco, holding out a teensy Japanese flowered bowl to uncle Lester.

"Fill 'er up," he said.

Erline banged the screen door shut. "Some people!" They could have their old peach ice cream for all she cared. Actually, she did care; she had looked forward to that ice cream. It had been her idea to start with, and she would have stayed in a minute if anybody had asked her to.

Nobody did, not even Audrey.

She stared hard, at nothing in particular, to see if she could cry. Nothing happened, so she went to her car and got in. She felt very alone, abandoned. Maybe if she didn't leave too fast, Mama Pearl might follow her and try to make up.

Erline knew that if Mama Pearl gave her half a chance, she would break down and cry. She needed to try to explain why she had acted so ugly and what was bothering her. Unlike Mama Pearl, Erline liked to talk things *out*.

Believe you me, she told herself, there's a lot in this family to talk about. We never talk about anything until it's too late. Erline knew that some of what needed to be talked about would hurt her, but she thought anything would be better than pretending that what had happened hadn't happened. Erline didn't think she could live that way much longer.

She started the car and gunned the engine to give Mama Pearl one last chance. The front of the farmhouse remained dark. Erline would either have to go back in and eat humble pie, or go home and mess around filling time until she could go to bed. She inched toward the driveway.

Already the road was deserted. She sat and stared at the empty road until finally she saw distant headlights. She decided to wait for the car to pass.

Erline had never known uncle Wiley, but he was on her mind. She did not understand how Mama Pearl could write him off without so much as a word after all those years. It was clear to Erline, though she had no evidence for it, that uncle Wiley and Mama Pearl had been secret lovers. That must have been why uncle Wiley went off west, to Muleshoe, Texas. At the time, Mama Pearl had been married to uncle Omer, who had looked like he was never going to die, and when uncle Wiley finally wrote to her again, Mama Pearl had taken to living with uncle Rosco.

What a mess. Nothing turned out right for anybody. And now, uncle Rosco, who had competed, whether he knew it or not, with an Absent Hero all these years, would have to compete with a Ghost for what remained of his life. And Pearl would probably never marry him, just as Francis would never marry her. Erline would have given a pretty to know the details of Mama Pearl's love life, but her woman's instinct assured her of the truth of the main lines.

A VW van, its muffler shot, choked past Erline. Her headlights picked up its psychedelic designs. Hippies, thought Erline. They all seemed to find Owen County sooner or later, and half of them stayed. She had told Mama Pearl that half the hippies living together in little rented shacks weren't married—at least not to each other. Uncle Rosco had started blushing and had to leave the kitchen with a coughing fit. Erline hadn't meant to say anything wrong, and she colored up too, but Mama Pearl was just as cool as you please.

"Well, Erline," she said, "maybe they are not ready for marriage. Maybe they are waiting for something."

That was just like Mama Pearl. Some things she would not name, or even admit the existence of.

Erline pulled out onto the road. She was sorry now she had let the other car get in front of her. She would have to poke along behind it all the way home. Maybe she had been waiting for something to happen, but, as usual, nothing did.

Erline's beauty shop, which doubled as her living-quarters, was on the other side of Gratz, across the road from the sawmill and a quarter mile from the quarry. She lived in what passed for the town's outskirts.

She was moving up on the VW van. Impatiently, she flicked her lights from bright to dim and back to bright by way of warning that she intended to pass. She read the license plate (New York State, hippies for sure) and the bumper stickers.

The bumper sticker on one side asked "Have You Hugged

Your Kids Today?" and the other simply said "Passing Through."

Erline groaned. "You can't forget a blessed thing a solitary minute," she told herself.

She did not recall when she had last hugged Audrey, though she must surely have done so at some time. Audrey was all elbows and teeth and eyes, and Erline did not want to hug her even if she could get close enough to try. Audrey was always squinting at people—studying them, she said, for character traits.

Everything lately seemed to make Erline think about death, though she tried to avoid the subject. She was scared stiff, now that she had begun to think about the difference between dying and being dead. Dying was what people did in the movies, but when they were shot or died of something dreadful, it meant something and you knew that you would see the same Star dying of something different next week.

Being dead was not like that. It did not have to mean anything. It just was. Thinking about being dead excited Erline and made her want to do crazy things just to prove that she was alive.

If she was passing through, she wished that she had come equipped with credit cards.

At the first "Pass With Care" sign, Erline lurched around the VW van. No sooner had she done so than she saw the oncoming car. She got back in line in front of the van just seconds before the eight-cylinder Impala swooshed into the darkness from which she had come. She breathed heavily, realizing how close she had come to hitting the other car.

She had been driving too fast, and so had the driver of the

other car. But if they had hit, the people in the VW would have been wiped out too. How many people would have died? And what would it have meant? She knew the Impala. It belonged to a schoolteacher who called himself farming the acres Mama Pearl's family used to own. She wondered what he was thinking about right now, and how he felt about the idea of being dead. For good.

The VW was tailgaiting her, and the driver was blowing his horn repeatedly as if trying to beat out some rhythm. What could the damn fool want? Erline speeded up; heroically, the VW kept up, still tooting away. —Of course, Erline knew what the horn-blowing was about. The idiot had seen her bumper sticker, which said "Honk If You Love Jesus." It had come with the car.

She blew her own horn savagely, almost blasphemously, and told herself it was not Jesus's fault at all. She pushed her car to sixty, though the roadside signs specified forty-five, and the VW van fell behind; even when she could no longer see its shape, only the glare of its headlights, she could hear the horn. It lapsed finally into a kind of gargling, reminding Erline of someone deathly sick, trying to catch their breath and throw up at the same time.

The drive was short, but Erline could not make it even three miles without a Herbert Tareyton. Besides, all that honking had unnerved her, to say nothing of the brush with death. She pushed in the cigarette lighter and found her pack. Three left. She lit one, and decided to drive to Monterey for more. For all she knew a customer might show up at her shop for a shampoo and set the next morning and she'd be caught without cigarettes.

Now that she was the talk of the county, she expected business to pick up. A few old biddies, and a few young ones too, would come to her shop and try to pump her.

Let them, she told herself. Fat lot of good it would do them. She wasn't saying anything to anybody about what had happened at the funeral home the night uncle Wiley lay in state. None of their business.

She slowed down at the bridge leading into Gratz, and thought about the stories she had heard about pirates on Severn Creek. They would hide out in the creek waiting for river traffic and then swoop down on whatever boat came along and take everything of value. Sometimes, they disappeared on the creek for days and days. What a life, Erline would always say.

People used to say that Hatton Cobbs might have been a pirate when he was young, but Erline did not believe Hatton had ever been young. And now Hatton was dead. Of an ulcer. The only real riverman she had ever known. Erline used to dream about floating down the Kentucky River on a barge, sitting out on the open deck in summer and inside, next to an oil-drum stove, in winter.

She still liked to watch the barges and the wake they left behind, but she was thirty-four years old and had never been on any kind of boat, summer or winter.

The houses in Gratz were dark. A group of men and boys leaned against a pickup truck at the Gulf Station, but otherwise nothing was doing in Gratz. She passed her house. The way she'd left the lights on made it look like someone was there. Mama Pearl would expect her to call as soon as she got home, but she had no intention to do so. Mama Pearl could just stew a little.

If the Monterey Cafe was closed, she would drive on to Frankfort. That should give Mama Pearl time to work up a good worry. In a few minutes, Mama Pearl would start calling. Maybe she'd have to break down and leave a message with Erline's Ansafone. Thus far, Mama Pearl had refused to leave a message though Erline had had her Ansafone for over two months. Mama Pearl said she would not talk to a machine even if it did sound like Erline.

Erline was half a mind to discontinue her Ansafone Service. She had let Francis talk her into getting it, for he said he wanted her to know he was thinking of her even if she was not at home when he called. Francis said he had got his Ansafone so his mother, who was deaf, would not have to answer the phone. When Erline called him, the phone did not ring; it just kind of clicked, and then Francis (or the recorded Francis) would identify himself and say for whoever was calling to leave a message when the recorder beeped. Erline always wondered what the old lady, Francis's mother, was doing.

Francis carried a little pocket radio with him that was supposed to beep whenever he got a call. He said that no matter where he was, he would know when somebody—Erline, for instance—was trying to reach him. They tried it out one night at Erline's. She dialed his number, and he held the radio to wait for it to beep. The recorded Francis answered at once, but the radio didn't beep. Francis said Gratz was probably outside his radio range, and as it turned out, Francis was out of Erline's range.

Francis told Erline that he used his Ansaphone strictly for business before meeting her, but Erline had later told him that she thought all his business was Monkey Business. That was after she learned the truth and again gave up men forever.

Erline had met Francis at a retreat at Gethsemane, and almost exactly three glorious weeks later she had learned that what he was retreating from was a wife and four kids. That had taken the air out of her sails and she no longer knew what to believe. He had told her he was an ex-priest and had never felt that way about a woman before.

He said that when the Pope began to open the windows of the Church, all kinds of things had flown in and he decided to fly out, but that he knew that he was still a priest deep down. Once a priest, always a priest, Francis had told her.

Francis said his Church had changed so much he could no longer remain a priest, but that he was determined to live and die a good Catholic. He said it was the least he could do for his mother. Erline asked him what was the difference between being married and—doing what they had done. She could not say it out loud but Francis knew what she meant, for they had just done it. Francis told her they could both confess what they had done, but that he, for one, could not profane the Holy Sacrament of Matrimony, for not only was he an ex-priest, but she was divorced.

Finally, Erline decided she was so happy it didn't matter that they could not be married, but she got pretty sick and tired of talking to Ansafone all the time. She would probably still be talking to Ansafone, if she had not lost Francis' telephone number and called long-distance information in Frankfort.

The number she got did not sound familiar, but she dialed it anyhow. Instead of recorded Francis, a woman answered. A young woman.

Erline asked for Francis X. Lighter, and the woman said he was not home and what was new.

Erline was certain there was a mistake, and asked, very distinctly and properly, was this the residence of Francis X. Lighter, the developer. Francis had told her he speculated in land which he sold to builders of subdivisions and that he sometimes invested in the subdivisions themselves.

When Erline said Francis X. Lighter, the Developer, the woman on the phone laughed an ugly laugh.

"Some of the Developer's developments are crying, honey, and I can't talk, but my advice to you is to forget whatever he's trying to develop with you."

Erline gasped.

"And if it's already developing, forget it anyhow. He's got four already and one on the way, and, as God is my witness, you're not getting a dime."

Then, she hung up.

Erline was wild. She called the information operator and tried to get an address, but the operator, one of those prim and proper types, would only say "Sorry. That is against reguLAtions." "Hell," said Erline, "what isn't?"

She dialed the number again, and again the woman answered. This time, she laid the phone down and went about her business, which seemed mostly to involve yelling at the kids. A television or radio was playing. Once a child picked up the phone and mumbled something. Erline tried yelling, and when that failed, she cried awhile; then she heard Francis' voice in all the racket. He picked up the phone, said "Hello" once or twice, and hung up.

Erline told herself her world had collapsed. She drove to Mama Pearl's instantly, and Mama Pearl put her to bed with cold cloths on her forehead, and when she woke up, everyone was solemn and whispering because uncle Wiley was dead. Erline told herself that Francis and uncle Wiley died at the same time, and the only difference was that uncle Wiley had the consideration to be buried.

Not Francis—he showed up at the funeral home, and when Erline saw him, she just about went crazy. She threw a good-sized gardenia at him and missed. She tried to throw him out of the funeral parlor, but later when the undertakers tried to get him to leave, she took his side. The next day at the funeral, one of the undertaker's assistants had fingernail scratches all over him. Everytime Erline moved, he skipped out of reach.

Erline guessed everybody was talking about her—everybody but Mama Pearl. Only Mama Pearl would refuse to talk. She would store it all up to use against Erline. And Mama Pearl knew more than anybody else.

Everybody at the funeral home that night knew that Erline ended up leaving with the same man she had thrown the gardenia at, and everybody who wasn't there had heard it by midnight that same night. But Mama Pearl knew what time Erline had come home, for Erline had left her car and clothes at Mama Pearl's and meant to spend the night there. As it turned out, she got to Mama Pearl's just about in time to get up and dress for the funeral.

Erline did not slow down in Monterey to see if the cafe was open. She was headed for Frankfort. She had an address now. At the very least, she meant to get a look at his house and see the woman. If Francis was there, why so much the better.

Mama Pearl came back upstairs from answering the phone and told uncle Rosco he had to get up and go to Frankfort and identify Erline. It was after midnight.

"Why?" asked uncle Rosco. "Is Erline dead too?"

Mama Pearl explained that Erline was not dead and that she was not *exactly* under arrest, but there had been some trouble. The police would not believe who Erline said she was, though she had told them they could look up her telephone number and call it and hear her very own voice on the Ansafone. The police said that Ansafone was not admissible as evidence.

Mama Pearl had not asked what Erline was doing in Frankfort or why the police wanted to know who she was. She knew that Erline would just get mad and hang up or something, and uncle Rosco would have to go to Frankfort anyhow.

All she said was "Well, Erline, how will Rosco find the police station in a town the size of Frankfort?" and that was enough to make Erline mad.

"Tell him to drive down Main Street sixty miles an hour," she said, "and the cops will show him where the station is."

Just on a hunch, uncle Rosco took a peek into Lester's room. Somehow, he was not surprised to discover Lester was not there. He decided that what Pearl did not know wouldn't hurt her. Augie and Audrey were in bed, and uncle Rosco decided Lester hadn't gone off to spring his sister Lurline from the Women's Detention Center as he and Augie had planned to do.

The night was misty and chilly. A barge was blowing its whistle when uncle Rosco crossed the bridge into Gratz. He was driving slow, for he hoped to see Lester walking home. Somebody was standing at the intersection of highway 22 and highway 253. It was Lester.

Uncle Rosco stopped the car, and the boy got in silently. Neither of them said anything for over a mile. Lester was clearly uncomfortable.

"Where you going?" he asked finally. "If you come looking for me, you've found me and we can go back home." When uncle Rosco said nothing, he repeated, "Now you've found me, why don't we turn around and go home?"

Uncle Rosco explained where he was going and why.

"That's where I was going," Lester said, "to Frankfort—to get even with Francis X. Lighter."

"Francis who?" uncle Rosco said.

"Lighter," repeated Lester. "Francis X. Lighter—the man who jilted Erline."

"Oh," said uncle Rosco. "What did you mean to do?"

"I don't know," admitted Lester. "I already used the snakes."

"What snakes?" asked Rosco.

"The ones I caught," Lester said wearily, as if anybody ought to know what snakes.

"How—?" uncle Rosco hesitated. "How did you use them?"

"Turned them loose in the Holiness Church," said Lester. "The door was open when I got there, and I left it open when I left. The snakes can leave if they want to."

Uncle Rosco groaned.

"What kind of snakes?"

"Good snakes. Ones they like. Copperheads, I hope."

They were coming into Monterey. Seventeen more miles

to Frankfort. Uncle Rosco felt pulled in both directions. All that kept him headed toward Frankfort was that he did not know what he could do about copperheads in the Holiness Church.

"What made you do a thing like that?" he asked. It was not a reprimand; he just wanted to know.

"I don't think I want to tell you," said Lester. "Besides, I told you I left the door open. The snakes can leave if they want to. Their preacher asked me once could he buy some good rattlers or copperheads. These were free. He should of known the best you can do around here is copperheads."

Uncle Rosco nodded. Even a Holiness preacher ought to know there were no rattlesnakes in Owen County.

Near Swallowfield, uncle Rosco asked again, as if the question had just come to him, why uncle Lester would go and do a thing like turning a bunch of snakes loose in a church.

"It wasn't a bunch," said Lester matter-of-factly. "It was two, all I could find." The way he said it, Rosco knew he had tried hard to find more.

At Peak's Mill, with seven miles to go, Lester said, "They've got no business praying for you and Mama Pearl. It's none of their business. What right have they got?"

"I see," said uncle Rosco.

They found the police station easy. Erline's car was parked right out front.

They saw Erline through the big front windows. Maybe she was not under arrest, but every policeman in Frankfort was watching her. She seemed to be having the time of her life.

"Oh," she said, "hi, there" when uncle Rosco and Lester came in. She made it sound as if they had just happened to bump into each other. One of the cops was trying to find out where she lived and she was saying over and over "Wouldn't you like to know?" The policeman said he sure would like to know, and if she wouldn't tell him, he'd just have to look it up in the records.

"What record?" Erline blared. "That nice officer, the Captain over there, said there wouldn't be any record."

The desk sergeant grinned and shook his head; you could tell he liked Erline's horsing around. Then he saw Rosco and Lester and nodded for them to come to the desk. Rosco pushed Lester before him, so Lester would have to do the talking. He thought it would be a whole lot easier for Lester to explain his relationship to Erline than it would be for him. Rosco wasn't sure he understood himself how he was related to Erline, or whether he was kin to her. He had wondered all the way to Frankfort what good it would do for him to tell the police he lived with Erline's great-aunt by marriage. All Lester had to do was say he was Erline's brother and this was his and her uncle.

After Lester said that, the desk sergeant said Erline could go if she wanted to. All she had to do was pay the tow charges on her car. Erline bristled and told everybody in earshot that she never asked no police to come and tow her car to the station. "If I'd wanted it here," she said, "I could of driven it here, if I'd had a chance."

Nobody said anything, and Erline struck up again.

"You mean that's all there is to it?" she demanded. "Lester and Rosco waltz in here and say who I am and I can go— AFTER you've detained me UNLAWFULLY for two hours?" Uncle Rosco told himself Erline was hitting her passing gear, and that he wouldn't be surprised if they paid her to leave.

She whipped a little handkerchief from her dress front, but she got so interested in what she was saying that she forgot to use it. "All I was doing," she said, eyes wide and innocent, "was waiting for my friend Francis to come home, and your—your—HOODLUMS all but arrest me, haul my car off, put me in a squad car—I have NEVER been in a squad car before—, and I'm supposed—meekly, I guess—to pay up for the honor of your company and let bygones be bygones?"

The way she said *Francis* made it sound like a woman's name, and the way she said that about bygones made it sound like she intended to sue everybody there. The desk sergeant was getting worried, and he said if it was that simple why didn't she call her friend Francis and save her kin folks the trip to town?

Erline saw her chance.

"Call Francis—?" she demanded. "Don't you think it's humiliating enough for my own little brother and my uncle Rosco and aunt Pearl to know I was practically arrested, without broadcasting it to everyone I know?" She told them her civil rights had been violated, and that she thought it was a sorry pass in the land of the free and the home of the brave, when any crowd of communists, of every color imaginable, got police protection, and a poor girl from just across the county line could not come to her own state capitol without being arrested and insulted to boot.

The policemen were clearly on her side, and the desk sergeant decided to give up. He said it looked to him like some of his men had made a mistake and why didn't he tear up that tow ticket and give Erline her car keys. She must be tired, the sergeant said, and he for one wanted to do everything he could to make her understand that the police of America were on her side.

Erline took her car keys from him as if she was doing him a favor, and uncle Rosco put his wallet away. He had been holding it up for the desk sergeant to see so that he would know that he was ready and willing to pay the tow fine.

Erline told the room in general that they just might hear from her yet, and the young cop grinned at her to let her know he wouldn't mind that at all. They got to the door, and, mostly for the young cop's benefit, Erline turned and said, "If you're ever in Gratz, Kentucky, don't expect any favors from Erline Waters Grissom."

Outside, Erline announced that she had had a TERRIBLE experience and was ABsolutely EXhausted. She said why couldn't Lester drive her home, but Rosco said he and Lester had something to discuss, and Erline better come on out to the house and see Pearl, for he imagined they had a thing or two to discuss also.

"Why, Rosco," said Erline, "you make it sound so AWFUL. All I did was drive by this friend's house—you remember Francis, a man I used to be interested in—and wait for him to come home. Somebody saw me and decided I was a thief-by-night, or Lord knows what and called the police."

"That's all," she concluded airily. "Just some nervous old woman, and ALL this trouble." She did not add that the woman who called was Francis' wife, or that Francis himself had come home just as the police were making her get in the squad car. She did not know if she was madder at Francis

for staying out so late (she wondered who with) or for standing there staring at her and doing nothing.

"You better come by the house anyway," said uncle Rosco.
"You tell it better than I could."

Erline sniffed and crawled in her car.

"I'll go first," said uncle Rosco. "You follow."

"See you around," Erline sang out and tooted her horn before doing a U-turn and scratching off in the direction of
Gratz. The policemen inside the station cheered.

Erline's car was parked in its usual place when Rosco and
Lester got home. They had not decided exactly what to do
about the snakes, but they had decided against 1) poking
around in a dark church looking for copperheads and 2)
turning on the lights and being arrested for church-breaking.
Maybe the next day they could go look, and, if anybody saw
them, they could say that Lester had seen a snake crawl into
the church.

Uncle Lester thought of the lie first, but uncle Rosco said
it first.

"Imagine old Mr. Hightower reaching for the song book
and pulling out a snake," said uncle Lester when they drove
past the church. His mouth twisted to stop a smile.

"How big was they?" Uncle Rosco asked, as if he needed
an exact size in order to imagine the enormity of Mr. Hightower's surprise.

Lester measured an indeterminate length in the air.

"Copperheads don't get very big," he said. "They don't
need to."

They found Mama Pearl and Erline settled down in the
kitchen drinking coffee as if that were the most natural thing

in the world to do at 3 A.M. Erline was smoking a Herbert Tareyton and telling Mama Pearl about one of the policemen she had met.

"He had on a name tag," she said, "and I'll bet I can get his number from Information." She puffed thoughtfully. "Maybe I'll check him out in the City Directory," she said. "It's supposed to give address, occupation, everything—even marital status."

Mama Pearl said that was a good idea, and Erline said she wasn't likely to put her hand in the same fire twice.

Mama Pearl blinked when she saw Lester, but uncle Rosco said he had found Lester walking back from Erline's where he had gone looking for her. The look Lester gave uncle Rosco meant that he had caught him in two lies in one night, and that he hadn't even thought of that one yet.

"Well," Mama Pearl said, "who is ready for breakfast?"

Lurline wrote from the Women's Detention Center that God had reached out and touched her and she would never be the same. Erline said, "Thank God for that," and Augie asked where God had touched her. "Where?" he asked urgently. "Where?"

Mama Pearl leaned over the page to see if Lurline had told where God touched her. By the time she found what she was looking for, Augie was crying about what Erline had said and because he wanted his mother to be just like he remembered her. He said Erline was hateful, and he knew what he would change her into if he had half a chance.

"Here," Mama Pearl comforted. "Here it is. You stop crying, Augie, and I'll read it to you."

After a while, she read it anyhow: "God has reached out and touched me and I will never be the same."

"You read that already," Augie complained.

"I'm getting to it," said Mama Pearl. "She says, 'It was between Goshen and Pee-Wee Valley (that's where the Detention Center is) that it happened.' There, Augie, He touched her between Goshen and Pee-Wee Valley."

"But where on *her* did God touch her?" Augie demanded, beginning to cloud up again.

"In the heart, I guess," said uncle Lester, who was squatting behind the woodstove. He had stacked the stovewood he had split the night before, and the woodbox looked like a picture out of a geometry book.

Lurline's letter had got uncle Rosco in trouble, for he had taken it out of the mailbox and later forgot he had put it in his back pocket. He was not sure what day it had come, but Erline wrinkled her nose and said from the smell of it he had been sweating on it at least a week. Mama Pearl frowned at uncle Rosco and asked when did he last change his pants, and he colored up and took to coughing so bad uncle Lester had to whack him on the back.

"Never mind, Rosco," Mama Pearl kept saying, and uncle Lester went to find the magnifying glass to see if they could figure out the parts which were too blurred for the naked eye.

The part about God touching her between Goshen and Pee-Wee Valley was clear as anything, but they could not read the most important part. She wrote that she would be coming home to visit, and that she expected everybody to put the little pot in the big pot for the occasion. ("Huh?" said Augie. "Put the what . . . ?"

The sentence saying what day she would come was the biggest mess of all. They could not be sure even of the month, though they thought it was July. Lester said the date had two

95

numbers in it, and Erline said, "Great, that can be anything from the tenth to the thirty-first."

Uncle Rosco said he did not think July *had* thirty-one days, and Erline began trying to remember the rhyme everyone learns in school. She did not get very far before Augie finished it up for her. "Everybody knows *that*," he said triumphantly. Erline looked fit to be tied. "Rosco didn't," she said sourly.

Uncle Rosco had caught cold out in the night air when he went to Frankfort to identify Erline and had a sneezing fit when he came indoors. He had reached into his back pocket for a handkerchief and pulled out the letter. Mama Pearl like to have let the bacon scorch while she puzzled over it.

Uncle Lester said that if they would read slow, he would type out what Lurline said and leave blanks for the words they couldn't make out. Audrey said there was no need for that; she would just memorize the letter as they went along.

Audrey said that how many days were in July had nothing to do with anything. "We know she's coming on a weekend," Audrey said, "so all we have to do is make sure the little pot's in the big pot every weekend until she shows up."

Uncle Rosco looked as if he was about to get up and go look for the little pot, but Erline said her sister was just using an old expression which meant having a celebration. "Huh?" said Augie. "That's dumb. Are you sure that's what it means?"

Uncle Lester nodded, and said vaguely, "It comes from the African."

"Huh?" said Erline staring at uncle Lester as if she had never seen him before. Then, she came to herself and said everybody knew that was what it meant and that she, for one, had never said that what *her* mama said was dumb and Augie had better look out. She said that she wanted to be ready for her only sister's homecoming. To do so, she said, they had to know when Lurline was coming, and wise-mouthed kids were not helping very much.

"Maybe," said uncle Lester, "she wrote 'the week of,' not 'the weekend.' That's what it looked like to me—through the looking glass—'the week of.'"

Erline and Mama Pearl huddled over the letter, sharing the magnifying glass.

"Well, Lester," said Mama Pearl at length, "it could be 'the week of July 16.'" Horror struck her. "She may be on the way home this very instant," she said, "for today is Monday, July 16."

"Where do you keep the fatted calf?" asked Erline spitefully.

"Well," said Mama Pearl, "Lurline always favored chicken, and if she wants beef, Rosco will just have to drive to Owenton for it." Rosco hitched forward in his chair to indicate his willingness to head for Owenton on a moment's notice.

Augie had gone to the living room and was kneeling on the sofa looking out the window. When Audrey followed and asked what he was doing, he said he was waiting for his Mama to come home. Audrey went back to the kitchen and told the others.

"Poor baby," said Mama Pearl.

"There'll be no living with him," said Erline. "What we'll do," she added brightly, "is call the Women's Detention Center and ask *them* when Lurline is coming. *They* ought to know." Everyone turned and stared at the telephone, but no one got up to call.

"Read it all the way through again," uncle Lester said after a while. "We may have missed something the other times."

"There's no need," chirped Audrey. "I have memorized it all, even the blurs. Ready?"

Audrey recited while Mama Pearl followed.

"Dear Pearl, Rosco, Lester, Audrey, and most of all, Dear, Dear Augie," she began in her schoolteacher, persnickety voice Augie hated. "It has been one whale of a week for me; there was a time I would have said something other than 'one whale of a week,' but all that is past, and I am a different person."

Augie came back from the living room and said Audrey had to start over, for he wished to hear the part about "Dear, Dear Augie." Without arguing, Audrey said it again but so fast that the words all ran together, and Augie said that was no fair, she hadn't read it that way before. Mama Pearl pulled him into her lap and he settled down to listen.

"You know," Audrey continued in her best expressive manner, "I have been made a trusty, and, to start with, I took advantage of that so I could sneak off to the pizza parlor I called you from that night, and raise a little cain."

"I thought that sounded like a rough place," remarked Mama Pearl. "A road tavern."

"Oh, good grief," said Erline.

"Go on, Audrey," said uncle Lester.

"Thank you," said Audrey.

"Last Thursday I drove one of the guards home to Goshen, Ky. He was my so-called friend, but on the way from the Center, he got out of line (if you know what I mean), and when I told him where he could go and what he could do (Remember—that was *before* I changed!), he said he could make it hot for me. I almost changed my mind then, for I en-joy being a trusty and like driving that new car around, but when I let him out at this little run-down shack with a bunch of kids (absolutely RUNNING WILD) and a wife big as the side of a barn with Another One, the sixth I believe, I knew I had done right."

"Poor thing," said Erline, "He's probably as unhappy as Francis, but women don't go and make men marry and we don't make them stay married either."

Mama Pearl said with all those children, much less with one on the way, he ought to *stay* married, and Erline blared her eyes as if to say Mama Pearl did not understand men at all.

"God has reached out and touched me," Audrey resumed.

"I've already heard that," said Augie. "Twice."

"And I will never be the same," Audrey chanted, glaring at Augie. "It was between Goshen and Pee-Wee Valley (where the Center is) that it happened. I felt so bad when I left Clyde at that Awful Place, I picked up a hitchhiker, which is strictly against the rules, and he made it happen."

Audrey paused for effect, and Mama Pearl, thinking Audrey had forgotten the rest, took it up and began to read:

"I was listening to the country and western station out of Louisville—too bad you can't get it out there at Gratz, it's great, and there's a dee-jay called Brother Love—when I saw this tall, gawky fellow with a guitar and a knapsack. He held up his thumb for . . ."

Smooth as a whistle, Audrey broke in,

". . . a ride. At first I passed him up, but something made me stop down the road. He come running up like he was good for maybe twenty more miles. He wasn't as puny as he looked to start with. He stood there looking at me, and I took the chance to look him up and down. After a minute, he said 'You look okay, but I won't get in unless you turn off that radio.' 'Who asked you?' I said, but I turned the radio off. 'And put out that cigarette,' he said, and, before I thought twice, I'd done it. 'Anything else?' I asked, sarcastic like. 'Yes'm,' he said, 'you could button up that shirt a little higher.' When I'd done that, he got in and began talking."

After a while, he shifted around until he got his guitar out of the case and began strumming on it. It was all Sacred Music. Then he sung for me; the sounds that came out of that man, it was enough to break your heart."

"Haven't there been any blurs yet?" asked Augie.

"Yes," said Audrey, "but I have put in the words, for they were obvious. Lurline says that directly the man with the guitar 'started to fiddle with the blank blank and asked me what blank it was'—Do you get that, Augie?" Audrey simpered.

"'When I told him it was five after seven, he said he was glad it was no later, for there was still time. The way he said that made my blood run cold. Time for what, I said. He told me I was in for a treat if my soul was ready and he turned on the radio."

"I know what those blanks were, Smartie," said Augie. "Don't I, Mama Pearl?"

Lurline wrote that what was on the radio turned out to be an evangelist from Waddy, Kentucky, who said he hadn't studied at any seminaries and couldn't speak any foreign languages. He said God's Message, the Good News, was enough learning for him and the language of the Bible, good old English, was all he needed. He said he could get through to any man, woman or child irregardless of their language, race, or national origin, and they would know what he said.

His name was Brother John, and he said his name put some people in mind of the Catholics and that was just all right with him, for Some of That Persuasion had been good men and women, especially the martyrs. He said children he knew had learned to play a little tune on the piano about Brother John, which they called *Frère Jacques* in the French tongue; he sung some of it, and Lurline remembered she could once pick it out on the piano.

He said he was like the Watchman in the Night, trying to find out who was sleeping and wake them up in time. He said he was a Voice Crying in the Wilderness. "Are you sleeping?" he asked.

Lurline wrote that when Brother John said that about the wilderness, she looked out the car window at the empty road and all she saw was one big wilderness. She thought of the Women's Detention Center where she was going, and it was worse. She realized she was just rushing through one wilderness to get to another one.

She pulled the car off the road and sat there staring at the wilderness outside. She had never felt more awake in her life, but she wasn't sure she liked it. She looked at the man with the guitar (she did not even know his name) to find out what to do. He told her to lay her hand on the radio and renounce her sins.

Afterwards, the man with the guitar, whose name turned out to be Wilburn, told her he would help her if she stumbled. He said he had been sent to her, and already, Lurline wrote, they were swapping letters. She had written him about being allowed to go home for a visit, and he had said he would meet her at Mama Pearl's.

"Isn't that lucky," she wrote, "for that way all of you can have the benefit of what I just stumbled into."

"Where will the man with the guitar sleep?" asked Augie, and before anybody could answer, he said, "Not in my room."

Audrey said it didn't sound like he would need a room, if he didn't ever go to sleep, and he'd probably keep everybody awake prowling around to keep watch.

"There's always room at my place," offered Erline.

"I've almost done," said Audrey. "Do you want to hear the rest or not?"

"Why not," grumbled uncle Rosco, who was more than half asleep. "We have spent the day with that little bitty letter and might as well finish it off in time for supper."

"The part so hard to read comes next," said Audrey, and Mama Pearl nodded and frowned at uncle Rosco who was to blame. "'Like a blank out of the blue,'" Audrey recited, adding matter-of-factly, "That must be *bolt,* 'I was called in to see the woman who would be the warden if this was a jail and not a Detention Center. She told me that I had *blank blank blanked* the responsibilities *blank* and I could now go home—lots of blanks at the bottom where uncle Rosco sat on the letter—and I picked the blank of blank.' That's the part that may be 'week of' or 'weekend.'"

Audrey took the letter from Mama Pearl and turned to the last page. "At the end," Audrey told them, "she says 'See you Blank,' with about a dozen exclamation points. It looks like Tuesday, or it could be Thursday."

Mama Pearl put down the magnifying glass. "You never

know when anything will happen until it does," she said, "and then, most likely, it's too late."

"Let's skip the part about the old Mexican woman," said Audrey, though everybody could tell she was dying to recite the whole letter. "All it says," she paraphrased before anybody could say anything, "is that Lurline began to have doubts about Brother John and decided to test him. She says Wilburn warned her the devil would not let her rest, and so she was prepared. She listened to Brother John on her Philco transistor radio and got it all down on her Sony tape recorder. She remembered what he said about being able to talk to anybody irregardless of language, so she tried it out on Rosie."

"Who's Rosie?" said Augie. "She's not coming here too, is she?"

"There's no telling," said Mama Pearl weakly. "The Lord knows who all your Mama will bring in on us. Or when they'll get here."

"I wonder is Brother John a Holiness preacher," mused uncle Lester. He was studying the dial of the kitchen radio trying to decide where Brother John and Waddy, Ky., might be.

"More likely a Jehovah's Witness," said Erline. "Didn't you hear that about keeping watch? They'll probably build a watchtower right here, if we let them."

What Lurline had done was play a tape of Brother John to Rosie, an old Mexican woman whose family had left her in Indiana when they finished picking vegetables and went back where they came from. She had somehow got to Louisville, and got herself arrested for armed robbery when she tried to get away with a bottle of Tequila. Lurline said the gun she waved at the liquor store clerk was rusty and wouldn't shoot, but that Rosie was given time anyhow. She said it was a "rotten shame" and "went to show that God had planned it all out and Rosie was part of His plan."

Audrey stopped short. "Huh?" she said.

She had been so busy memorizing what Lurline wrote and trying to fill in the blanks, she had not thought much about what most of the letter said.

"Does Lurline mean God *wanted* that old woman to go to prison and that He put her there just so Lurline could play a dumb old tape recording to her?" Audrey shook her head.

"My Mama is not in prison," wailed Augie. "She's in the Women's Detention Center. You read it yourself, Audrey."

"You know what 'detention' means, stupid?" asked Audrey.

When Lurline played the tape recording to Rosie, the old woman sat smiling and nodding as if she understood. She always did that, Lurline wrote, no matter what anybody said to her. But then, Lurline said, "She took to twitching and shaking and fell out of her chair and thrashed around. A guard had to come in and prise her mouth open so she would not bite her tongue clean off."

Lurline wrote that she had never seen anything to beat how that old woman took on, and she guessed it was the Spirit did it. "That proves it," she added triumphantly, "for Rosie cannot understand more than two or three words of our lingo."

"It sounds to me like a epileptic fit," said uncle Rosco.

"I wonder when they'll get here, and how long any of us can stand it," said Erline.

Mama Pearl got up and went to the stove for the big iron kettle she had put at the back for dishwater. She moved toward the sink with the heavy kettle.

"While they're here," she told them as she poured scalding

water in the aluminum dishpan, "Wilburn might as well sing something at the wedding." Steam enveloped her, and she blinked behind her clouded glasses.

"But no matter what Lurline says about Brother John, I guess Reverend Howell will perform the ceremony, for I am still partial to the Baptists."

"Wedding?" echoed Erline. "Ceremony?" She stared wildly about her. "Who in the world that we know is getting married?"

Audrey began to hum the wedding march, and uncle Rosco colored up and started to cough, but uncle Lester was there to pound him on the back. Augie went and stood close to Mama Pearl and asked would there be a wedding cake, and Mama Pearl leaned over and hugged him and said why not?

"It's not every day your Mama comes home," she told him, "or that I feel like a wedding. Why put it off? I said to myself just now, for we are, after all, just passing through."

Erline shivered and said somebody was walking on her grave again, and then she clapped her hands to her face and said, "Me and my big mouth, talking about graves at a time like this."

The Day
that Elvis Presley Died

At 11:09 on the morning of August 16, 1977, Erline Waters
Grissom realized with sudden and awful clarity that life is
hell. The day was downhill from there on.

Until eleven o'clock, she had been wholly out of it. If it had
thundered, she would not have known it. It did not thunder,
but the telephone did ring. That was what woke her up, but
she did not answer it, for she could think of practically nobody on earth she had much of anything to say to.

A half-empty bottle of gin sat on the table next to her
clock-radio. She did not like to think how much she had
drunk the night before, and she especially did not like to recall that she had spent the evening alone, socking down gin
like it was going out of style. She had gone to Frankfort, and
the night had been a real bummer. She bought the gin when
she realized she was looking for Francis and that she was
not likely to find him.

Sitting alone in a bar she had once gone to with Francis
and peeling the label off a bottle of Miller's High Life, Erline
decided she was fed up. She did not find anyone in the place

remotely interesting. Two or three boys from around home, just barely old enough to buy beer, were trying to work up their courage to come over and talk to her, and a middle-aged man, with bushy sideburns and a bad cough, was staring at her from the bar.

Though Erline was not looking at him, she knew when the man decided to come over to her table. He stood looking down at her, one eyebrow slightly raised in what he must have thought a provocative look. Erline sighed and looked at her watch.

"You waiting for something?" the man asked, leaning familiarly over her.

"Yeah," said Erline. "A good excuse to leave this joint, and, boy, do you ever fill the bill." She swept her cigarettes and lighter into her bag, snapped it shut, and left. She locked her car door when she got in, and sat considering where to go next. She drove around for a little while, and one place looked seedier and deader than the last.

Audrey and Augie were right; they did take up the sidewalks in Frankfort at ten o'clock. She bought her gin just as the liquor store owner turned off the neon lights which spelled out "Last Chance Liquor." Erline headed home. At least her air conditioner would have it cool there, and she would not have to see all those slack jaws and beer bellies. At home, she began with a Tom Collins—frozen lemonade, gin, and ginger ale; then she moved on to shot glasses of gin with ginger ale on the side.

She moved restlessly about her house and beauty shop. She had begun to itemize all her beauty shop equipment, so she could advertise it for sale. Hell, she might even sell the house and the trailer and the lot too—if she could get her price for it. She'd take Audrey off somewhere with her, maybe to Florida, maybe even California.

Nothing or nobody was holding her here, in Gratz, Kentucky, for God's sake.

Erline had never actually decided to close up her beauty shop. One day, she just upped and did it. The way she told it, she had been "stood up" one time too many. Old Lady Grider called her exactly two minutes before time to walk in the door for a permanent and said something had come up and she couldn't make it. "Seventy-nine, going on dead, and already crazy as a betsy-bug," Erline thought, "and something comes up—what could possibly come up unless her fat, equally crazy, daughter refused to drive her to get her hair fixed?"

Erline kept her temper. The old lady was so deaf she *had* to yell to make her hear. "When?" Erline screamed, "When do you WANT to COME?" "I'll call when I'm free," Mrs. Grider said, and hung up. That did it. "When *she's* free," Erline fumed. She went straight to Owenton and bought herself an orange-glow sign that said CLOSED.

She propped the sign in the window and walked outside to study the effect. She came back inside, and underneath the word, she added in her best Palmer script—

(Just in Case You're Interested).

Underneath that, she put her initials: EWG.

"If God is good," she had told Mama Pearl, "I will never again wash, or curl, or comb anybody's hair but my own."

The telephone rang again, and, for a minute, Erline thought wildly that it might be Francis. Then the thought died and she let the phone ring unanswered. At 11:30 she got up and managed to get coffee water to boil. She decided against spiking her black coffee with gin, and she put the bottle behind the organdy curtain on the bedside table and turned on the radio. The first thing she heard was the hushed voice of the disk jockey saying that Elvis was dead.

She just sat down on the bed and cried. Everything had been bad enough before, and now this. The announcer said they would be playing Elvis hits all day. How was she going to get through the day doing nothing but crying and listening to Elvis hits? She turned the radio off and went to get some breakfast. A can of V-8 juice, two slices of bacon, and an egg on toast made her feel good enough to think about getting dressed.

Erline had decided that what she needed to do was get outside and do some good, hard work. She put on her jeans and sneakers and an old blue workshirt. She tied her head in a faded blue bandana, and checked herself out in the mirror. Before going outside, she put on an enormous pair of lavender-tinted sunglasses. She was headed for Mama Pearl's house, and whatever she found that needed to be done, she intended to tackle the job. And whatever she could not do by herself, she intended to see that Audrey and Augie helped her do. She was ready to carry on—even if Elvis *was* dead.

Her car was like an oven and frying pan combined. The seat was too hot to lean back against, and the steering wheel burned her fingers. Erline could not remember when it had rained last; maybe a good hard rain was what she needed. The creek along the road had disappeared into the rocks, and the Kentucky River dwindled daily. Trash of all sorts littered the banks and clung from the limbs of dead trees, where the last high water had left it. The smell was muddy, fishy, sour, and dry, all at once. Erline began to wish she had poured herself a little gin to bring along in a flask.

The twelve o'clock news was all about Elvis, and Erline listened again to the details. She thought, then, of the two tickets in her wallet for the big Elvis Presley concert at Freedom Hall in Louisville. She had meant to take Audrey to the concert, and now neither of them would ever hear him in person. Still, she fished around in her bag until she found her wallet and made sure the tickets were still there.

Everything looked quiet at Mama Pearl's. Too quiet. Rosco's truck was not in the yard under the walnut tree. What if something had happened? What if they had been trying to call her and she hadn't answered the phone? She imagined some of the awful things that might have happened—her own Audrey killed by a car, or worse. Guilt and hangover made her sweat. She leaned hard on the horn, which wailed piteously.

She popped a Certs in her mouth. Gin was supposed to be odorless and she had already brushed her teeth hard, but she wanted to be on the safe side. Mama Pearl was hard to fool. She gave the horn a final jab and set off, at a half-run, for the house.

Without knocking, she threw the door open and glared around her. Augie sat, open-mouthed, at the dining table. He had a large book propped against his cereal bowl. Audrey, swathed in scarves, crouched before the hall mirror where she could see herself. She had a flower in her hair, and she was reciting something.

"Shhhh," said Augie. "This is the big scene."

"Didn't you hear me blowing?" demanded Erline.

Audrey withered her with a look, and then, satisfied with what she had done, tried it out on the mirror a few times.

"Good grief," said Erline. "Where's Pearl?" Nobody answered. She went to the empty kitchen and felt the coffee pot before pouring herself a cup. On and on Audrey went—her voice conveying a multitude of emotions, none of which she had ever felt. Outside, the world looked blistered with heat; the sun seemed permanently stopped at noon. Audrey was saying something now about the winter of our discontent.

Erline covered her ears. She almost wished that something awful had happened, for, then, there would be something for her to do. She stared at the luxuriant rhubarb growth at the edge of the garden, trying to make Mama Pearl materialize. Thinking about the rhubarb made her mouth water, and she wondered if what people said was true: the stems of rhubarb are wholesome, but the leaves will kill you. She wished she had the nerve to put the saying to the test. Somebody had said that death was a home remedy, and she wished she could find the courage to discover what ills it cured.

No matter how hard Erline stared, Mama Pearl would not appear. Erline recalled sitting alone in this same window years ago, late in the afternoon, when the skies had suddenly clouded up, and a light rain had begun to fall. Three rabbits had come from the fields into the short-clipped grass to play. They were not hungry and they did not appear frightened. All they had to do was play, and they did—until, suddenly, as if at a signal, all three sat up briefly, listened, and ran away into the weeds. Erline never knew what had interrupted their play. She decided they just knew when to stop, and, for a long time, she would sit in the window and watch for them to come back and to resume their game. They never did, and, after a year or so, Erline forgot to look for them.

She was not looking for them now, but it was almost as if she saw them anew, running and leaping in the glistening grass.

Augie came in carrying the big book. "Audrey has memorized practically the whole book," Augie told her. "I didn't have to help her but once."

"Huh," said Audrey. "A big help you were—you couldn't even find the place." She drooped into the kitchen as if art had depleted her.

Erline tapped a cigarette. She decided to try again: "Where's Pearl?" she asked.

"Off," said Augie noncommittally. Audrey pursed her lips impatiently, and drew a deep breath before answering.

"She and uncle Rosco went to Owenton—though uncle Rosco did not want to go and said it was a waste of time and money," Audrey said briskly. "It was not even eight o'clock when they left but I was already up, and we knew they were going and would not be back before this afternoon (which it is now) and I am supposed to be looking after HIM—." Augie scowled, and Erline rolled her eyes wondering when, if ever, Audrey would get to the point.

"—which is more than anybody else around here even tries to do," Audrey continued. "But thank the Lord, HE did not get up until about an hour ago, and then he wanted to eat up what Mama Pearl had left us for lunch instead of having breakfast, and when I made him eat breakfast, he got mad and he has left half his Cheerios in his bowl, which (as usual) is right where he took it to eat."

Erline shook her head warningly at Audrey. She could see Augie was beginning to cloud up.

"Mama Pearl went to the doctor," Audrey said in her normal voice. Erline was so accustomed to hearing her daughter speak in what Audrey called her "expressive range" that the words made her shiver.

"To the DOCTOR?" Erline said blankly. She knew it. Her premonition had been right. Nothing awful had happened yet, but it doubtless would. Pearl had never been sick, or gone to the doctor either.

"The doctor," Audrey echoed hollowly. Augie began to cry now.

"Mama Pearl is not sick," he told them. Then, he said it over and over.

"And that man," shrilled Erline, "had the nerve to say it was a waste of time and money—. You wait and see if I don't blister his ears when I get half a chance." Erline had the feeling her world was fast falling apart. She looked around wildly for something to do, but of course Mama Pearl had left the kitchen in apple-pie order.

"Come on," Erline said. "Let's get out of here. Let's find us something to do, and, later, I may drive you kids to Frankfort. How's that?"

Erline's first idea of something to do was to get out uncle Rosco's Snapper Mower and cut the grass and weeds around the garden. On the way to the shed, she told the children about Elvis. The way she told it was like a mother telling the children their father would not be coming home again. She was a little disappointed at their reactions, especially Audrey's, for they had been planning for ages to go to the big concert in Louisville.

"How old was he?" Audrey wanted to know. It sounded as if you just might as well expect anybody past twenty to haul over and die any minute. Audrey showed more interest when Erline said there had been talk of drugs.

"You've got to expect it," Audrey said. "All the Great Entertainers do it."

"Not the King," said Erline. "I'll never believe it, no matter who says that he was a dope-fiend." After a minute, she said softly: "I have listened to his records almost since I can remember, but now I will never hear him live." She had never thought before exactly what *live* meant; before, it had just meant the difference between a record and the person. She wiped her eyes with a finger, and hoped that maybe she could cut loose and really cry.

"Won't you get your money back," Augie asked, "—for the tickets?"

Audrey hooted. "Who'd want to?" she said. "They'll be worth their weight in gold—tickets to Elvis's Last Concert."

"I guess they will," Erline said. Her eyes narrowed. "Unless everybody else gets the same idea and keeps theirs too," she said.

Erline could not get the Snapper Mower to go. She propped her foot in the right place and pulled the crankcord until the veins stood out in her neck and she was seeing dancing spots before her eyes. It did not even sound as if it *might* start. While Erline rested, Augie tried a few times, and then they hunched down and stared at what Audrey said uncle Rosco adjusted when it did not start the first try. Finally, they pushed it back in the shed and Augie kicked it and they went off to the barn to see what they could find to do.

All they found in the barn was a half-dozen chickens taking dust baths. Augie decided to feed them some corn, and when he opened the feed bin a big blacksnake, with a lump in its middle, wiggled sluggishly into the haypile. Erline and Audrey squealed and ran, but Augie fed the chickens anyhow.

Audrey was telling her mother about snakes. "They cannot chew," she said, "but they can unhinge their jaws and swallow things whole. That one had probably swallowed a mouse live and was resting while he digested." Erline shuddered.

"Probably a baby rat," corrected Augie. "That lump was too big for any mouse." He watched the chickens eat. "Can we have lunch now?" he asked.

"Yuk," said Audrey, turning up her nose delicately.

Erline felt sick again. She closed her eyes and saw a gigantic snake with its jaws unhinged. When she opened her eyes, they fell upon a rattletrap truck.

"Does that thing go?" she asked.

The key was in it, and though Augie said that anybody who could not get a little power mower started, for sure couldn't get a truck to go, Erline crawled in and turned the key. It ground away—and Augie, who wanted to go eat the fried chicken Mama Pearl had left, laughed like crazy—and then it started—died, and started again.

Erline gunned the engine a minute, and then turned the key off.

"I have had a bright idea," she told the children. "We are going to make ourselves *really* useful around here and surprise Mama Pearl and Rosco."

"They'll drop over dead," Augie announced. "You never do anything around here."

Erline continued to fake-smile; she was not about to have her bright idea discouraged. Neither Augie nor Audrey asked her what the idea was, but she told them anyhow. "We are going to pick the watermelons," she told them, "and take them to that fruit stand in Frankfort and sell them." The children did not appear enthusiastic, so she improvised. "And with some of the money," she said, looking at Augie, "we are going to go shopping for 'something special' for supper tonight. We will have it cooked and waiting when Pearl gets home."

Audrey said they would never make it back before Mama Pearl came home, and Augie said before he picked any watermelons, he wanted to know what Erline considered "something special" to eat. "If you mean tuna fish salad," he said, "you can just forget it." Still, the idea seemed to be catching on.

Augie ran back to the house to get the fried chicken so they could have a picnic lunch, and, with Audrey directing her, Erline backed the truck out of the barn and onto the edge of the watermelon patch. Audrey came up with the bright idea of using the wheelbarrow to haul the melons from the ends of the rows to the truck, and Erline decided to fill the bed of the truck with hay to cushion the melons. She stood way back from the haypile, for she remembered where that blacksnake had gone.

Augie came back with the platter of chicken, and they all began to eat. "Which ones do we pick?" Augie wanted to know. He was chewing on his second piece of chicken and squatting over to thump the green-striped melons. He did not know what he was listening for, but he thumped them just like uncle Rosco did.

"Oh," said Erline breezily, "just the biggest ones—they'll bring the best price."

She pushed a wheelbarrow of melons to the truck, where Audrey helped her nestle them in hay. Augie's job was to pick the melons and lay them at the end of the rows, and when Erline returned from the truck, he would go and help her load the wheelbarrow again. The pickup truck filled rapidly, and Erline's spirits soared.

"There is nothing like a little bit of good, hard work," she told the children.

She threw more hay on the truck, and they started a second layer of melons. This time, she did not worry about the snake at all. Her face was flaming from the unaccustomed exertion, but she enjoyed being in charge and getting things done.

The tailgate of the truck did not have a catch to hold it shut, but Erline figured that one out fast. "Go find a stick, Augie," she said, "and when I hold these two pieces of metal together and line up the holes, you push the stick down hard." She considered calling him back to say he should look for a piece of iron, but the stick he brought was a perfect fit. They jammed it in so tight that, as Audrey said, they would never get it out.

"Who cares?" Erline sang out. "Having it shut is the point, isn't it?"

They all got tired at the same minute and decided to quit before they completely filled the truck. "This way," Erline explained, "we'll have plenty more for another load—maybe even two. And we don't want to flood the market, do we?" They had maybe a hundred melons on the truck.

"How much will we charge?" Augie asked.

"At least a dollar apiece," Erline said in her no-nonsense voice. Augie was rooting around in the hay trying to see how many dollars they were going to make.

"These will go for a pretty-penny," said Erline, "I have not seen any watermelons at the store." She threw another fork of hay on top of the load. "To keep them from blistering in the sun," she said wisely.

They all piled in the front of the truck, and Erline wondered out loud why Rosco let a perfectly good truck sit rusting in the barn. "Starts like a charm," she said, starting it. She was feeling so good, she decided she ought to torture herself a little.

"Go get your transistor radio," she told Audrey. "They are playing nothing but Elvis Hits on the radio all day and we can listen to 'The King of the Road' on the way to town."

A car they did not know stopped at the mailbox, and they saw Mama Pearl get out and wave goodbye to whoever was driving. "Shoot," said Erline, "Pearl is back already, and will not be all-the-way surprised."

Mama Pearl looked surprised enough when Erline rattled up to her and hung out the window and called gaily "Want to go to market, lady?" The children screamed with laughter, and Mama Pearl said, "Well, Erline, I tried to call you to see if you wanted anything in Owenton, but I guess you did not answer the phone."

Erline did not hear that, but she cut the engine and, looking hard at Mama Pearl, said, "Are you okay, Pearl? I mean really okay?"

Mama Pearl fanned herself briefly and said, "Well, Erline, I have been cooler in my life, but other than that I am fine."

She let that sink in. "Rosco," she said, "is worried sick about the drought. He has gone to look at the tobacco he is growing on the Gaines place, so Mrs. Eubanks said she would drive me home." She nodded absently toward the mailbox, where Mrs. Eubanks had stopped her car. "We met her at the drug store in Owenton," she said.

Erline's eyebrows shot up to her hairline. "What were you doing at the drugstore?" Erline wanted to know.

"Getting ice cream," Mama Pearl told them, though she instantly realized her mistake when Augie asked where *his* ice cream was.

"Well, Augie," Mama Pearl soothed, "we will get you one right now—won't we, Erline?" She peered into the truck to see if there was room for her. "We will just drive to Gratz," she said, "and get all of us something."

Erline had another bright idea. She would get Mama Pearl into the truck without telling her where they were going and, then—she would just hijack Mama Pearl. Erline told Augie to scrooch up, and he said he would ride in the back of the truck but Mama Pearl said no, there was no reason in the world she could not ride in the back. It was not all that far to Gratz.

"Many's the time," she said, "I used to ride on the back of the wagon, and, later, the back of a truck." The children squirmed, for they were horrified at the idea of Mama Pearl riding in the back of the truck.

"Many's the time," Mama Pearl said, trying to figure out how to get into the back of the truck. "Many's the time, when I was young." She had laid her pocketbook on the hay, and, standing on the running board, she was easing herself first onto the fender and then into the truckbed. Augie jumped out to help her "make a nest" in the hay, and Erline started the engine.

Erline drove slow and easy, and the kids knelt on the seat to stare at Mama Pearl. She held onto the side of the truck with one hand and to her hat with the other. She was smiling fixedly to show how much fun she was having.

"We are going to trick Pearl," Erline said happily. "We are not even going to slow down in Gratz."

"What about my ice cream?" Augie demanded.

"Oh, you'll get your old ice cream," Erline said. "But won't it be fun to make poor old Pearl ride through downtown Frankfort on top of a load of watermelons? She'll be fit to be tied." Erline laughed her nervous laugh, and Audrey began to giggle and wave to Mama Pearl, who could not wave without turning loose her hat or the truck. After awhile, even Augie decided the joke was worth waiting for his ice cream.

Everytime they met a car, Mama Pearl would smile and nod regardless of whether she knew the people in the car. She looked as if it was the most natural thing in the world for her to be sailing down the highway on the back end of a pickup truck.

But when they did not slow down in Gratz, she began to look inquiringly at the children. She had not stopped smiling, but she no longer looked happy or comfortable. Her nest of hay was blowing away, and she had taken off her hat and weighted it down with her pocketbook. *What is Erline doing? She will be the death of me yet. I am having a stroke. A heat stroke. I will die in the back of a truck, trying to pretend I am having fun.* She looked like she was trying to find something better to hold onto. She was backing her way toward the cab of the truck where she saw a metal pipe screwed into the truck's side. She caught hold of it at last, and frowned and shook her head at Audrey and Augie.

"It's not fair," said Augie. "Her hair is getting all messed up." He had never seen Mama Pearl's hair messed up before.

"Oh, shut up," said Erline. "Pearl is loving this. She'll laugh about this the rest of her life."

Erline has no intention of slowing down, much less stopping, until she gets to Frankfort. The children keep waving at me. They are laughing to beat the band. This is their idea of a joke. Don't they see I am sick?

Stop her, Audrey. Augie—? Stop her. I did not mean to encourage her in this foolishness. I just wanted to show that this family can still have fun.

"She does not look to me as if she will ever laugh again," said Audrey.

"Worry warts," Erline said, pleasantly. "Look—we're almost there. That's the sign for Peak's Mill." She slowed down for the long winding hill that led into North Frankfort. "Another mile and we've got it made," she said. "Over the bridge and into town."

She cannot stop. Nobody can stop. All you can do is hold on until the ride ends. The worst can happen, I will be thrown off. If I can hold on, maybe broken bones will be the worst. Will they heal, at my age?—And who will look after the children and Rosco?

That hill, it will be the death of us. Lester made Rosco drive fast that day coming back from Shelbyville. I thought we were gone, but here we are—about to die on another road, another way. It all comes to the same thing. We never even went back, that day. No need to.

The little girl behind those enormous sunglasses, what if she had been killed? She and the others in those cars headed straight for—. They would all be dead now, the little girl always dead and always as old as she was then.

The curve coming up was a sharp one, and Erline lifted her foot from the gas and eased her other foot onto the brake pedal. The hill sloped almost straight down at the end of a double-s curve.

Erline pushed the brake pedal a little harder. Nothing happened.

They were beginning to gain speed, and Erline pumped away at the brakes. *Omer dead, and always old. As old as he was the day he died. I will soon catch up with him, one way or the other. Wiley dead, too. But not the man I seen in the casket. Younger. Always younger. The man I knew died, not the one in the box in the funeral parlor.* Erline was hunched over the steering wheel wrestling to keep the truck on the road. She decided not to worry about staying on her side of the road, for hitting the bank or another car seemed preferable to plunging off the highway and into the river. The transistor radio blared away—Elvis, singing "Heartbreak Hotel."

Audrey planted her feet firmly on the floorboard and grabbed Augie to hold onto. "Stop it," Augie was saying. "Stop it right now, Erline."

Flailing around in the hay, Mama Pearl clutched the metal pipe with both hands now. Her mouth was open, but no sounds came out.

That day, coming back from Shelbyville, I closed my eyes and waited. Nothing happened, and I do not yet know if I was sorry or glad. Whenever I cross that bridge, I think of water closing over the top of a car. That's how I got Lester and Erline and Lurline. The closest I could come to being a mother come about when a drunk man went over a bridge.

He remains the same age, too, and as drunk now as when he set out that night to go get more booze so he could be drunker.

And now that same drunk man's daughter will go over another bridge and into the same river a few miles upstream from where her people went down thirteen years ago.

Then Lester and Lurline will be all that's left. Them and Rosco.

Rosco . . . .

She looked like a hen taking a dust bath.

At the final turn, Erline said a prayer—wordless but devout. The worst was over now, but the steepest part of the hill was yet to come. From here on, it was straightaway—and any cars coming up the hill would have plenty of room to pull over and let her get by.

I do not want to watch you die too, Rosco. I do not want to be in a room full of people, all watching me, and see you in a casket, hands too clean and folded on your chest, the way you will be in my mind from then on. And I do not want to care for you, waiting for you to die, the way I done Omer. Clean you, feed you, have to cry for you.

When Audrey opened her eyes, her first thought was of Mama Pearl. Sure enough, Mama Pearl was still there, though stretched out full-length and holding onto the pipe. Her hair was all in her face and her eyes were closed. Augie's eyes were wide open, fixed; he continued to say "Stop it, Erline" but the words no longer meant anything.

Audrey realized that her mother's eyes were closed now. She must have closed them when she realized how many cars were ahead of her—some in front and some, trustingly, crossing the road in front of them.

"Erline, open your eyes," Audrey cried. She leaned over to begin pounding the horn. At first, all the horn would do was gurgle but, at last, Audrey got it warmed up to warn everybody that they were coming. At the bottom of the hill, the railroad tracks slowed them down some and, then, they started up hill into Frankfort.

As soon as they hit the incline, the load shifted—all of it but Mama Pearl, who held on tight. *And I do not want to see if you are brave when I have to tell you you are dying, Rosco, and I do not want to see if you really are brave when you die.*

What Erline has done for a joke will spare me that.

The watermelons crashed backwards and knocked the tailgate loose. Everybody behind Erline was ducking watermelons and hay. Erline saw the sign which announced Jimmy's Fruit Stand, and she aimed for the parking lot. She turned off the ignition and hoped for the best—which was not very good. The sudden stop hurtled watermelons forward again.

When I do not open my eyes again, ever, I will know I have been spared. I will remain always an old lady sailing down highway 127 into Frankfort on a load of watermelons into the Kentucky River.

For a few minutes, all of them lay still and then, Augie screamed: "Mama Pearl!" They found Mama Pearl sitting up and trying to straighten her hair. Erline could not speak; she clung to the side of the truck staring at Mama Pearl. Some of the cars they had forced from the highway were turning into the parking lot now, and others followed to see what would happen. The road was littered with smashed watermelons.

Mama Pearl gathered a loop of hair and gazed down the road.

But I open my eyes; I will be spared nothing.

"Well, Erline," said Mama Pearl, "it is just as I thought—the melons are not ripe."

Erline groaned, and then began to gag. She shook, and it was all Audrey could do to hold her up. A dozen or more melons were smashed inside the truck, and the wasps had left whatever they had been doing and had come to light in the truck.

Audrey got Erline seated on the running board, and helped Mama Pearl get out of the truck. She went to get a Seven-Up for Erline.

A man in a dark blue suit approached the truck. "Are you okay now?" he asked. "Almost," moaned Erline. Augie was bored and began fiddling with the radio. He was sick of Elvis, and said so.

"Do you have a peddler's license?" asked the man.

"A peddler's license?" Erline said. "Of course not, what do you think I am? The nerve."

After a minute, the man spoke again. "I seen you come down the hill," he said. "That was some pretty fancy driving."

"Thank you," said Erline.

The man had opened his jacket to show his badge.

"The brakes give out," said Erline.

"Erline has done nothing wrong," said Mama Pearl. "It is a miracle any of us are still alive. The Lord chose to spare us."

The man took off his hat as a sign of respect.

"Hey, Erline," Augie yelled, "is that man a cop? I knew the cops would get you again."

"Again," said the officer. "Again?" Then, warily, "Lady, do you have a record?"

Erline was too mad to be sick. She spoke to the officer slowly, as if to a child. "No," she said, "I do not have a record, but I do happen to know my rights, so if you have any charges to make—why don't you get busy and make them and then *leave us alone*?"

Mama Pearl looked impressed, and Erline felt encouraged to go on.

"You would think," she said, "that the law would be interested in our safety and would try to help out instead of coming around to worry the very soul out of us after the Awful Experience we have just had, going hell-for-leather down that damn hill." She began to cry.

"Well, Erline," said Mama Pearl, reaching her hat out of the truck and putting it on, "you do not need to swear, but I think you are right about what the Law should be doing." She gazed reproachfully at the officer, who averted his eyes and went to his car.

He returned with his citation book. "I am letting you off easy," he said. "I could throw the book at you, but I will not."

"Thank you," said Mama Pearl.

"Forget about the peddler's license," the officer said, "and forget the reckless driving and speeding and running a stop sign—"

"Thank you," Mama Pearl said again.

"But," the officer said, raising one eyebrow, lowering his

voice and fixing Erline with his gaze, "but—that wreck you're driving does not have a Safety Sticker, and anybody with a grain of sense would know better than to try and drive it."

He wrote the ticket and handed it to Erline. Sputtering with rage, she accepted it.

He tipped his hat to Mama Pearl, who told him he was a credit to the force and to have a nice day.

Erline stuffed the ticket in her shirt pocket. She marched, silently, to the fruit stand. "You wouldn't want to buy what few watermelons I've got left, would you?" she said to the woman behind the counter.

The woman shook her head.

"You saw they were green, huh?" said Erline.

The woman nodded.

"The telephone," Erline said. "Where is it?" The woman jerked her head toward the corner of the store. It was a pay phone, and Erline had trouble finding a dime. She got the operator and gave her the name and number—a collect call to uncle Rosco.

"Rosco," Erline said. "Erline."

"Get in the car," she told him, "and come to Frankfort to get us."

"What do you mean 'again'?" she said. "That was ages ago—and, no, I am not in jail. I have never been in jail. That was a misunderstanding from the word Go—that time you had to come and identify me."

The fruit stand lady moved closer to her cash register as if to protect it.

"Look, Rosco," Erline said. "We're at Jimmy's fruit stand

on the way into town—Mama Pearl, the kids and me. They are waiting outside at the truck.—Yes, I said *at the truck*. I KNOW the brakes are shot. *Boy*, do I ever know that those brakes are shot. Look, just get us. I want to get out of this place; pick us up at the Rexall's on State Street. We'll walk there and have an ice cream."

Erline listened briefly. "Forty minutes," she said. "Come on, Rosco, you can do better than that. Hell, I made it in no time flat."

At the Rexall's, Mama Pearl and Erline sank down into a booth while Audrey and Augie went to the counter to order. Mama Pearl looked as fresh as she had when they set out from home.

"Are you really okay, Pearl?" Erline asked. She reached out to touch Mama Pearl's hands which were folded on top of her pocketbook.

"Well, Erline," said Mama Pearl, "I am as well as could be expected."

Erline winced, but Mama Pearl went on.

"Rosco and me went to Owenton today," she began.

"And I heard that he said it was a waste of time and money for you to see the doctor," said Erline. "Who does he think he is, anyhow, and who does he think will pay the bill?"

"He is as good as my husband," said Mama Pearl, "and he will pay the bill." "But you do not understand," she continued. "I knew he would never go to the doctor unless I went too—and what I learned was no worse than I expected."

The children were heading back from the counter with a menu. Mama Pearl looked delighted to see them. Erline's neck no longer seemed capable of supporting her head; she sat with both hands clapped up against her face. Her expression was neither disbelief nor anxiety. She looked eager to know at once the very worst that there was to know.

She managed to extend one finger and waggle it for silence. The children looked impressed. "Get anything," she said. "Buy any damn thing you want, and bring me a black coffee and bring Pearl two scoops of vanilla ice cream, but leave us alone a minute."

The children squealed their pleasure. "A banana split with everything on it?" asked Augie.

"Sure," said Erline, "why not?"

Audrey and Augie raced back to the counter.

"Pearl—," said Erline. "I am coming home. You need me."

Mama Pearl looked baffled. "You are always welcome, Erline," she said with her customary good manners.

"He does not know," Mama Pearl said. "He does not know the worst. We will not have him much longer." Erline gasped.

"Rosco?" she asked.

"For a minute," Mama Pearl said, "coming down that hill, I thought I would be spared having to tell him." She shook her head. "But that was too easy, and the Lord decided I would have to do it. I will tell him."

Erline was busy trying to sort out her feelings when the children headed back to the booth. Their banana splits bled pink with cherry juice in their Whip Top. They set down Erline's coffee and Mama Pearl's ice cream.

"Jesus," said Erline, "I will never forget the day Elvis Presley died."

Mama Pearl was craning her neck to see outside to the street.

"We better hurry," she said. "He will be here any minute."

"Who?" asked Erline looking around her wildly.

Audrey and Augie ate their banana splits in quiet, until somebody put some money in the juke box and played Elvis's "I'll Do It My Way." And then, uncle Rosco came and everybody went home.

Bright Star

Mama Pearl woke up at 2:30 in the morning, and leaned on her elbow to look out the window. It was light as day outside; the moon was full, and Venus hung, uncertain, over the ridge. A chill had dropped over Sawdridge Creek, and Mama Pearl felt cold. She lay back and pulled the covers up, but she did not have time to go back to sleep before Lester began to scream.

The first scream did not end before the second one began to well up behind it, and it sounded to Mama Pearl as if Lester was determined to keep that second scream going for as long as he had breath in him. She and Rosco were up at almost the same time, and Mama Pearl said, "It's Lester." Together, they hurried down the hall.

Lester was sleeping in a room back under the eaves on the east side of the house, all the way down the hall from Mama Pearl's and uncle Rosco's. You had to go through Augie's room to get to it. It had lots of windows, and all of them were open, for uncle Lester liked air moving where he slept. The door to Augie's room was shut.

Augie had begun crying before uncle Lester finished the first scream. Augie was still asleep, whimpering and crying, and with all the racket, Audrey was not sure, at first, who was screaming, uncle Lester or Augie. Audrey stepped out of bed onto the floor about the time uncle Lester started winding down. It sounded like he was gargling or something, and then he began to build up again.

Audrey put her hands to her ears. "Shut up, Augie," she said. "Shut up." She meant to go see about uncle Lester, but it sounded as if somebody was killing him. Maybe she would be next.

Mama Pearl floated silently through the room, and, without lights, found her way to uncle Lester's door. Uncle Rosco hung in the doorway; he did not want to go into the children's room wearing nothing but his underwear. Audrey followed Mama Pearl, made brave by her presence.

"Lester," Mama Pearl said, low but clear. "Are you all right, Lester?"

Uncle Lester was sitting up in bed. He looked younger than his fourteen years, but he looked as if he had lived forever. "I meant it," he said. "I meant every word I screamed."

"Lester," Mama Pearl said, "you did not scream any words. You just screamed—and nearly scared the life out of me. What was it that you meant?"

"That's all right what I meant," uncle Lester said darkly. "I just wanted you to know. That's all." He looked about him defiantly.

"You meant it all, Lester," Mama Pearl soothed. "Now, go back to sleep. We do not need to talk about it."

The sheets were bunched up about uncle Lester's body.

Audrey stared at him outlined in the window. He had been sitting up and now he slumped back against the headboard. He looked like a picture she'd seen somewhere, maybe at school. He raised his head once and looked at her. Audrey thought she had never seen anybody look more tired in her life.

"What's Augie crying about?" uncle Lester asked. "Do you want me to go see about Augie?"

"No, Lester, you go to sleep. I'll see about Augie."

When uncle Lester was still again, Mama Pearl pulled the spread up over him, and sat for a minute on the bed. She just barely touched him. From the doorway, it looked to Audrey as if the morning star was descending into Mama Pearl's head.

"Goodnight, Lester," Audrey heard Mama Pearl saying.

Erline, who had slept through everything, could not wait for uncle Lester to come downstairs the next morning. Audrey had told her about how uncle Lester had screamed and almost stopped and then set out all over again and ended up with a blood-curdling whoop. She also told her what he had said to Mama Pearl. By the time Lester came downstairs, Erline was certain she had heard it all herself.

It was Sunday morning, and nobody, not even uncle Lester, had to get anywhere by any special time. Because of the chill, Mama Pearl had made a fire in the wood range and had made the coffee there and was frying sausage. But because it was Sunday, she had mixed up waffles which she would bake in the electric waffle iron.

She had beaten six egg whites to fold into the batter, and she was waiting to do that until everybody was up. The syrup was bubbling with melted butter on the back of the stove, and the light on the waffle iron had gone out, which meant it was ready.

Erline was seated at the head of the kitchen table. She was wearing her kimono and drinking coffee. "Lord, what a night," she said, and lit her second cigarette of the morning.

"Well, Erline," said Mama Pearl, "I hope you do not intend to say anything to Lester. You cannot help what you do in your sleep, and I, for one, do not begrudge anyone a nightmare once in a while." She lifted the bowl of beaten egg whites, ready to pour.

"Did you say you were going to Mass at Shelbyville?" she asked Erline.

Erline shook her head impatiently. "You know I'm no better Catholic than I was a Baptist," she said. "I'm not going anywhere for awhile."

Erline took her third cigarette of the day from the pack and tapped it on the kitchen table. "What we've got to do," she said, "is get at the underlying cause of all this."

"All what?" asked Audrey.

"These nightmares troubling Lester," said Erline. "The boy needs help."

Erline had been reading some books on psychology and dream interpretation. She was dying to see if she could match up uncle Lester's dreams with anything she had read about.

"He's holding something back," she told Mama Pearl, "and the only way it can get out is when he is asleep and the 'censor' is off-duty." She had read that, and was disappointed when nobody, not even Augie, asked her what the 'censor' was.

"We all hold something back," Mama Pearl said reasonably. "And it always finds a way of getting out—in dreams, or drinking—or in changing religion and smoking cigarettes." Erline narrowed her eyes at Mama Pearl, who was by now innocently pouring a waffle into the iron.

They heard footsteps on the stairs, and Erline church-whispered, "Here he comes—. Act natural."

Augie went to get in line for the first waffle and Audrey tried to look as if she couldn't care less, but while Mama Pearl wasn't looking, she mouthed the word *pig* at him and poked her cheeks out and crossed her eyes.

"You do look like one, you know," said Augie.

"Like one what?" asked Erline.

Mama Pearl was watching the puffs of steam escaping the waffle iron, for when they stopped the waffle would be done.

Uncle Lester came in whistling. He stopped abruptly, when he saw Erline. Normally, she took her coffee back to bed with her and forgot to drink it until it was cold.

"Aren't we having eggs?" he asked Mama Pearl.

"You can if you want, Lester," said Mama Pearl, "but I thought Audrey and Augie would enjoy waffles for a change."

Uncle Lester sat down at the table. "I'll wait for uncle Rosco," he said. "Him and me will have scrambled eggs."

He got up to get himself a cup of coffee. "Mama Pearl," he said, "I am sorry I woke you up last night. And Audrey, thank you for coming to look after me. Augie, I didn't mean to scare you. It was just a dream."

Audrey gaped. Mama Pearl beamed, and Erline sulked. Lester had said nothing to her.

"I wasn't much scared," said Augie. "It's okay."

"How long has this been going on?" asked Erline as soon as uncle Lester sat down. "The dreams, I mean."

"What dreams?" he asked.

"Why, you just now said 'it was just a dream,'" Erline snapped. "Didn't he say 'it was just a dream'?" she appealed to the room at large.

"It was the only dream I've had," uncle Lester said. "At least, the only one I remembered—and I knew I was dreaming, but, somehow, it seemed important to do something and the only thing I could do was yell, so I did."

Erline leaned forward. "Tell us about your dream, Lester," she said.

"I can't tell you all about it," uncle Lester told her, "but I can tell you the main lines of it. Is that okay?"

"Anything you want to tell," Erline assured him. "It'll be good for you to talk about it." She looked smugly at Mama Pearl.

"Somebody," said uncle Lester, "was doing something awful to somebody, and I couldn't help it, so I thought the least I could do was yell and let it be known that it hurt."

As if he'd just thought of something, he said, "Mama Pearl, I might as well have a waffle while I'm waiting for uncle Rosco."

"Soooo," said Erline. "Then what happened?"

"That's all," uncle Lester said. "Then Mama Pearl and Audrey came in and Augie was crying, and I asked if I should go see about Augie."

"That's all?" Erline stormed. "What kind of dream is that?"

"It's the kind I had," uncle Lester said. "And I can't help what kinds of dreams I have, can I?"

136

"Who was the *somebody*," Erline demanded, "and what were they doing, and who were they doing it to?"

"I won't tell you," uncle Lester said.

"YOU won't tell me?" exploded Erline. "How can we help you if you won't tell anything?" She rolled her eyes despairingly.

Uncle Lester looked sorry, and, in a minute, he said, "There is a little bit more about how I felt. I began that first yell, and, somehow, it didn't seem enough, so I just sort of let it die out and began another. I knew I was doing that, and I said to myself, 'There is not much I can do about anything, but I can let them know that it hurts.'"

"Aha," said Erline. "Who are *they* and what is *it*? That's where we'll find the answer."

Lester was holding his plate up for Mama Pearl to take. The next waffle would be his.

"They is all of us," uncle Lester told Erline, "and it is what we all the time do to each other." He ladled syrup on his waffle, and speared a sausage patty from the platter.

Augie was ready for another waffle. He eyed uncle Lester seriously and said, "Was it me they were doing 'something awful' to?"

Uncle Lester looked Erline full in the eye. "I'm not saying who it was," he said. "We were doing something awful to all of us, and nobody meant to do it and nobody knew how to stop doing it." He began to eat.

After a while, Erline could not stand the silence.

"Don't I get a waffle, Pearl?" Erline asked. Then, to everybody, she said, "It would never stand up with a real psychologist. I'll tell you that much. There is nothing like it in any of the books."

Uncle Rosco came in saying the woodchucks had been in the cabbage again but that he hated to set traps. Erline told him that the woodchucks were also eating away the foundation of the house, and she guessed one day he would just turn the property over to them. And uncle Lester said, "They have been here longer than we have—so why not?"

Erline sputtered, and Augie said, "We're having waffles, uncle Rosco, and you can have my next one," and uncle Lester said uncle Rosco could have his next one too, but he was going to catch up—and didn't Mama Pearl want him to cook the rest of the waffles?

"Well, Lester," she said, "if you are sure you do not want scrambled eggs, I will sit down awhile and you can cook the waffles."

Uncle Rosco said waffles sounded fine to him, and uncle Lester changed places with Mama Pearl, who laid her hand on uncle Rosco's shoulder as she sat down.

Uncle Lester gave her the next waffle, which she said was perfect.

Ching-Ching.
Whuff-Whuff.

Lester had a special place he would disappear to when things got too much for him. He would stop at the woodshed for the ax and a wedge and then head to the back corner of the woodlot where somebody had hauled a gigantic sycamore round from the creek bottom. The sycamore round had been there since before Lester was born.

Lester would disappear and, after while, you would hear the ax go three or four sharp licks, and then there would be a pause while Lester positioned the wedge. Then, there would be the ring of metal on metal and, finally, the *whuff-whuff* of Lester trying to work the wedge loose so he could start again.

For a long time, the sycamore round endured more or less undiminished, but it began to wear down the summer uncle Rosco took sick. Whenever Lester was not off at work, he was likely to be out back worrying that sycamore round. To herself, Mama Pearl said that she would give a pretty if somebody hauled the sycamore round off somewhere.

It was a waiting time of year. Farmers had done what they

could, and the corn and tobacco had to do the rest. Rosco worried about what a hailstorm would do to the tobacco. He had crop insurance, but he did not want to collect on it. He expected his to be some of the best tobacco at the market.

The doctors were seeing what they could do for Rosco, but it did not sound as if they could do much. Still, Rosco saw first one doctor and then another. Pearl thought she could maybe stand it better if Rosco would complain. Even when she rode with him to the doctor's, he would act as if getting home in time for supper was his biggest concern. He did not want the children home by themselves.

Sometimes Rosco would come indoors in the heat of the day, and would go to the sink for some water. At such times, Pearl wished she could disappear so maybe Rosco would take out his bottle of Old Heaven Hill from his toolbox on the back porch and mix some of it with his springwater. She knew the bottle was there, Rosco knew it was there, and Pearl thought maybe Rosco knew that she knew, but they acted as if the bottle did not exist. Rosco's illness was like the bottle. They both knew it was real, but neither would allow it to assume its proper degree of importance.

Even when Rosco told her that Dr. Brown, in Frankfort, wanted him to see a specialist in Louisville, he maintained the illusion that the new doctor merely wanted to find out what's what. He effectively denied what both of them knew, for he did not say cancer specialist.

Mama Pearl told herself she already knew what was what. Rosco was dying a little at a time and, while he was at it, he might just as well admit it and let himself go a little bit. But that was not the kind of thing she would ever say to Rosco.

Rosco was at the kitchen sink, and Mama Pearl could not even say to him what the sound they both of them heard— the *ching-ching* of metal on metal—made her think of. Rosco had pulled the wooden bucket of springwater out from the cool dark under the counter and had dipped the gourd into it when the *ching-ching* began. Pearl kept talking about the blackberries she aimed to freeze and those she aimed to can.

The *ching-ching* stopped, and Rosco lifted the gourd to his mouth. At the first *whuff-whuff*, he poured the water down the drain.

"Aren't you thirsty, Rosco? You look hot enough—" She had started to say "hot enough to die." If Erline was there, she would clap her hand over her mouth and roll her eyes. Mama Pearl started over. "You look hot enough to drink that water you just poured out, Rosco. Do you want some ice in it?"

"What's Lester cutting wood for, in this heat?" Rosco wanted to know.

Mama Pearl did not know what words to use to tell Rosco.

"The woodbox is full," challenged Rosco, "and the woodshed, too." These hot days Mama Pearl cooked in the fry-skillet Erline had once gotten with green stamps. Erline had told everybody she was dying to see what they would have in a place called a Redemption Center.

Rosco continued to look hard at the woodbox, and directly they heard a half-dozen more sharp licks of the ax. Rosco winced, and Pearl began talking about how the grapes needed picking. She said they should pick the scuppernongs first, for already bees and wasps had settled on the arbor. She said she would make Rosco plenty of scuppernong-hull preserves, and they would eat or give away the rest. Rosco said he would take a peck to the Thompsons tomorrow, but the Lord knew what Mrs. Thompson would make him bring back in return.

Mama Pearl told him if it was something that had to be cooked, canned, or frozen, he had just better float it on down Sawdridge Creek to somebody who maybe needed it, for she had more than she could do to keep up. She wished the Lord would hold back some of His plenty and let things be for awhile. She said what passed for a prayer that she could have some rest and if Rosco could not get better, he would at least not get worse for awhile. She thought of Lester's sycamore round, which she knew would hold up as long as he needed it.

Rosco said he had to get back to work—that is, unless Pearl wanted him to begin picking scuppernongs, and she said no, he should do whatever needed doing. She heard him pull the crank-cord on the mower, and then it started up. Pearl shucked a dozen ears of corn and sat down to cut and scrape them into a dishpan. Tonight, she would cook on the woodrange—corn, okra, butterbeans, maybe even biscuits to go with the last of last year's scuppernong-hull preserves. There was no sound now from the woodlot, but she listened to Rosco cutting wider and wider circles around the walnut tree.

A few days later Lester came home early from the feed-store. Mr. Bascomb's truck had broken down, and though Lester let it be known he could fix it, Mr. Bascomb had let somebody haul it off to Owenton. Then, Mr. Bascomb took his wife and girls off to run their boat up and down the Kentucky River for the twins, SueAnn and SueFan, to water ski.

They had asked Lester if he wanted to go, but he said he'd rather be all the way in the water or all the way out of it. It didn't seem natural to be on top of it. Mama Pearl was snapping beans for soup mix when he came in. She was doing her best to keep the woodbox empty.

Lester sat down at the kitchen table to have him a cup of coffee. Thirty-two pints of scuppernong-hull preserves glittered on the counter in front of quarts of tomatoes and gallons of soup mix. Despite all, the back porch smelled like over-ripe tomatoes, and bees, a little drunk on scuppernongs, buzzed in the baskets. Mama Pearl stirred her coffee thoughtfully, and half-groaned. Outside, the summer squash and zucchini were swelling. The cucumbers were getting warty, the beans tough. There was no keeping up with the Lord's bounty, she told Lester.

It was the perfect opportunity to tell Lester that she and Rosco would be going on Wednesday to see a specialist in Louisville, but she had just begun to work around toward the subject when they heard the first sharp lick of the ax. They waited for the sound of the wedge being driven into the sycamore. Rosco was in the woodlot taking up where Lester had left off.

Mama Pearl plunged into what she had to say. "I know Wednesday is your day off," she told Lester, "but Rosco couldn't help when we have to go, and we will hurry back as quick as we can."

"Where are you going?" Lester asked. "Is Lurline getting out of the Detention Center Wednesday?"

"No," Mama Pearl told him. "We will try to call Lurline while we are there, but the trip has nothing to do with her.

It is a doctor—a specialist. Dr. Brown thinks a doctor in Louisville can maybe help your uncle Rosco. The appointment is for eleven o'clock."

The sound of the ax rang out, and Mama Pearl raced on. She said she would leave potato salad and chicken already cut up, salted and floured, so that even Erline could fry it, but, with any luck at all, she expected to be home in time to cook it herself.

Lester stood up. Without their saying anything about it, they agreed that Rosco could not hold up long at the rate he was working on the sycamore round. Lester did not want to be sitting there when Rosco came in. "Tell Lurline hello for me," Lester said. "And I will fry the chicken for you."

Pearl felt the weight of the word she had not said. "Maybe a cancer doctor will not be like the others," she said. "Maybe he does not see so many people that we will have to wait all day."

Lester considered this. "You never can tell," he said. He rinsed both their coffee cups and skeedaddled. Mama Pearl put the beans in the refrigerator before, almost furtively, she skeedaddled too.

A few minutes later, Rosco, red-faced and sweating, came in the kitchen and headed straight for the water bucket. He listened hard to the still house before sipping the water. He poured more water and added an ice cube. At his tool box, he listened again before taking out the bottle of Old Heaven Hill and pouring some of the reddish liquor into his cup. He drained the cup and, after thought, poured and drank more before he put the bottle away.

From her upstairs window, Erline watched Rosco go to the chicken yard and empty the bucket of springwater into the chicken trough. She narrowed her eyes to watch him wind his way up the hill toward the spring—the same direction she had seen Lester go a few minutes earlier. She decided to watch and see if they came back together. When they did, Rosco was still carrying the bucket, now full, and both of them looked as if they had poured water over their heads. Rosco set the bucket down, and Lester dipped the gourd in so he could pour more water over their heads.

"That doesn't look like a halfway bad idea," Erline decided.

On Wednesday morning, Lester was the first one up, as usual, though he did not have to go to work. For some reason nobody can remember, the stores around Owen County have always closed on Wednesday afternoon, and some of them finally took to closing all day. Lester had brought the old Remington typewriter home from the feedstore, and he intended, if he could get Erline out of his hair long enough, to write some letters.

Mama Pearl had told him the name and address of the cancer specialist in Louisville, and she told him also that the doctor operated early every morning and is in his office only between eleven o'clock and two. Lester said if the doctor knew what he was doing he would not have to operate on so many people. He said he planned to write the Jefferson County Medical Association to see how some of those operations have come out.

Lester decided he might as well cook breakfast. He and uncle Rosco both liked scrambled eggs. Mama Pearl would eat eggs with them, and he did not expect to see Erline for another hour or two. Lester knew Audrey and Augie would rather have cereal than eggs but that their favorite breakfast was pancakes they got to cook themselves. While the coffee perked on the hotplate and the bacon began to sputter in the fry-skillet, he mixed up pancake batter. Then he broke eight eggs, one at a time in a mixing cup, and poured them in a large bowl. From one, he dipped a blood spot with a fork. He beat the eggs, added salt and a splash of fresh cream, and beat them again. Beside the electric griddle, he set the pancake batter and two spatulas exactly the same size. With luck, Audrey and Augie should cook their pancakes peaceably.

Lester had taken the bacon up to drain when Erline surprised him. She rushed in, clutching her kimono to her as if the house was on fire and she had to get out quick, but Lester noticed she had taken the kerchief off her head and had combed her hair.

"What in the world are you doing up so soon, Erline?" Lester wanted to know. He opened the refrigerator to get two more eggs.

"I came down to cook breakfast for poor Pearl and Rosco," she snapped, easing herself into a chair and reaching for the bacon. "What do you think would get me up so soon after I cried myself to sleep last night?" She fumbled with her package of Herbert Tareytons. "Poor Rosco," she said. "Poor, poor Rosco."

Lester put more bacon in the fry-skillet and turned it on. He poured coffee and brought Erline the kitchen matches to light the cigarette she held. For a few minutes, she sipped and smoked in silence.

"O—Lester," Erline yelped suddenly and tragically. "The children—their lunches." She struggled as if to rise.

"It's okay, Erline," Lester said. "They're in the refrigerator—the lunches." He almost smiled at the idea of Audrey and Augie in the refrigerator. "Mama Pearl and me made them last night."

Erline subsided. "The poor children," she said. "Who will look after them when—Rosco is gone?" She stared at Lester darkly. "I said I would make their lunches," she told him, "and I meant to, but you and Pearl have already done it." She looked bleakly around the kitchen. "Peanut butter?" she accused. Lester nodded. "I meant to make them tuna fish sandwiches," she said. "A real lunch—with potato chips."

Lester had sat down at the table now. "There are some things we need to talk about in this family," Erline told him. "The right hand does not know what the left hand is doing." Her two hands raised aloft summoned up the difference between peanut butter and tuna fish. She waved her hands, dismissing both tuna fish and peanut butter.

"This is a time, Lester," she said bravely, "that we Waterses have to stick together."

"We are sticking together," Lester said reasonably. "We will all have breakfast together and Audrey and Augie will go off to Vacation Bible School and Mama Pearl and uncle Rosco will go to Louisville, but we will all be here for supper." He made a stiff gesture as if to summon up the supper scene, but Erline was not paying attention.

"We never talk about things," she said. "Here's Rosco going off to some *cancer* doctor, and Pearl never said peaturkey about it until yesterday." She rolled her eyes expressively. "Pearl said you were going to cook the chicken if she didn't get back in time," she said.

Erline blinked her eyes hard, and Lester said she could make the children's sandwiches tomorrow. She waved her hands impatiently. "Why, Lester," she demanded, "wouldn't

Pearl get back in time?" Then she answered herself: "Because Rosco is—terminal, Lester. Do you know what *terminal* means?"

Lester got up abruptly to turn the bacon and pour more coffee.

When he returned to the table, Erline surprised him a second time. She was crying and doing nothing to wipe away the tears.

"When they leave, Lester," she said threateningly, "if you go out to that woodlot and chip away at that old tree all day and leave me to stew by myself—I, I don't know what I'll do." She concluded with a little hiccough. "You and me can at least talk some."

"I got a better idea, Erline," said Lester. "I got to make a phone call before I can tell you about it." He disappeared toward the hall.

Rosco and Pearl came downstairs and then the children. Augie looked in the refrigerator and said, "Goodie, peanut butter sandwiches," and Erline said everybody would have to excuse her a minute but for them to go ahead and eat without her. She told everybody she never ate breakfast, though she had already eaten so much bacon that Lester was considering cooking more.

Audrey and Augie cooked their pancakes while Lester scrambled the eggs. The plates were full and Mama Pearl had just said "Well, Lester" in preparation to praise him for the fine breakfast, when Erline appeared wearing her seersucker pantsuit and plastic high-heel shoes.

"We are going with you, Pearl," she said. "That is, if you don't mind." She cut her eyes at Rosco, who looked pleased as punch.

148

"Charlotte says the children can go home with her after Bible School," Lester explained. To the children, he said, "We'll pick you up at five, if that's okay."

Mama Pearl looked at Lester a minute and then, questioningly, at the typewriter he had put on the floor when he set the table.

"The woodbox is full," Lester told her, "and my letters can wait."

Augie and Audrey got their sandwiches so they could go wait for their ride.

A Miss Is as Good
as a Mile

School would be starting in another week, and Augie, for one, thought the summer had been a total waste. They had not *gone* anywhere, and except for that one day they set out to see aunt Muddie and she was not at home, they had not even *tried* to go anywhere.

"Why don't we go on a vacation?" Augie asked at least once every day.

"Maybe we will, maybe we will" was the best he could get out of anybody.

Augie was mad because he had not even got to go to Louisville with Mama Pearl to see Lurline, though, as he told everybody, it just stood to reason if anybody got to go it ought to be Lurline's own son. The whole day was ruined, and Augie did not intend to do much to improve it. Erline had taken Audrey to Owenton to buy school clothes, and she had tried to make Augie go too. When he stuck his tongue out at her and told her to go to hell, she said she was going to tell Mama Pearl exactly how he had behaved while she was off seeing Lurline.

Augie did not care what Erline told Mama Pearl, but he

did not consider it much fun to have to be mad at *everybody* all at once. As he had told Erline and Audrey repeatedly that morning, he was bored stiff. Lester, of course, was at the feed store, and uncle Rosco was off in his pickup truck looking at the tobacco crop, which he did every spare minute, and, with Mama Pearl gone, there was nobody even to talk to.

Early that morning, uncle Rosco had driven Mama Pearl to the bus station at Frankfort. She was to take a Greyhound to Louisville, where Brother John, the radio evangelist from Waddy, Kentucky, would meet her and drive her to the Women's Detention Center to see Lurline. The night before, Augie had thrown what Erline called his "special deluxe variety of fit," to see if he could not make Mama Pearl take him with her, but it had not worked. You would think Lurline was not his mother at all, the way other people could go see her whenever they wanted and he could not.

Mama Pearl had left that morning before Augie got out of bed, and he was a good mind to go to bed before she got home. The way he saw things, he might as well go to bed right now, for the day was a loss and Erline had said she would fix supper for them—he knew from experience what *that* meant: tuna fish and potato chips.

Even uncle Rosco had not been himself lately, but Augie told himself uncle Rosco was worried he would have to irrigate the tobacco fields. Neither he nor uncle Rosco liked doing that. Uncle Rosco went around looking up at the sky all the time, studying the clouds. When he was not doing that, he was squatting down in the tobacco field to dig at the earth with his big freckled hands. Already, the tobacco in the creek bottoms was headhigh and beginning to turn color a little.

Mama Pearl did not understand how Augie and uncle Rosco felt about irrigating the crop. She thought uncle Rosco was worried about the cost. Augie had heard her tell uncle Rosco that, for once, they could afford to irrigate the whole county if they needed to. Augie knew that Mama Pearl meant that with the money she had inherited from uncle Wiley, she could pay for almost anything. Augie knew uncle Rosco would not let Mama Pearl spend her money on his tobacco crop.

Later that same night, Augie had heard Mama Pearl tell uncle Rosco that they could afford to take a vacation trip, too, if he wanted to go. Augie hoped uncle Rosco would not mind whose money they spent to go, maybe, to Florida.

"I got to look after the crop," uncle Rosco said.

The highlight of the summer had come when Lurline and Brother John showed up just in time for Mama Pearl's and uncle Rosco's wedding. They had come exactly when Lurline had written to say they would, but, naturally, nobody was expecting them because uncle Rosco had sweated on Lurline's letter until nobody could read it. One day, Mama Pearl looked up from the stove and said, "Why Lurline, there you are." Behind Lurline, Brother John stood, uncertain, but eager to please. Everybody liked him from the start—even Augie.

Augie especially liked the way Brother John's eyes crinkled and he'd laugh and, then, draw his mouth down straight and serious as if he'd caught himself doing something he oughtn't. Augie laughed along with Brother John, and tried to see if he could change his expression as fast as Brother John could. He couldn't.

Then Erline began making cracks. "Why don't we make this a double wedding?" she said. And when Lurline blushed, Erline squealed and said, "O my, I guessed a secret, didn't I?"

Everybody but Augie laughed, and Erline said, "Whassa matta—lil' Augie?—You don't like your new Daddy?"

Brother John agreed to sing a couple of gospel songs at Mama Pearl's and uncle Rosco's wedding, but he said it wouldn't be right to play his guitar. The occasion, he said, was too serious. The wedding took place in the living room in front of the fireplace where Erline and Lurline had put two big pots of daisies and a pair of giant candleholders.

Lurline and Erline both cried during the ceremony, and Augie later heard May Evelyn, the postmistress, telling the preacher's wife that they were probably recalling their own weddings—"which was enough to make anybody cry." Mama Pearl wore a long pale-lavender dress, which Erline said was the color for penitence in *her church*. Lester broke in to ask did Erline mean *penitence* or *penance*. Erline stared at him blankly. "Whatever," she said. Mama Pearl shrugged it off: "To each his own," she said. "Lavender has always been a happy color for me; when the wisteria comes out I know winter is done."

If anybody thought it was funny for Mama Pearl and uncle Rosco to be getting married after living together in the same house so long, they did not say so around the family. Uncle Lester told Erline that the Holiness preacher claimed that his congregation's prayers had "touched the hearts of two living in sin."

"How could that be, Erline?" uncle Lester wanted to know. "Uncle Rosco did not even know they were doing it until he found out I had put the snakes in their church to get even."

"You did what?" said Erline blaring her eyes at him. "Good Lord, do they know you did it?"

"Uncle Rosco made me get them out," uncle Lester said sadly. "But we could find only one of them. The other may still be there."

More people had come to the wedding than were invited. Some came out of curiosity to see Lurline, and others came to see Brother John. It turned out that a good many of them belonged to his Radio-land Congregation and expected him to know them.

To everybody, Mama Pearl said the same thing. Standing next to uncle Rosco in the dining room doorway, she looked around the room where Erline and Lurline served punch and coffee at opposite ends of the table and Audrey passed cookies. "Well," Mama Pearl would say, "Rosco and me feel like we have raised two sets of children already, and it seemed time to settle down."

Augie enjoyed the wedding until he got sick and threw up, and uncle Lester made him go lie down and he fell asleep, and when he woke up Lurline and Brother John and everybody had already left. Mama Pearl, back in her regular clothes, had explained that Lurline would be in trouble if she did not get back to the Women's Detention Center by six o'clock. But Augie said they should have woke him up so he could tell his own mother goodbye.

Augie scuffed his shoes in the oil-soaked dirt where Erline's car normally sat. Uncle Rosco kept trying to tell her what she should have done to stop the oil leak, but she said she was sick of the old car anyhow and was thinking of getting herself a new one. "The ashtrays are already full," she said breezily. Privately, Augie wondered what she would use for money to get a new car. He stopped under the walnut tree and looked around for nuts. He did not intend to eat them, but to throw them at whatever he happened to find to throw at.

In the distance, he saw uncle Rosco bobbing up and down at the edge of the tobacco field next to the barn. He was feeling the ground to see how dry it was, and while he was at it, he was probably pulling off any worms he saw on the plants. Augie thought maybe he should go help. Once, uncle Rosco had paid him and Audrey a penny a worm to collect them and drop them in jars of kerosene. Both of them had got tired and quit before they had collected a full dollar's worth.

Earlier in the summer, uncle Rosco had offered to pay them to clip cedars out of the pasture. "A nickel a head," he told them. "Big or little—it don't matter." So, Augie and Audrey had picked the smallest ones, the teensy little seedlings they could get with the shears. Because they did not use the saw or the hatchet, they forgot and left them in the pasture where uncle Rosco found them a day or two later. They had quit cutting cedars as soon as they had enough nickels to go to the movie.

Augie felt a little guilty, so he angled down the hill to see if he could help uncle Rosco do anything. He saw the old red-blond rooster marching toward the hens where they were scratching in the straw. He let fly with a walnut. Uncle Rosco's head bobbed up when the rooster let out a squawk, so Augie bent over a rock where he knew a blue lizard lived.

He ended up chasing the lizard into the buckeye thicket, and when he caught it, he took it to show uncle Rosco. Uncle Rosco cupped his big hands for Augie to put the lizard in, and he stroked the lizard's head with his thumb until it lay relaxed in his hands. He laid it flat in one palm, belly up, for Augie to stroke. It lay mesmerized, eyes unblinking.

"After while," uncle Rosco said, "I'm heading to Red True's place. You want to go? Maybe we'll get a hamburger for lunch."

Augie knew what uncle Rosco was up to. Red True owned the best irrigation equipment around. Uncle Rosco had decided it was time to irrigate the tobacco, and he was trying to cheer Augie up about it. Both of them hated to pump the water out of Sawdridge Creek. Augie did not answer uncle Rosco's invitation.

"It's going to rain, uncle Rosco," he said.

Uncle Rosco didn't exactly shake his head, but the way he looked up at the sky meant that he did not think it was ever likely to rain again. The skies blazed blue without even a white scud of cloud. Augie would not look up, for he had been predicting rain for the last six dry, scorching days.

"You wait and see," he said now. "I know. I know it'll rain—the moon had a ring around it."

"When?" asked uncle Rosco. "A week ago?" He spoke slowly and deliberately. Uncle Rosco did not do anything in a hurry, and he said that he never had to take back anything he said because he didn't say much. Even Audrey admitted you could count on what uncle Rosco said.

"What'll the cows drink if you drain the creek?" Augie countered.

"What do they always drink?" Uncle Rosco said. "We'll pump them a trough of cistern water every morning and another at night."

"Mama Pearl won't like the flies with the cows that close

to the house," Augie told him. "She won't like it a bit." The trough was near the smokehouse, and Augie remembered the swarms of flies and horseflies on the porch last summer when uncle Rosco had opened the gate to let the cows into the yard to drink. He remembered, too, that last year the cows had kicked down the metal screen in front of the spring so they could get to the water. Normally, the cows drank the run-off water and did not try to get into the spring.

Last summer, while Red True pumped, Augie had gone from hole to hole in the creek to collect the fish and crawdads from the almost empty pools. He transferred them far downstream where the water still stood. Uncle Rosco ended up helping him. Together, they watched snakes and turtles moving downstream. A trickle of water crossed the rocks, but the sand drank it thirstily. When Red True drained one pool, he moved quickly, efficiently to another.

Augie hated the sound of the pumps. The hoses which led to the irrigation pipes looked like bloated snakes. They writhed and throbbed with the life of the water, and sometimes their suction pulled snakes and fish into the fields where they clogged the pipes. Red True would unscrew some pipe, and out would come a bass, or a trout. If it was a fish, he left it where it landed; if it was a snake, he tried to kill it.

"It'll rain tonight," Augie repeated. "It's got to."

Uncle Rosco considered.

"I'll tell Red True to come tomorrow afternoon," he compromised. "That gives it twenty-four hours to rain." As if by way of answer, sheet lightning played in the west sky.

"Did you see?" Augie asked.

"That lightning's been working a week," uncle Rosco told

him, "and not getting the job done. That's dry lightning. Don't get your hopes up."

He headed up the hill toward his pickup truck. He still held the blue lizard cupped in his hands. He walked with his hands held out in front of him, like somebody in a procession carrying something precious. "You coming?" he asked.

"I don't think so," Augie said. "Uncle Rosco—don't forget the lizard."

Uncle Rosco stopped to put the lizard down at the base of a large fieldstone. It darted from his flattened hand into a shadowed crevice, and, then, as if not believing its good fortune, stuck its head out, eyes glittering, throat throbbing.

Augie had decided to walk to the mailbox and wave good-bye to uncle Rosco from there. Then he would wait for Leroy the mailman. He did not expect any mail worth mentioning. The interesting mail had stopped when uncle Wiley killed himself. Lurline wrote every once in a while, but she always said pretty much the same thing. Uncle Wiley's cards had been different. Augie had not yet forgiven uncle Wiley for killing himself before he got to Gratz so Augie could meet him.

Once, a long time ago, before Augie even knew that uncle Wiley existed, uncle Rosco had said that somebody had *committed sideways,* and Augie wanted to know what he meant.

"It doesn't mean anything," uncle Rosco said. "People around here just say *sideways* when they mean suicide." Augie knew what suicide meant.

Uncle Lester had piped up then, and said that people must say *sideways* for suicide because they know that even if you think you want to die, you don't really mean it at the last minute.

"So," he said, "You kind of go into it sideways, instead of front-on."

After word came that uncle Wiley had killed himself in his motel room in Louisville, Augie wondered if maybe uncle Wiley had changed *his* mind at the last minute. One day he asked Mama Pearl what she thought. They were out on the back porch surrounded by baskets of vegetables Mama Pearl had picked in the garden early that morning. Mama Pearl thought so long about it that Augie thought maybe she had forgotten to answer him.

"Well, Augie," she said finally, "if uncle Wiley changed his mind at the last minute, he let the Lord's plenty of last minutes go by before he got to that final last one. The telephone was two feet from his head, but when they found him, he was lying straight and still as if he was posing for his picture."

After a minute, Mama Pearl added, "And he had written my name and number on a sheet of paper under the phone, and he could have called that number any number of times during the time it must have taken him to die."

Mama Pearl's hands lay idle on top of the basket of beans in her lap. Then, without looking down, she pinched the end of a tough-shelled bean and drew its string to the other end, like a zipper, and shelled out the pale-blue seeds inside.

"He had bought himself all new clothes," Mama Pearl said, "and he had got a shave and a haircut and paid up his motel bill just before he took all those pills. He laid down and fixed himself the way he wanted to be found." Augie was fidgeting. It made him uneasy for Mama Pearl to say so much all at once.

"Augie," she said, "I do not know what you would call a 'last minute' for a man like Wiley. He could have changed

159

his mind any time that day—or even any time for the Lord knows how many years."

Augie did not understand how anybody could decide *not* to kill themselves years before they did it. He did not ask her to explain, for she was still not done with his first question.

"Erline says it is a sin to kill yourself," Mama Pearl said, "and I told her I would not argue with her about it, but that it seemed to me just as much of a sin to let everything go by you and not really live when you could. I said that once you'd decided not to accept a blessed thing the Lord offered you, you wasn't going too much deeper in sin if you just killed yourself all the way."

"Killed yourself all the way—?" echoed Augie.

"Yes," said Mama Pearl, "you do not have to take a knife—or maybe a razor—or a gun or pills to deny your life. You can just not live it."

"Oh," said Augie.

"Erline said she would bring me a book to read on the subject, so I would understand my error, but I told her it did not matter what I thought of what Wiley did. What matters, I told her, is keeping on thinking what good we can of him and keeping on reaching out our hands for what life has to give us."

What Mama Pearl had really told Erline was that she would keep on loving Wiley as she had always done, now that he was further away even than Texas.

Augie had another question, and he blurted it out.

"If you've got to die," he said, "like the preacher said at uncle Wiley's funeral, what's the use of anything? What does it matter what you do?"

"Well, Augie," said Mama Pearl, "what's the use of that tray of banana ice cream in the freezer if you and me don't eat it up?"

Augie was on his feet. "Lots or little?" he asked.

"Lots," said Mama Pearl. "And push the coffeepot over where it'll warm up. When your uncle Rosco comes in, he may want some coffee with his ice cream."

"Just charge it to Pearl," Erline said negligently. The woman in the boy's department at Goldman's began writing out a charge ticket. Erline and Audrey had picked out a suit for Augie.

"Won't he look cute?" Erline kept asking. "A little vest and necktie—I didn't know they made three-piece suits for kids."

"He's not going to like it," Audrey said.

"Not like this suit?" demanded Erline. "Of course he'll like it—once he gets used to it." Erline operated on the assumption that sooner or later children like anything they cannot avoid.

"I mean he's not going to like any of it," Audrey told her.

Erline waved her unlighted cigarette airily. "He'll get over it," she said. "Kids always do. They forget they were mad and end up having a good time in spite of themselves."

"Says who?" muttered Audrey. Then, aloud, "I, for one, intend to be in my room with the radio turned on loud and the door locked, when they tell him."

Erline lit her cigarette, and when the clerk turned to tell her for the fifth time that she could not smoke in the store, she smiled broadly and said, "That's okay, we're leaving." Audrey followed her with their packages.

Francis X. Lighter was sitting in his car in front of Erline's house. Repeatedly, he had tried to get Erline on the phone and had finally driven out from Frankfort to see her. A sign in the window said "Closed," and, from the looks of things, Erline did not even live here any more. The oil spots in the driveway, from where Erline's car leaked, had dried up, and all the venetian blinds were closed tight.

Francis drove back to Gratz and wondered whether to ask about her in the feedstore or the bank. He decided to go into the People's Bank, and stood in line at one of the two counters. The woman in front of him was putting money in her Christmas Club Account. The youngish woman behind the counter eyed Francis curiously. She was thinking that he, for sure, didn't come from around here. He was dressed fit to kill, on a Thursday morning.

He leaned forward slightly, and asked in his sexiest voice, "Do you know where I can reach Mrs. Erline Grissom?"

The clerk's lifted eyebrows dropped. "Sure," she said. "That's her brother right over there." Francis considered leaving right then, but everybody in the bank was listening—everybody, that is, but uncle Lester. He was concentrating fiercely on the figures the other bank clerk was adding up on a machine. He was making the feedstore deposit, and he did not want the bank to be able to catch him in a mistake. He had itemized all the checks and added them up, and to that sum he had added the cash.

He gave Agnes the deposit book and his adding machine tape. "Just mark off the checks on my tapes and count the money," he told Agnes, "and you will see I am right." He regarded it a waste of time for her to check his figures. He hoped to impress the bank so that next summer, he could have a job behind the counter of the bank instead of at the feedstore.

"Right on the button," said Agnes finally. "Exactly $567.32."

"What did I tell you?" Lester asked.

"Lester," the other clerk repeated. "Didn't you hear me, Lester? This man is looking for Erline."

"What does he want with her?" uncle Lester asked.

"Why don't you ask him, Lester? He's standing right here."

Uncle Lester still had not looked at Francis. "I am looking for Mrs. Grissom on business," Francis told everybody. Then, needlessly, he added, "Strictly business."

Lester swung his eyes to Francis X. Lighter and looked him over carefully. Then he picked up his deposit book and little canvas pouch. He nodded to Agnes, and said to the room at large, "Well, why don't you write her a letter then? A business letter." With that, he left.

Francis shook his head and started to say something to the clerk Lester had called Agnes, but she had bent her head over her work. Francis left the bank and got in his car to drive out of town. He saw uncle Lester in front of the feedstore, pencil in hand, waiting to write down his license number.

Again, Francis shook his head. "Wonder what he'll do with it, now he's got it," he said to himself.

Uncle Lester had a special book in which he wrote license numbers. Usually, he wrote down a brief description of the car and sometimes of its occupants, where he saw it, and when. Today, he simply wrote down on a fresh page the day, Thursday, August 21. He would fill in the details later.

In the feedstore, he gave Mr. Bascomb the deposit book.

"My figures," he said, "were right on the button. As usual. It took me longer than usual because some fellow was asking questions." Mr. Bascomb looked up from an order book. "What about?" he asked.

"I didn't tell him anything," said Lester.

Francis thought he might as well go back to Frankfort. Then he remembered the road Erline had shown him which led to her people's place. The name was Waters, like Erline's middle name, though as Francis understood things, nobody much who lived there was named Waters. Some old woman, who had once been married to somebody in the family, and her husband or boyfriend, and Erline's kid and her sister's kid. He could recall nothing about Erline's child. Francis knew that if he had any sense, he would drive straight back to Frankfort and forget Erline Waters Grissom.

Instead, he drove toward what Erline called "the home place." A man in a pickup truck was pulling out of the road onto the highway. He lifted one finger in greeting, and Francis did the same. Within a half mile, Francis saw a mailbox with "Waters" painted on it. No house was in sight, but a little boy stood next to the mailbox. Francis pulled off the hardtop, and rolled his window down.

"You're not the mailman," Augie challenged. "Where's Leroy the mailman?"

"Beats me," said Francis. "I am looking for someone, too. Is Erline Grissom here?"

"Nope," said Augie. "She's gone."

"Gone?" said Francis. "Where?"

Augie lifted his shoulders as if the possibilities were too immense to list.

"She's been gone a long time," Augie mourned. "I'm all by myself."

"Are you her little boy?" Francis asked, his voice suddenly gentle.

"Shoot, no," Augie said. "My mother is Lurline, and she's been gone even longer than Erline." Francis recalled something about Lurline's being in prison for forging a check or something. He nodded encouragement to Augie. "Erline took Audrey—that's her daughter—with her when she left," Augie concluded.

To indicate he had said all he meant to say, he took aim and threw a walnut at a distant crow wetting its wings in the creek.

Francis thanked him and said goodbye, but the boy did not look at him again. Why would Erline go and move away without telling him anything? Francis closed his window and began looking for a place to turn around. At the intersection, he saw the mailman's blue, three-wheeled car. Leroy raised one finger in greeting, which Francis returned. Maybe he should ask the mailman if Erline had left a forwarding address. He thought better of doing so, and while the mailman turned into the road beside him, Francis flipped open his indexed address book. He opened to G, and drew a heavy line through the initials EWG and the phone number underneath.

"That's life," he told himself as he swung the car onto the highway and headed back toward Frankfort.

"Hi, Augie, how's it going?"

"Terrible. Everybody's gone but me, and there's nothing to do."

Leroy the mailman nodded. He expected Augie to ask if

he could ride around with him and help deliver mail, and, though it was strictly against regulations, Leroy expected to let him do so.

"Say," he said, "is your mother home?"

"You know she's not," Augie said, beginning to cloud up. "Why should Mama Pearl write her all those letters if she was here?"

"That's what I thought," soothed Leroy. "Just what I thought."

He pulled a letter from the stack beside him. "What should we do with this?" he asked Augie. It was a letter addressed to Lurline. It was addressed in pencil and the handwriting looked old-fashioned, so Augie guessed it must be from aunt Muddie.

"Is it from Shelbyville?" Augie asked. "If it is, it's from aunt Muddie, and she ought to know where Lurline is, for she is always writing to her—at Louisville."

"Half the time, you can't tell any more," said Leroy. "Used to be, you could look at a letter and not only tell what town it come from but the day and the hour it was postmarked. Now, mostly they say 'US Postal Service,' which don't tell you much of anything." He studied the letter briefly. "Sure enough," he said, "it must be from your aunt Muddie, for the postmark says Shelbyville."

Augie took the letter so he could look at the postmark.

"Do you want me to forward it to your mama in Louisville?" Leroy asked him.

"No," Augie said. "I will just keep it for her."

Leroy hesitated. "Well," he said finally, "you be sure to ask Pearl what she thinks you ought to do about it."

"She's not here," Augie said.

"Say," Leroy suggested, as if he had just had a good idea, "why don't you hop in and help me deliver the rest of this mail?"

"Nope," Augie said. "I got to stay here and look after things." Studying the letter, which he held close to his face, he headed back toward the house.

Erline and Audrey were sitting in the Court House Cafe in Owenton. Erline was smoking another Herbert Tareyton and occasionally sipping her coffee, and Audrey was making her coke last as long as possible. For lunch, Audrey had ordered nothing but a coke, though she had later eaten Erline's potato chips and pickle which came with her chicken salad sandwich. Miss Nell, in the Junior Miss department at Goldman's Department Store, had said Audrey was big for her age, and Audrey had decided she would quit eating for awhile.

"Look," said Erline, when the waitress brought her sandwich. "Pringles."

The waitress stared at Erline and then at the potato chips as if she had never seen either of them before. "You don't want them, you don't have to eat them," she told Erline and returned to her stool behind the cash register.

"Stuck up thing," the waitress was thinking to herself about Erline, who leaned across the table to whisper to Audrey. "Stuck up thing," she mouthed. "You'd think we didn't go to high school together—and that I don't know perfectly well why she quit going."

"Why?" Audrey asked. "Why did she?" Audrey was practicing her Elizabeth Taylor look and voice—the one she had learned from watching *National Velvet* on late TV.

"O, you know," Erline said, rolling her eyes. "I've explained all *that* a million times." The fact was, Audrey did understand, but not because Erline had explained anything. Audrey had found a book under uncle Lester's pillow. She tried hard not to believe any of what she read, but she finally asked uncle Lester about it and he told her it was true and she better look out.

Audrey had tried to tell Augie some of it, but, as she suspected, he told her she was crazy and he was going to tell Mama Pearl on her. Some parts of the book were crazier than others, and Audrey had finally decided that she, personally, had nothing to do with any of it.

Erline had purposely put off having lunch until late— "when the crowd thinned out," as she put it. She had succeeded, for there was no one in the cafe but the waitress and themselves. Her reason for avoiding people, she said, was that everybody was dying to pump them to find out what was going on in the family. Audrey wondered why anyone would pump them to find out anything, for she regarded their lives as unpleasantly public. Everyone had read about it in the paper when Lurline was convicted of forging uncle Lester's name on a check for $1,000. And, later, after uncle Wiley had killed himself, that had been in the paper, too. And, though the county newspaper had not reported the fact that Erline had thrown a potted plant at Francis X. Lighter, while uncle Wiley was lying in state, everybody and his brother knew about it.

Now, she guessed Lurline's wedding would make the society page.

And what people couldn't read about in the paper or find out by asking anybody on the street, they could just wait for

Erline to announce to them two minutes after they ran into her. Erline had talked nonstop to everybody who had waited on them in stores that day, and even Audrey had learned a few things she hadn't known before.

"People like that," Erline said now, jerking her head toward the sullen waitress, "are fit to be tied now everybody knows how rich we are."

"How rich?" said Audrey in her Elizabeth Taylor little-girl voice. "And who are *we*? I haven't noticed there's any *we* to it; it's Mama Pearl who's got the money."

"It's all the same," Erline insisted. "It's in the family, and the way Pearl is holding onto it, there'll be more tomorrow than there was yesterday. We're just helping her get rid of a little of the surplus today—after all, I figure we're entitled to a little of it now."

Audrey didn't bother to answer. Instead, she leaned her head slightly to one side and opened her eyes wide at her mother.

Erline flustered. "Who's it doing any good?" she demanded. "And hasn't Pearl lived with us all these years—absolutely rent-free?"

Audrey leaned her head even further to one side and kept her gaze on Erline. "Say," her mother said thoughtfully, "you know who you look like when you do that—? What's-her-name, that floozy-looking actress married to Richard Burton . . . that's who. Did you ever see a movie called *National Velvet*?"

Audrey pursed her lips. "Thank you very much," she said. "I, for one, do not regard Elizabeth Taylor a floozy."

The way Audrey saw it, *they* had been living with Mama Pearl, not the other way round, and, until lately, Erline had not even lived there at all, though she had shown up for meals often enough—food grown and picked and cooked by Mama Pearl. First, Erline had closed up her beauty shop and then, before anybody knew what was happening, she had packed up her bags and moved back home.

"I have moved back to stay," she told Mama Pearl, and, in the next breath, she was saying what all was wrong with the house—not enough closets, not enough bathrooms, and no shower. "Oh, well," she would say, "nothing's perfect, but this old house can be a dream—with a few dollars here and there."

She went around the house with a tape measure and a clip-board, trying to decide what to do to the house. Sometimes, she would say that she thought they should all move out and just start over. And then Mama Pearl would narrow her eyes at Erline, and Erline would return to her measuring and sketching. She had been thinking lately about what a good idea it would be to ask Francis X. Lighter for help with what she liked to call "extensive remodeling." Boy, she thought, wouldn't that burn Francis's wife—to have him working for her on a really big job. . . .

Audrey was thinking about what Erline had said about getting some of Mama Pearl's money *now*. It sounded as if Erline was waiting for Mama Pearl to die. "Won't it be uncle Rosco's money," she asked, "if Mama Pearl dies? After all, they are married now."

"That was a mistake," Erline conceded. "We should never have let them do a silly thing like getting married. Still, it could be worse." She laughed briefly and mirthlessly.

"Rosco," she said flatly. "What would Rosco do with money? He'd sit on it worse than Pearl does." She drummed her fingernails on the tabletop, impatient at the idea of Rosco's being allowed to sit on any sum of money, much less the sum she had decided Mama Pearl must be worth.

The waitress got up from behind the cash register and, heaving a massive sigh, punched the no-sale key and took out a coin. She shuffled toward the juke-box and studied the songs a long time before making her selection. Johnny Cash came out loud and clear. Erline winced.

"If she can't run us out," she said, "she'll drown us out."

The waitress heard, and raised one finger to the front of her nose, which she tilted upwards. Audrey giggled. The waitress came over to collect their dishes, and paused long enough to frown at Erline's overflowing ashtray. She finally picked it up with two fingers and held it far in front of her. She made a special trip back to get Erline's coffee cup, which she did not offer to refill.

"What *is* that girl's name?" Erline mused. "Something with an H—. Something simply awful to be stuck with for a name. What on earth was it? Maybe Havoline?"

"That sounds like a motor oil," Audrey said. "Nobody could be named Havoline."

Loretta Lynn was singing now—something about wearing miniskirts and how great it was to have the pill. "They ought to ban that song," said Erline. When the third record turned out to be Johnny Cash again, Erline decided it was high time they left. She put a quarter on the table. "More than she deserves," she told Audrey, and they went toward the cash register.

A bright orange pickup truck stopped in front of the Court House Cafe. Two shirtless men were in the cab, and a half-dozen more were riding in the back. The ones in the back still wore their hard hats; they were construction crewmen for the powerline going up. They knotted around the truck for a minute, obviously deciding whether to put their shirts on. Most of them had their shirts tied around their waists, and the others had to root around in the truck to find theirs.

The waitress behind the counter paid no more attention to the sunburned men outside than to Erline, who waited, haughtily, to pay her check. The men began to file inside, and Erline cut her eyes at them as they passed, looking for the slender, dark-headed one who had first caught her eye. The waitress was reading a movie magazine, running one finger down the page to tick off each line as she finished it. Erline and Audrey had to wait for her to finish the page, which she eventually did.

The waitress was examining Erline's and Audrey's check suspiciously, as if she would not put it past Erline to change the total. Negligently, Erline had tossed a ten-dollar bill onto the counter and stood, pretending to say something to Audrey, though really making sure the men got themselves an eyeful.

"Hey, Havoline," one of the men called, and Audrey began to giggle. "Havoline, come over here. We got something to ask you."

Erline was certain she knew what they wanted to ask Havoline. They would want to know who *she* was, and, boy, wouldn't that burn old Havoline up? She took her change as if she was doing Havoline a favor, and laid one hand on Audrey's shoulder to steer her outside.

Audrey shrugged her hand off and whispered, "Did you hear? Her name *is* Havoline."

At the door, Erline cut her eyes back, and, sure enough,

every man jack of them was following her with his eyes. She could have sworn that the cute little, dark-headed one was the one who had called to Havoline.

"Hey, look," said Audrey, "here comes uncle Rosco. He must be headed to the cafe."

"Lord, let's hurry then," Erline said. "I wouldn't go back in there for anything—not even if he begged us."

They waited in front of the cafe window, while Erline looked for her car keys and, by the time she had gone through her purse twice, uncle Rosco was there. It turned out he was headed for the Gulf Station. Erline half listened to what he was telling them about a spare part he had asked Elmo to find for him. When he finished, Erline told him how hot and tired he looked and that he should get himself something cold to drink. But he did not take the hint.

"Audrey and I were just saying," Erline lied, "that we hoped you would treat us to a coke or something."

"Well," said Rosco, "that's all right with me, if you want to."

"Not me," said Audrey. "I hope I never have to see old Motor Oil again as long as I live." She headed for Erline's car.

"Some other time, Rosco," said Erline, waving at him as if he were off on a long journey and wondering how well she could be seen from inside the cafe.

Uncle Lester got home early and nobody was there. The feedstore had closed early because old Mrs. Grider, the mother of the feedstore owner's wife, had finally died. For two years Mrs. Grider had lived with the Bascombs, and they had talked constantly about how to get her off their hands. She had already worried the life out of two husbands and an older daughter before she came to live at Gratz. Now she was dead, everybody made it sound as if she had spent her life spreading joy.

Mr. Bascomb hung a wreath of artificial white lilies on the door, and everybody tiptoed and whispered while they closed up. Lester decided they must have had the wreath a good while and were waiting for a chance to use it. He did not know Mrs. Grider, but had heard lots about her; he had seen her glaring from the back seat of Mrs. Bascomb's car and had wondered whose idea it was for her to sit there.

Erline had sometimes fixed Mrs. Grider's hair, and she said the old lady was a hell-cat, whose language would not bear repeating. The Bascombs had tried to hush it up when Mrs. Grider somehow got to Frankfort and was found under a culvert finishing off a six-pack of beer. Nobody could say how she had got there, but Erline said, in her opinion, Mrs. Bascomb had better take to locking up the broom.

Lester had tried to find out how old Mrs. Grider was without coming right out and asking. He wanted to compare her age with Mama Pearl's and uncle Rosco's. He worried about them and about who would look after them when they were old. If Mrs. Grider, who had six children, was not wanted anywhere, what about Mama Pearl? Erline and Lurline were always saying she was not even a member of the family, and she had never had any children. It was not a question of money, but even with Mama Pearl's money, who would look after them unless he did?

He could tell nobody was at home even before he went into the cool of the hall. The house *felt* empty, and he shivered a little bit, thinking about how it would be someday when none of them lived there any more. He hated to think how the old house would change if Erline got her way and started to remodel it.

Lester was not hungry or thirsty either one, but he went straight to the kitchen and got a dipper of water from the stoneware crock of springwater in the back porch refrigerator. He raised an eyebrow when he saw three bottles of Miller's High Life on the rack. Erline's, he guessed. Uncle Rosco always kept a bottle of Heaven Hill hidden somewhere, which Mama Pearl pretended to know nothing about.

When Lester saw the envelope with Mama Pearl's name on it, he wondered how he had missed it the first thing. He guessed he hadn't expected it, and that was why. It was propped up against the cut-glass sugar bowl in the middle of the kitchen table. The envelope was sealed, and Augie had written Mama Pearl's full name—Mrs. Pearl T. White.

"Lord," thought Lester, "what has Augie decided to do dumb this time?" There was no telling what Augie had done to get even for not getting to go to Louisville with Mama Pearl to see Lurline.

Lester glared around the kitchen. "Where is Audrey?" he said out loud. "And Erline?" Had they gone off and left Augie all day when they knew as well as he did that Augie had cried himself to sleep last night? He had the envelope open. "Dear Mrs. White," Augie had printed. "O Lord," said Lester, "he must be really mad."

The letter continued:

Aunt Muddie wrote to Lurline, and I have read what she had to say.

I am going to Louisville to see Lurline, for she has lots to explain.

So do you.

Augie

PS

Do not try to stop me.

Lester had both hands on his head and looked like he was trying to pick himself up by the hair. He looked around for aunt Muddie's letter, but he knew already that Augie would take that with him to show his mother. Anyhow, Lester had a pretty good idea what the letter said. It said too much, but not enough to let Augie know there was no point in going to Louisville.

Lester *knew* they should not have tried to fool Augie. By now, Lurline and Mama Pearl were probably through signing the papers which would get Lurline out of the Women's Detention Center on probation. Brother John would be with them, or he would be waiting in his car—which Lester suspected Mama Pearl had given him the money to buy. Lurline and Brother John meant to get married, and the Counselor at the Detention Center said that was okay, for she thought Brother John was a good influence on Lurline.

They had meant to surprise Augie—that had been Erline's idea. Erline said Augie would be happy as pie to see his mother and his new daddy if they promised they would have another wedding with cake and ice cream like they had for Pearl and Rosco.

Lurline had doubtless written to aunt Muddie, who had answered her at Gratz, instead of Louisville, saying just enough to let Augie know he had been tricked but not enough to let him know the details. Lester went to the telephone and stared at the number for the Women's Detention

Center. He could call and maybe Lurline and Brother John could look for Augie on the way home.

He knew that Lurline would get hysterical at once, but that Mama Pearl would worry more than anybody. "Lordy Lord," he said turning away from the phone. He folded up Augie's letter, and went to the big Bible open on the table in front of the living room window. He put the letter inside the Bible, carefully noting the place. If anybody decided they just had to read the third chapter of John before he got home, they would find it.

He closed the door on the house's emptiness, and looked around him quickly before he set out running.

SueAnn and SueFan Bascomb were sitting in front of Erline's house in their VW. Their mother had sent them to Erline's when Erline did not answer the phone. They were to see if Erline could drive to the funeral home at Owenton to fix Mrs. Grider's hair before 7:30, when they expected people to begin showing up to call on the family.

"Tell her that Mama swore by how she fixed her hair," Mrs. Bascomb instructed, "and tell her we wouldn't want anybody but her to fix Mama's hair—the last time."

"Erline GRISSOM?" the twins exploded. "Gram couldn't STAND her, and BESIDES, she has a big orange CLOSED sign in her window—and EVERYBODY says Gram made her so mad she nearly popped and drove sixty-miles-an-hour to Owenton to buy the sign."

"Your grandmother bears her no ill will," Mrs. Bascomb told them. "She was not that kind of woman, and surely Erline will not begrudge her a little time to make her look nice this last time." After a minute, she added, "If Erline doesn't want to do it, just tell her the job is included in the funeral bill and she can name her own price."

On the way to Gratz, the twins agreed that money would talk; Erline Grissom would do anything for money. "How much would *you* charge to curl a dead woman's hair?" Sue-Fan asked her sister. "Fifty dollars at least," said SueAnn, "and if it was Gram's hair, I would add another ten—for there are all those bald spots to cover up."

SueFan giggled. "But at least Gram will be quiet for a change," she said.

At Erline's house, they agreed nobody was home even before they got out and pounded on the door. They were dripping sweat, and thought that the simplest thing to do would be just to close the top of Gram's casket so nobody could see her, or her hair. They knew their mother would never agree to that, for then everybody would make up terrible stories about how the old lady died. People would say she had been beaten, or something. The twins got back in the VW and talked about what to do.

"Where do Erline's people live?" SueFan wondered. "The ones not in prison, I mean."

"Hey, look," SueAnn said. "Isn't that one of their kids over there?" She pointed across the highway, where Augie had suddenly appeared. He did not look toward Erline's house, but was staring down the empty highway. What cars came along were going the wrong way, and Augie thought he would never get a ride to Louisville.

Some dumb girls were blowing their horn at him and waving at him, and he pretended he did not hear them. He was glad to see a car coming from the right direction. It just *might* take him to Louisville. Augie put up his thumb. The car passed him at first, and then stopped and began to back up. He began to run toward the car and saw that the license plates said Jefferson County, which was where uncle Lester said Louisville was.

Behind him, two blond heads stuck out of the VW windows and the girls were calling to him to wait a minute. Let *them* wait, he thought; this was his chance to get to Louisville.

"He's actually getting in that car," said SueFan. "Write the license number down."

"What for?" said SueAnn. "He's not our kid."

"Just do it," SueFan said. "You never can tell. Let's see— CMP-810, Jefferson County."

"Okay," SueAnn sighed. "Sometimes we do the dumbest things." She wrote the number on her palm with a felt-tip pen and waved her hand in SueFan's face. "What do we do about Gram's hair?" she asked.

"How about a home permanent?" SueFan said. "We'll split the fifty dollars."

"Ugghh." SueAnn collapsed on her side of the car. "Count me out," she said.

Erline and Audrey were finishing up their shopping. The back seat of the car was filled with boxes and packages, and Erline looked very satisfied with herself. "What good is money anyhow, if you don't spend it?" she had asked more than once. So far, she had spent no money but had charged everything.

"Just one more stop," she told Audrey. "Then we'll be home in a flash."

"Tuna fish," said Audrey. "I bet you're getting tuna fish and potato chips for supper."

"How'd you guess?" Erline fake-smiled and braked the car inches short of the plate-glass window of the Minit-Market. She left the engine running. "If I'm not back in a minute," she said, "just turn the key."

Audrey yawned. She was listening to the radio and had no intention of turning off the engine. She knew Erline would find SOMEBODY to talk to. Audrey wished Augie was along. He would set up a howl to stop at the MacDonald's, and Audrey bet Erline would give in after about two good howls.

Augie had written Lurline's address on the back of the letter from aunt Muddie. As soon as he got in the car, he took the envelope out of his pocket so it would be handy in case the man driving the car wanted to know exactly where he was going. Sure enough, the first thing the man said was "Where you going?"

"Louisville," said Augie.

"*Where* in Louisville. It's a big place."

"Oh," said Augie indifferently, "out near Pewee Valley will be fine." He was not at all sure he wanted to tell somebody he did not know that he was going to see his mother at the Women's Detention Center. The big car was moving fast, and Augie craned his neck to see if he could tell *how* fast they were going.

"I'm cold," he said suddenly. "Can I open the window and let some of the cold out?"

"Cold?" the man said. "Okay, we aim to please. I'll turn the air conditioner off." They were already nearing Bethlehem, and, after that, they would be in Pleasureville in no time, then Cropper and Shelbyville.

Augie began to squirm around and leaned over to look in the back seat of the car. A metal bar across the back seat supported about twenty hangers, each draped with plastic covers. Two or three bulging briefcases and leather folders lay on the seat. On the floor was a metal ice chest with *Pepsi Cola* printed on top. Jammed up against it was a bag with bottles in it. A tall recloseable bottle of Canada Dry rolled around on the floor. Augie squirmed some more.

The man had been watching Augie in the long mirror on the windshield. "Now what?" he asked.

"I guess being cold has made me need to go to the bathroom," Augie said. He was shaking slightly, and now the air conditioner was off, he was beginning to feel hot. He felt as he had once when he had caught a virus.

"Can you hold it six more miles?" Augie shook his head vigorously. The car slowed down and swerved, and, miraculously, Augie thought, nosed comfortably between brick and concrete markers beside a winding country road. Gigantic oaks lined the road, which led toward an unseen house.

"It's all yours," the man said, gesturing toward the expanse of grass and trees.

"Here?" Augie asked. "I don't think I have to go after all." The man leaned across and opened the car door. "Git," he said. Augie got out and then reached back in for aunt Muddie's letter. He fully expected the man to drive off and leave him. He walked into the trees and got behind one of them, and, at first, he thought maybe he really didn't have to go, and then he felt better.

From behind the tree, Augie could see that the man had got out of the car too and had watched where he went. He stood for a minute as if he was going to go to the bathroom too, and then he opened the back seat of the car. Augie waited a minute longer and then walked around the tree and into the road. The man had put ice and ginger ale into two styrofoam cups when Augie returned, and he was pouring something else into one of the glasses.

"Everything come out all right?" the man asked him. When Augie said nothing, the man handed him a cup of ginger ale. "Have some ginger ale," he said. Augie shook his head. "Take it," the man said, so he did. The man started to put the bottle back into the back seat, but thought better of it and laid it instead on the front seat, where only the neck stuck out of a paper sack. They got back in the car.

"What's your name, anyhow?" the man asked.

"Augie," said Augie. "What's yours?"

"Chuck," the man said, and held out his hand to shake. Augie took his hand, and said, "Chuck what?"

"Just Chuck," the man told him, withdrawing his hand and letting it rest casually on the seat behind Augie, who turned on the seat and stared at his hand. "Where'd you get the ring?" he asked. Chuck was wearing an enormous silver and turquoise ring.

"Arizona. The Indians made it," Chuck told him, dropping his hand close to Augie so he could see it better. "Ever been to Arizona?"

"No," Augie said, "I've never been much of anywhere, I guess."

"Well," said Chuck, "you and me are going to Louisville, aren't we? That's somewhere." He did not start the car, however, and, after holding his ring under Augie's nose again, he opened the bottle beside him and poured more liquor in his cup.

"You're not supposed to do that," Augie said. "Drinking and Driving Equals Disaster." He had not tasted his ginger ale.

"Hey, that's pretty good," Chuck laughed. "I'll remember that. But I'm not driving—am I?" He lifted both hands to demonstrate that fact. He took a sip of his drink, and again leaned across Augie to open the glove compartment. He found a package of cigarettes, and solemnly offered Augie one before he lit his own.

"If you like the ring," he said suddenly, "you'll love this." He pushed back his sleeve and removed a turquoise-studded bracelet from his slender wrist. He handed it to Augie, and added: "And this?" He twisted suddenly on the car seat and pulled up his loose shirt to reveal a gigantic belt buckle, which was comprised of looping silver snakes whose heads and tails held in place another large, heavily-veined greenish-blue stone.

"See the snakes?" Chuck asked. "They're sacred to the Indians." He tried to guide Augie's hand over to feel the belt buckle, but Augie withdrew his hand and, wordlessly, gave Chuck back the bracelet.

"Tell you what," Chuck said thoughtfully. "You like the ring—it's yours." He slipped it off his finger and passed it to Augie. He was still slumped over in the seat. Above the buckle, his stomach was pale and hairy. Augie held the ring and turned it in the light.

"It's too big," he said finally and hung it on the top of his thumb to hold back toward Chuck. "I got to be going," he said suddenly, and laid the ring on the seat between them. "I want to be in Louisville before dark."

"How come?" Chuck wanted to know. "You can stay with

me tonight and I'll get you wherever you want to go—first thing tomorrow." Augie hesitated, and then began to open the door.

"Okay, okay," Chuck said. "You win." He started the car, backed it into the highway, and zoomed forward, faster than ever. "What's wrong," he asked, "you don't like me?" Augie stared at him silently, then he took a small drink of his ginger ale. "Thanks for the ginger ale," he said. "It's good."

"Sure," Chuck grinned. He still held the styrofoam cup. He took a deep drink. "Here," he said, "hold this," and freed of the cup picked up the bottle; with his teeth, he removed the cap. "Hold the cup over, buddy," he said, and when Augie did so, he let the bottle gurgle a long time before he stopped pouring.

"How 'bout yours, buddy?" he said. "Need freshening?"

"No," said Augie. "No thank you." He wondered if Chuck had forgotten his name, and he wondered also if Chuck had put whiskey in his ginger ale. Chuck handed him the whiskey bottle, and Augie considered letting it slip from his hands and spilling it. "Get the top, and put it on," Chuck told him.

"Hand it to me," Augie answered. The cap had fallen from Chuck's mouth into his lap. "Pretty smart, aren't you?" Chuck said matter-of-factly. Augie shook his head no, and put the top on the bottle, which he placed on the seat between them. Then, on impulse, he pulled it over closer to him.

"Pleasureville, buddy," said Chuck, "and I am feeling no pain." They slowed down at the traffic light at the Gulf station, and turned left, following the signs which said Shelby-ville. "Pleasureville," repeated Chuck. "Wonder why they named it that?" He grinned crookedly, and Augie said he didn't know why anybody named anything what they did.

"Take Gratz," he said. "Nobody I know can say why they named Gratz *Gratz*."

"Forget it, babe," said Chuck.

Soon, they were on the highway again, and Augie asked how far it was to Louisville now.

"Miles," said Chuck. "Miles to go before you sleep."

Mama Pearl and Lurline sat in the front of Brother John's 1975 Corvair, while Brother John filled up the trunk and part of the back seat with Lurline's things. "I did not know I had accumulated so much," Lurline kept saying, and Brother John would say, "You ladies just relax. I believe in the equality of the sexes, but there are some things the man ought to do."

"Am I making another mistake, Pearl?" Lurline whispered. Brother John was nowhere in sight, and Mama Pearl wondered why Lurline was whispering.

"Only you and he can answer that," she told Lurline. "But if you are not certain how you feel, you do not have to do anything. Rosco and me want you back home, with or without a husband."

"How I feel," Lurline moaned, "is half the problem. I do not know any man I have ever loved as much as I want that tall skinny preacher."

Mama Pearl stared out the window and would not look at Lurline. Finally, she coughed a little and Lurline jumped and said, "Yes, what is it?"

"You are talking about two things," Mama Pearl said. "You are talking about wanting and loving, and I have lived a long enough time to know that they are not the same."

"Am I?" said Lurline. "I thought I was talking about whether I loved Brother John enough to marry him and stay married this time."

"Well, Lurline," Mama Pearl sighed, "they may be mixed up in your head, but for me, wanting and loving are two different things." She transferred her gaze to the horizon. "And I have done both things," she said. "Once, both of them together; once, the wanting without the loving; and, lately, the loving without the wanting."

Lurline ducked her head to see if she could find the distant point Mama Pearl seemed to be trying to memorize.

"With Rosco?" she breathed.

"It is not my life we are discussing, Lurline," said Mama Pearl, snapping open her pocketbook and pulling out a tiny handkerchief. "We are talking about what you are going to do with your life, and before *he* gets back in the car, I think we had better decide so that he will know what to tell Augie when we get home."

Brother John appeared in the door carrying a potted plant with multicolored peppers on it and hundreds of tiny white blossoms.

"Where you want this, Lurline?" he called. Wordless, Mama Pearl lowered her window and took the plant. She held it on her knees and examined the peppers, some green, some yellow, some speckled, and others purpling toward maturity.

"That's what Rosie give me," Lurline told her. "You remember Rosie—the epileptic Mexican lady."

Mama Pearl nodded. She kept her eyes on the pepper plant.

"These purplish fruits," she said, "are where you've been.

186

The taste of them burns your tongue. The speckled ones put me in mind of mixed feelings, and the yellow and green ones are things that haven't been decided yet. But the blossoms are all the things that can be."

Lurline's eyes were stretched as wide open as they could get. She regarded Mama Pearl as if she was a person from another planet. Lurline reached over and touched a blossom with her finger. It shook on its tiny twig, and she prodded it again. The petals fell away like dry butterfly wings, leaving a tiny green protuberance which was a new pepper.

Brother John swung open the car door on his side. "All set?"

"—and raring to go," Lurline said. She ran her fingers under his chin and up the other side of his face toward his left ear.

"Pearl and me have just decided something," she said. "You're the man for me—but what do we tell Augie?"

Uncle Lester loped across the bridge to the filling station-grocery store on the Henry County side of the Kentucky River. He had run all the way to town, and burst into the grocery store's smell of fresh-ground coffee. He could hear the exhaust fans pumping away, and, after the glare outside, the cool and darkness seemed to wrap around him. He wished for a minute he could just buy himself a Dr. Pepper and go home again.

He wound his way through piles of canned goods and islands of breads and cookies. At the cash register, he saw Mrs. Youngblood, her head wrapped in a chiffon scarf which did not hide the plastic curlers crimping her hair. She was looking down, talking to somebody.

Moving closer, Lester saw the Bascomb twins seated on

Coca Cola flats and eating sandwiches they had made at the back of the store: pimiento loaf and cheese on Rainbo bread. Lester felt suddenly tongue-tied. The Bascomb twins were a year ahead of him in school; they never spoke to him there or at their father's store, which they visited infrequently—mostly to get money. Secretly, Lester thought they needed to be taught a lesson, and, sometimes, he imagined how he could teach it to them.

"Mrs. Youngblood," he began now, "I'm looking for Augie—and I thought maybe you . . ." The twins gasped, and SueAnn waved her hand in his face. There was something written on her hand. Both twins had jumped up and were talking, both at the same time.

"That's just what we . . ."

"So we wrote it down, and MAYBE . . ."

"We're so GLAD that you . . ."

"You never know about STRANGERS, do you . . . ?"

"What about Gram's hair?"

"Where's Erline?"

"And so, what are we going to do?"

Lester was staggered. "What has your Gram's hair got to do with anything?" he asked.

"Erline is supposed to be fixing it right now," SueFan said, "so she can lie in state."

"But now—with Augie kidnapped and all," snuffled Sue-Ann, "I guess everybody will just have to take her the way she is, bald spots and all."

Suddenly, both girls were crying and Mrs. Youngblood said, sternly, "Now look what you've done, Lester—they're upset again."

"What is all this?" Lester demanded. "Who says Augie has been kidnapped? It's the first I've heard of it."

"He got in a car—an Oldsmobile," said SueAnn, "and this is the license number." She held her hand steady while Lester copied it down in his license-number book. "CMP-810," he wrote.

He headed for the door, and then he recalled old lady Grider's hair. "Erline is in Owenton, shopping," he yelled to the twins. Then, on an afterthought, he said, "Shopping for Lurline's wedding."

"Lurline's wedding," the twins wailed. "But we've got to get GRAM buried."

"That's gratitude for you," SueFan told her sister.

"How bad does her hair look?" Mrs. Youngblood wanted to know. "Maybe she'll get by in a pinch. Have you thought of putting a hat on her—or maybe a kerchief?"

Lester galloped back in. "Change for a dollar," he said, waving a bill at Mrs. Youngblood. "I got to call the State Patrol."

"Use my personal phone, free," Mrs. Youngblood offered, "but call the Owen County Sheriff and let *him* call the State Patrol. That's what we pay taxes for."

"How long ago was it?" Lester asked from the phone. "How long since Augie got in that Oldsmobile?"

The telephone rang at that very minute, and Mrs. Youngblood answered it and took down a fifteen-dollar grocery order before she hung up. By then, the twins had told Lester that it was "ages and ages ago" that they had seen Augie trotting down the road to get in a late-model Olds. SueFan said the Olds was blue, and SueAnn said it was black.

"Will you both agree that it was 'dark'?" asked Lester.

"More light-dark than dark-dark," said SueFan.

Then Lester had the operator begin trying to get the sheriff on the phone, and Mr. Bascomb came into the store. He had seen the twins' VW out front, and they all talked to each other at once while Lester tried to tell the sheriff about Augie. Then everybody left but Mrs. Youngblood, who stood close enough to listen to what all he was telling the sheriff.

"The license number," Lester shouted into the phone, "is CMP-810."

"No, it's not," Mrs. Youngblood said. "That's not what the girls told you. You've got it wrong."

"What was it then, Mrs. Youngblood?" Lester asked, staring hard at his license-number book.

"I don't know," said Mrs. Youngblood. "How should I know? But that doesn't sound right to me."

"Sheriff Conway," said Lester, "I have two license numbers here—and one is, for sure, the right one, but I'm not sure which. Let me give you both of them. Okay?" Slowly, he read both numbers and Mrs. Youngblood nodded approvingly.

"That sounds more like it," she told him.

Uncle Rosco sat in the Court House Cafe stirring his coffee like crazy. Havoline propped companionably on the table, watching him. The juke box was silent, and the construction workers had cleared out.

"You trying to break that cup, Mr. White?" Havoline asked.

Rosco frowned more deeply than before. He slowed his stirring but did not stop.

"A man," Rosco said, "has a lot on his mind people don't know."

Havoline nodded. "A woman, too," she said. "I don't tell half what I got on my mind."

Rosco leaned back and forward approvingly.

"That's right," he said. "Keep something back, for it is what you keep back and wrestle with by yourself that makes you *you,* and not somebody else. Our thoughts are all that make us different, and nobody can take them away."

Havoline eased herself around and sat down in the chair opposite uncle Rosco. "What's worrying you?" she asked. "Sometimes you need to tell, and what you tell lets somebody else know who you are."

Rosco let up on his stirring. "The children," he began, and then he repeated "the children" as if that was all that needed to be said.

"I know," Havoline said, "I got two myself, and no daddy." She looked vacantly at the cloth she held, and began to scrub away at the table top. Uncle Rosco watched the blue-flecked formica begin to glow.

"But it don't matter—I mean, about the daddy. I love them all I can, and I guess that's enough."

Rosco tasted his coffee. "Me, too," he said, "but mine aren't mine, and if ever I had any of my own, I don't know them and they never knew me."

"Do you miss them?" Havoline asked. "The ones you didn't have, or don't know if you did have them?"

"Yeah," Rosco said, "but I got others. Audrey and Augie and their crazy mothers, whatever kin they are to Pearl, and Lester. They are all I got."

Havoline had stopped wiping the table, and together they watched it turn dull again. No amount of wiping would make it shine long.

"Augie give me a lizard today," Rosco volunteered. "I walked toward the house, holding that blue-tailed lizard, and I thought how I could throw it on a rock, or I could lay it down somewhere and it would run off and do whatever lizards do."

The cafe door opened, cutting off what Rosco was telling. Red True came in. He was taller than most men, and his hair was redder and his eyes bluer than you would believe possible two minutes after seeing him. Everytime you saw Red True, you had to start all over and make yourself believe that he was that tall, that red-headed, and that blue-eyed. But for twenty years or more, Red True had not thought about how tall he was, or how red-headed, and he probably thought everybody's eyes were as blue as his own and his Daddy's.

"Well, Mr. True, come in and have some coffee," Havoline said. She knew Mr. True was meeting Mr. White at the cafe, but she made it sound as if she was surprised and glad to see him. She went for the coffee, and Red True sat down.

The two men exchanged no greetings, made no preliminary conversation. Uncle Rosco got right to the point.

"I got to irrigate," he said, "but I don't want to do it until tomorrow afternoon."

Havoline had brought the coffeepot, and Red True included her in his gaze. Finally, he said, "Tomorrow'll be too late, Rosco. I expect Sawdridge Creek will be up by then. If you meant to irrigate, you should have done it yesterday."

"It's going to rain?" said Rosco. "When?"

Havoline went to the window and looked out. "Any minute now," she said. "It's building up for a real gully-washer."

"Just like Augie said it would," Rosco told them. "Augie said so, and I wouldn't believe him."

Havoline came back to the table. She seemed troubled.

"Mr. White," she asked, "which did you do—throw it down on the rocks, or lay it down easy?"

"It run away—like it couldn't believe it was free," Rosco told her, and she smiled as if she was glad.

Thunder rattled, and Red True said, "I, for one, had better get home or Somebody will want to know Why Not."

Lightning split the sky. "Lord," said Havoline, "I hope the children are inside." The first rain was hitting the roof. "Augie said it would rain," Rosco told them again, "and it is starting now."

The telephone rang. "That'll be the children," Havoline said, hurrying to answer it.

"The children," Rosco said. "I got to get on home. Augie is by himself." He and Red True walked together into the rain.

Mrs. Bascomb hurried toward the produce section of the Minit-Mart. What a day. It had been almost too much for her. She had not cried when they found her mother dead that morning, but she had cried from sheer exasperation during the course of making arrangements. Well, she had done everything she could do and she did not want to see another single, solitary person until she had to. She aimed her gaze at the ceiling and watched her reflection in the gigantic circular mirror. The closer she got to it, the harder she frowned. She looked like a floating yardgoods display.

She meant to buy a big sack of fruit. With plenty of fruit salad on hand, she would resist the ham and fried chicken, potato salad, cakes and pies which she knew had been accumulating at her house. From the looks of her kitchen, every woman in Owen County had been frying and baking at least a month in preparation for her mother's death. Neighbors had taken over the house for Mrs. Bascomb early that morning, and when she called to get the twins to go looking for Erline, she had to listen to a detailed report of how many chickens and cakes and pies had already showed up.

Well. She just wouldn't eat it—not any of it. Grief was hard enough to bear without putting on an additional forty pounds or so. People might mean well—sometimes she was almost certain they did—but one look at her and her husband should convince them that coconut cakes and lemon pies were *not* what they needed.

Mrs. Bascomb tore off four plastic bags from the roller, and squinted at one of them to see which end opened. She selected two dozen apples, golden delicious and winesaps, and six lemons; she would squeeze lemon juice on her salad. No greasy, fattening mayonnaise for her. Bananas, though fattening, would help the flavor, and she took two big bunches of them. To make up for that, she dropped a stalk of celery in her grocery cart. Then a dozen pears—and, after sniffing them all, she picked out the ripest of the pineapples.

She steered toward the Express-Chek line, but someone she'd never seen before darted in front of her. Eight items or fewer was the rule for the Express-Chek. Well, she had just five items—two kinds of apples at the same price surely counted as one item. She craned her neck to see what the woman in front of her had. It looked to her like ten, at the very least. She pushed her cart as close to the other woman as she could, so nobody else would push in front of her, and drifted off to see what else she might need. Nothing came to mind.

When she returned, the other woman was laying her groceries on the counter in front of Minnie. Mrs. Bascomb shoved her cart forward again, and drummed her fingernails impatiently. Minnie's cash register clacked away, and then fell silent as Minnie weighed a bunch of bananas. Minnie looked funny, and was uncommonly quiet.

As if to make up for Minnie's silence, the woman ahead was talking nonstop. "Anything that costs fifteen cents a pound these days," she was saying, "me and my family will eat. I don't know how long since bananas been *that* price."

Minnie rang up the cost of the bananas. "I don't think I'll ever eat another banana," she said.

"Why?—You get sick on them once?"

Minnie shook her head. She was looking straight at Mrs. Bascomb, but did not seem to recognize her. The other woman was clearly interested in Minnie's opinions of bananas. "Why not?" she demanded.

"The last thing Mama eat," Minnie said, "was a half a banana. It was two o'clock in the morning, and she'd been fretting the whole night. I said, 'Mama, maybe if you eat something, you'll go back to sleep. I got to go to work tomorrow,' and she said, 'maybe some banana.' By three, I knew I had to call the doctor, and she died before he even got there."

Mrs. Bascomb clapped her hand up to her chest. She was not breathing right. She leaned hard on the cart. The other woman looked as if she did not believe Minnie.

"I ate the other half," Minnie said. "The other half of the banana—so it wouldn't go to waste." She half laughed then, and punched the cash register a final time.

"You think it was the banana killed her?" the other woman asked.

"I'm here, ain't I?" said Minnie. "That'll be four dollars and seventy-nine cents."

While Minnie bagged up the other woman's groceries, Mrs. Bascomb hurried back to the aisle she had just left. For a few cents more, Hellman's mayonnaise beat all the other brands. A big jar of maraschino cherries would color up her salad, and chipped dates and walnut pieces wouldn't hurt any either. Miniature marshmallows always made a hit, and were easier than the big ones you had to cut.

Laying her purchases on the counter, Mrs. Bascomb said, "If I've gone over the eight items this one time, Minnie, I hope you won't mind. I'm in a hurry to get home and fix supper."

Minnie rang up the order and bagged it. Mrs. Bascomb took the bag and then leaned forward to whisper to Minnie. "Don't look now—here comes Erline Grissom, just when I don't need her anymore."

Minnie looked at Mrs. Bascomb uncomprehendingly, and they both watched Erline disentangle a grocery cart and push it down the aisle with two perfectly manicured fingers. "Minnie—," Mrs. Bascomb faltered, "mine died today.—I'm sorry about your mother."

Minnie gave her dressfront a little twitch. "Coast is clear now," she said, and watched Mrs. Bascomb labor toward the door.

Aunt Muddie was moving her potted plants from the east end of the porch. The wind whipped her skirts around and had already broken the top out of her biggest begonia. She was a good mind to call the radio station, even if it was in

Louisville, and tell them what she thought of their so-called weather service. The twelve o'clock news had said "fair and hot."

"Say one thing and do another," she told the darkening skies.

Something crashed at the back of the house, and she picked up the piece of broken begonia to take indoors. Maybe she would root it. If what she heard crashing was one of her best dishes, the least she could do would be to write her United States Senator again. What with atom bombs and men walking all over the moon, it was no wonder the weather was out of hand.

Nothing was broken. The wind had turned over a big box of Oxydol she had left in the window. She stooped to brush the blue-speckled powder back in the box.

"If you ask me," she said to the window as she closed it, "the way this world is going, Judgment Day is way overdue." She turned on a couple of lights, but sat in the dark front room to enjoy the storm.

"We got to hurry," Erline told Audrey. "Windshield wipers don't work."

"What's new?" asked Audrey. Erline had been in the Minit-Market exactly twenty-three minutes. Audrey had timed her. When she came out, she threw a big package onto the seat. "What the hell," she said cheerfully. "Tonight is a sirloin night, and that is what we are having."

Audrey considered asking if Mama Pearl's credit worked at the Minit-Market as well as everywhere else in town, but then the first clap of thunder came and she put her hands over her ears and slid a little closer to Erline.

"Look, there goes Rosco's truck. I'm going to tailgate him,

and, if I can't see the road, I'll just follow his tail lights." She turned on her lights and fell in behind uncle Rosco. "Pretty soon," Erline said, "we'll be sitting in the kitchen waiting for these steaks to get done."

In a few miles, Erline flicked her brights at uncle Rosco. "Hell," she said, "won't that truck do more than forty?" But she did not pass. "Don't worry, Audrey," she said, "we're almost home."

Erline was looking forward to the evening. Lester would have the fire already made, and pretty soon Mama Pearl and the others would come driving in from Louisville. They would eat steak and talk about the wedding. Augie would be fine; she knew he would. She could hardly wait to see the children in their new clothes.

Sheriff Conway told Lester to go home and wait and see if Augie telephoned.

"How can he?" Lester asked. "He doesn't have any money."

"He can call collect," the sheriff said, "and besides, I may need to talk to you. I don't need to be looking for but one of you at a time. Get on home like I told you."

Lester got home before the storm started, but he could tell it was coming. All the birds were calling, and making little short flights from tree to tree as if uncertain where to light to ride out the storm. Lester let himself into the darker darkness of the house and tried to think what it would be like when they were all there again.

Uncle Rosco would be happy not to have to irrigate his crop, and Augie would be crowing about how he knew all along it would rain. Maybe Augie would be over his mad spell by the time Mama Pearl and Lurline got there with Brother John. Lester wished he could think of something good to fix for Augie to eat; tuna fish salad was not likely to improve Augie's disposition. Lester wouldn't let himself think that Augie maybe would not be home for supper.

The wind banged the front door shut, and uncle Lester turned on lights, including the front porch light. He laid out some candles for just in case the power went out. He went to the woodshed for kindling, but then went back to prop the back door open so he could hear the phone in the event it should ring. He soon had the cookstove roaring and a kettle of water on, though he had no idea what he wanted boiling water for.

The telephone rang, and he ran to it and then let it ring twice more before he picked it up. It was Mrs. Bascomb who said he should tell Erline not to bother about fixing her mother's hair. They had taken Mrs. Youngblood's suggestion and had found the perfect hat, and, anyhow, the way the weather was acting up, not much of anybody would turn up to look at her anyhow.

Lester could hear somebody saying, "Ask about Augie, ask about Augie." That would be the twins, and he decided they were not as bad as he had thought.

"And how is your little brother, Augie?" Mrs. Bascomb asked. "Have you heard anything?"

"He is not exactly my brother," uncle Lester explained, "though sometimes he seems to be." He did not feel like explaining that he was Augie's uncle, and he knew that if he did, Mrs. Bascomb would say, "My, my—an uncle as young as you are." He decided to let it go.

"I hope Augie is fine," he said, "and is not out in this rain."

Francis X. Lighter was keeping to the back streets of Frankfort. He had run into an insurance company receptionist he knew named Trudy, and they had spent the late afternoon telling each other their life stories over a succession of Trudy's favorite drink, which turned out to be strawberry daiquiris. While Trudy called her mother to say she was going bowling, Francis called his wife to say he was taking a client to the Kiwanis Club supper-meeting. He told Trudy he was calling his mother also.

Francis intended to take Trudy to the Holiday Inn for supper, but, first, he would stop for a bottle of rum in case his luck held out and they ended up checking in at the Holiday Inn. The way things looked, the bottom would fall out any minute and Francis did not expect too much trouble in talking Trudy into sitting out the storm in comfort.

He passed the liquor store he normally used and stopped at one where the attendant was locked in, and you had to stop your car at a little window and order from there. "What is the world coming to?" Francis asked Trudy. "Crime is so bad, you cannot even go inside to buy what you want." He ordered a half-dozen cans of daiquiri mix and a quart of rum.

"My, my, Francis," Trudy mumbled, "You must expect to make a night of it."

"Indeed, I do," Francis replied. "It's not every day I meet a girl like you."

The blue lights came on behind him before Francis had gone a block. He pulled over at once, directly in front of his regular liquor store. The wind was beginning to blow hard, and he rolled his window down to wait for the policeman.

The policeman made him get out of the car and show his driver's license. Francis blustered a little, and was glad that, for reasons of his own, he had not let himself get drunk. He did not think he was showing the effect of the daiquiris at all.

"This your car?" the cop asked him. Francis nodded. "Then, you'll have to come with me."

"On what charge, officer?" Francis asked, flabbergasted.

"All-state alert," the policeman said. "They'll tell you at Headquarters, and you'll be told your rights. For now," he added ominously, "you're not under arrest—that is, unless you refuse to go quietly." He almost sounded hopeful that Francis would resist.

"But what about my wife," Francis said, lowering his voice. "Surely she can go home." The cop was shaking his head.

"What's wrong, Francis?" Trudy was calling. She slipped over the seat and stuck her head out the driver's side. She looked obviously drunk.

"Your wife," the policeman said levelly, "told Owen County Sheriff Conway that you had been gone all day and were taking a client to supper."

"His what—?" yelped Trudy.

"Owen County," said Francis dully. "That kid—."

"What kid?" the policeman wanted to know.

The policeman parked Francis's car at the liquor store. Then he put Francis and Trudy in the back of his car and locked them in. They sat as far from each other as possible.

To Headquarters, five blocks distant, the policeman said, smugly, on his radio: "It's him all right. He said something about a kid in Owen County. I'm bringing him in—with an accomplice. Forget that other license number."

Chuck was beginning to call for more whiskey and Augie would not give it to him. He had the bottle between him and the door now, and Chuck could not reach him or the bottle without stopping the car. Augie sat straight and alert, watching the road.

"Turn on your lights, dummy," said Augie. "It's getting dark."

Chuck did as he was told, but seemed puzzled. "Why?" he asked, "why is it getting dark?" He squinted into the windshield. "It's not time for it to get dark," he complained. "I don't like it."

"It's going to rain," Augie told him, "just like I said."

A tractor poked down the highway in front of them, and Chuck managed to slow down and avoid hitting it. Periodically, Chuck made a swipe at Augie. He was getting mad about the whiskey. He rattled his ice cubes at Augie. "Give me," he said. "Give."

"Ice," said Augie. "You need ice." He took the cup neatly from Chuck's hand and, taking the bottle with him, tumbled into the back of the car. They looked at each other in the rearview mirror.

"Don't you want to go to Louisville with me," Chuck wheedled, "and stay in a motel?—You never stayed in a motel before, did you?"

"Who needs it?" Augie asked. Chuck was looking for a place to pull off the road.

"Here's a little bit of whiskey," Augie said. "Go on, take it—or I'll throw it out the window." He extended the cup warily, ready to yank his hand away if Chuck grabbed it.

They were nearing the stop sign a mile outside Shelbyville, and Augie had his hand on the door handle. If Chuck really stopped, he intended to jump from the car. Seeing that the way was clear, Chuck took advantage of the tractor's stopping to swing around it and pass. They sailed into Shelby-ville at forty-five miles an hour, and Chuck was asking for whiskey again.

"I know a shortcut," Augie said matter-of-factly. "You ought not to be driving in Shelbyville. There's a lot of cops here." Chuck shot him a quizzical look in the mirror.

"What you do," Augie told him, "is turn right onto the next road, and you will miss town. That road takes you straight to the expressway."

At the intersection, lightning cracked. "Turn here," said Augie. "Jesus," said Chuck, "that was a close one."

"It missed us a mile," taunted Augie. "What're you afraid of?" He was watching the roadside and gauging the storm. "*That's* not dry-lightning," he said. "It'll get the job done."

"Huh?" said Chuck. The first raindrops hit the windshield.

"Turn on your wipers, dummy. It's going to rain buckets."

Chuck did not seem to know how to drive slow, and he swore every time they hit a pothole in the road. "If this fucker doesn't take us to the expressway," he told Augie, "I am per-sonally going to skin you alive."

Somewhere up ahead, a light was shining. If Augie had it figured right, the light was at aunt Muddie's house. He waited until they were close to it.

"Owwww," he howled, falling onto the floor and pulling one of Chuck's jackets off the hanger with him. Chuck swerved and then steadied the car. "Augie?" he said. "Augie, are you okay, buddy?"

The car was creeping along, and the light must be close now.

"I'm throwing your whiskey out the window," Augie

yelled. Chuck clapped a foot on the brake, but before he could turn around, Augie had thrown the jacket over Chuck's head and was out of the car.

He ran through the fields toward aunt Muddie's house. He was still carrying the whiskey. He hid outside and listened to Chuck call him, sometimes angrily, sometimes wheedling. Finally, the car drove off.

Augie went to aunt Muddie's door and knocked. When she appeared, he handed her the whiskey and said, "Hi, aunt Muddie—I got to use your phone and let uncle Rosco know it is raining in Shelbyville and tell him it will soon be there— like I said it would."

Uncle Rosco parked his truck under the walnut tree and got out to show Erline where to park so she would be close to the house. They left all the packages but the steaks in Erline's car. Uncle Lester held the door open for them, and Audrey went straight upstairs. She came down in a minute to say that Augie was not there.

"Who said he was?" said uncle Lester. "He'll be home directly."

Uncle Rosco went to the window and watched the trees slashing around in the wind and rain. "He's not out in this rain, is he?" he asked Lester.

"I hope not," said Lester.

To change the subject, uncle Lester told Erline about Mrs. Grider and about how Mrs. Bascomb had wanted her to come to Owenton and fix her mother's hair. "In this rain?" Erline exploded. "If that's not just like that old Hell-cat." After a minute, she said, "Maybe I should call them—after all, a death in the family and all."

Uncle Lester said he had explained to Mrs. Bascomb, and

then Erline said, "Shoot—wouldn't you know I'd be off somewhere? I could have made maybe ten, fifteen dollars."

Then, they saw carlights in the driveway and uncle Rosco broke the world's record getting out to see who it was, and while he was taking an umbrella out to get Mama Pearl inside, the telephone rang.

Everybody was in the hall talking at once, though Erline and Lurline were leading the pack, when all of a sudden everybody fell silent at once. Brother John hung, undecided, in the doorway; he had not forgotten himself and really smiled once since they got there.

"Where's Augie?" Lurline demanded. "Where's my baby?"

Uncle Lester, his face luminous, came in from the kitchen and said, "Erline, get those steaks ready to cook in an hour, for uncle Rosco and me have to go and get Augie at aunt Muddie's. She says he showed up there with a bottle of whiskey and said he had to call uncle Rosco and tell him it was raining."

Uncle Rosco was already at the door, and Mama Pearl was telling him to drive carefully. "Bring my boy home safe," Lurline told him. "And don't forget that whiskey," said Brother John.

"While you're waiting," uncle Rosco said. "I got a bottle of Old Heaven Hill somewhere, and Pearl knows where it is as well as I do. Make yourself at home."

Brother John forgot himself then and smiled the way Augie had always liked.

"Well, Rosco," Mama Pearl was saying, "you hurry back, and I guess I can look after the family while we wait."

"Cocktails before dinner," said Audrey in her throatiest Lauren Bacall voice. "What is this family coming to?"

The Miracle
the Whole Year Waited For

Autumn was a trial at best, and this year it was worse than usual. Getting the children outfitted and back to school was probably the least of it, though Erline, conscious of what she called Mama Pearl's "legacy," chafed at the limitations of Owenton's single department store. She had taken to ordering L. L. Bean catalogues, but when she showed pictures to Augie, he said "no way," and even Erline's own Audrey had nothing better to say than "yuk."

Neither Audrey nor Augie had anything good to say about the Owen County Consolidated School, but as long as they were going there, they wanted to look like everybody else. Sometimes Erline despaired of ever raising the family above its surroundings. Augie said he hated it when all the teachers wanted to know if he was any kin to Lester or Audrey. When he admitted he was, they would say "how wonderful," for everyone knew how smart *they* were.

"What about me?" Erline wanted to know. "Don't they ask if you're kin to me?"

"Nobody remembers back that far," Augie said innocently and ducked before Erline could swat him.

All summer, Audrey had memorized Shakespeare for Miss Green, which, as she said, turned out to be love's labor lost, for Miss Green had gone off to the University of Louisville to work on her Masters of Arts in Teaching and had fallen in love with a Special Education major. She was staying in Louisville to learn how to teach children with learning disabilities. "Shoot," Augie said, "she could've had a field day in Owen County."

The tobacco had been cut weeks ago and hung in the barn. Uncle Rosco wore himself out most days going up and down the hill to look at it. Mama Pearl said the tobacco wasn't going anywhere and that it would cure just as fast without Rosco there worrying over it. Uncle Rosco would look like he agreed, but, directly, he'd be up out of his kitchen chair and sliding toward the door. He would feel the tobacco and study the tiers it hung from. The barn was leaning downhill, and, though Rosco insisted the barn was structurally sound, you could see that all that weight was too much for it. Sometimes you could hear the timbers crack as they pulled away from the upright supports.

Mama Pearl said it was enough to give her an apoplexy to see Rosco, at his age and in his health, climb up the rafters loaded down with a hammer, nails, and a two-by-four to brace one of the tiers. What made this autumn worse than others for Mama Pearl was the secret fear that it might be Rosco's last. Then, there was the weather and there was Erline.

When Erline learned that Rosco was sick and maybe did not have long to live, she packed up and came home to live with Mama Pearl and uncle Rosco and Lester and Audrey and Augie. "You are my family," she told them, standing open-armed in the doorway. She looked as if she meant to hug them all and Augie hid behind Mama Pearl, but at the last minute, she wrapped her arms around herself instead. Erline made it sound as if she was making some kind of sacrifice for uncle Rosco.

Secretly, Mama Pearl thought Rosco deserved better. Aloud she said: "It is your home, Erline—and we are always glad to have you here." In a week, even Audrey stopped pretending to be glad to have her mother around all the time. Whenever Augie was in the room with Erline any amount of time, he would roll his eyes and tap his head expressively.

When Erline moved out of her mobile home combination beauty parlor and house, she brought one suitcase and a bag full of hair-rollers, cosmetics, and Herbert Tareyton cigarettes. Every few days she would drive back to Gratz and pick up one or two things. Soon, she could hardly get inside her room, and Lester told her she should have an auction sale.

Around the house she wore what she called a kimona and Mama Pearl called a housecoat. Sometimes, she put on jeans and a windbreaker and went outdoors to collect firewood. She said doing that brought back the good old days. "Not if you do it every day," Mama Pearl said.

From 10:30 or so until noon, Erline drank coffee and smoked Herbert Tareyton cigarettes. Then she turned on the radio so she could complain about whatever the weather was doing. Whenever Rosco came in, Erline would cast her eyes upward; as soon as he went out again, she would sigh and say "Poor Rosco." After a minute, she would add "Poor Pearl." Whenever possible, she made Mama Pearl sit down and drink a cup of coffee whether she wanted it or not.

Periodically, Erline would june around to find something useful to do, which nearly always meant trouble—something broken, a cow in the road because Erline left the gap open. Mama Pearl dreaded winter's setting in, for she said there was not enough room in the house for Erline to june around. Still, Mama Pearl looked hard at the calendar, for she knew it was time for cold weather. "If it doesn't go ahead and get started," she said, "it will never end." Rosco looked as if he did not quite follow her line of thought, but he agreed that a change in weather would make the tobacco come in case. When that happened, Erline would not have to june around to find something to do. They would all go to the stripping room where there would be plenty to do, and it would be what they had waited for all year.

One day Rosco would go into the barn and the barn would feel and sound different. It would not rustle; it would sigh, tobacco stalk against tobacco stalk. The stalks would be sensuous to the touch. A hand of tobacco dropped from the top rafters would not break. It would be like a miracle.

You do not expect miracles. You just wait and see what will happen and, likely as not, it will be something you can live with, and before you know it, because it is what happened, you have decided it is what should have happened. More often than not you will forget after a time even to wonder if what happened was good or bad, because its happening is all that really matters. That cannot be changed and you make the most of it, which to my way of thinking is all the miracle anybody has a right to expect.

Mama Pearl had not said any of those words. Erline and the rest of them would have swallowed their teeth if she had ever said so many words at one time. She had done lots of thinking this past year or so, and, although she had not thought the words themselves, she had summoned up the feelings that the words amounted to. Looking back at her life, which sometimes seemed to be just one set-back after another, one loss hard on the heels of the one before, she had come to understand that nobody can keep a credit and loss sheet and expect the two to balance out. What you do to balance your books is decide, once and for all, that the losses are really credits in disguise.

When the tobacco came in case, it would be like a miracle but it was a miracle many people had helped to occur. Mama Pearl decided that miracles required a good deal more than faith; the kind of miracle she was hoping for would occur only if she worked at it and nurtured it the way Rosco tended the tobacco.

Lester had been doing what he called research about tobacco. It was not enough for him to see and feel that, suddenly one day, the dry tobacco softened up and seemed to come back to life. He wanted to know why, and he wanted to know why it was called "coming in case." Rosco, on the other hand, took all on faith; he knew that if you waited long enough, the miracle would occur—and the name of the miracle was "coming in case." For him, the things of this world had their proper names, and none other. Before Lester's persistence, he sought more satisfactory answers.

"Pshaw," said uncle Rosco, "it stands to reason they call it 'coming in case' because then you can put it in boxes, or cases, and move it without breaking it."

He squinted at Lester and tried not to show how pleased he was with himself. Lester was not impressed. He said that in the olden days they used to take tobacco to market in barrels, not cases at all, and that desperadoes—holdup men—used to lie in wait for the farmers on the way home from market.

Erline had stood as much as she could. "Who cares any-how?" she asked. "What they used to do is dead and gone now." Then she rolled her eyes at uncle Rosco and clapped her hand over her mouth as if she had said something wrong, and uncle Rosco said he believed in living in the present, but, by Ned, he also liked to remember how things used to be done.

Stripping time was the highpoint of uncle Rosco's year. Going to market and holding in his hand the check which represented a year's work was nothing compared to the good spirits and conviviality in the stripping room. Rosco liked having an excuse to drive to Frankfort and buy some really big bottles of Heaven Hill bourbon whiskey. He liked having Will Living singing and fiddling while the stripping crew worked. This year, Rosco thought maybe he would keep Audrey and Augie out of school a couple of days so they could see how hand-labor should be done.

During stripping season, Rosco would be up early to get the fire started in the stripping room before he did the chores. After breakfast, he would start coffee and slide a bottle of Heaven Hill under the mountain of tobacco hands he had piled near the long table. By eight, everyone would be hard at work pulling the rich-smelling burley leaves from the stalk, sorting them into three grades, twisting them into bundles tied with a tobacco leaf. By ten or so, they would hear Will Living coming up the hill, fiddling as he walked, and sometime later, they would find the bottle of whiskey and uncle Rosco would pour drinks for everyone. They would begin loading the long wagon bed, resting from the close work and enjoying the music and whiskey. Rosco paid top wages, but some folks said they'd rather pay Rosco than miss the fun.

This year, Rosco was impatient. He felt time running out on him. The weather was not cooperating. The dry weather needed for cutting and housing the tobacco persisted, and Sawdridge Creek had not come up out of its banks all fall. Rosco told everybody that the humidity was high enough maybe to do some good, but he knew it would take a good general rain to bring the tobacco in case. Lester had told him that the government pamphlets said the tobacco had to absorb seventeen percent of its weight in water before it came in case.

Uncle Rosco could tell no difference, from day to day, in the condition of the tobacco. It never came in case a little at a time; just all of a sudden, it would happen to all the tobacco at once. It was like grace.

Still, Rosco walked under the sagging barn rafters and reached up to finger the golden canopy. He had a good deal on his mind these days, and he told himself he could get on with things better once he knew the tobacco season was all the way over. He'd be ready for winter then, and anything else.

On October 14, Rosco was up before five o'clock. He was troubled by the lights across the creek at the Thompson place. "Not good," he said, feeling for his clothes. No reason whatsoever for the Thompsons to be up at this hour, unless something was wrong. Rosco did not sleep now as he used to; ever since he had learned something was wrong with him—

something called Hodgkin's disease—he would wake up during the night and be unable to sleep again. He would lie still in bed, so he would not wake Mama Pearl. He liked to watch things outside take their proper shape.

There'd been a sprinkle of rain during the night and the sky promised more. Rosco could hear the creek raging, which meant somebody upstream had got a good rain. He wondered whether to take time to shave before going across the creek to find out for sure what was wrong at the Thompson's.

At the door, hugging his shoes against his chest, Rosco thought he had done the impossible and had got out without waking Pearl. He found the doorknob, and, silhouetted against the hall's forty-watt bulb, he froze in place when Mama Pearl spoke. She sounded as if she had been waiting for him to open the door.

"Rosco," she said, "you do not need to start the kitchen fire for awhile. I will do that when I get up, for you better get on over to the Thompson's. Their lights have been on since three o'clock."

"Two-forty-five," he corrected. "I mean to get over there right away." They did not have to say what they both knew was wrong at the Thompson's, but Rosco decided right then he better shave. Standing before the bathroom mirror, he thought back to an afternoon the past summer.

It was right after the call from Louisville about Wiley. Rosco had stood before the mirror trying to steady himself to shave before the drive to Louisville to make arrangements. He did not think he could help Pearl, for he had not dealt firsthand with death before and he and Pearl had never faced a death together. The solemnity of Wiley's death weighed heavy on Rosco; he felt helpless before the idea of the un-known dead man. He did not know Wiley, but he knew Wiley at one time had wanted to marry Pearl. He had the idea Wiley had gone to Texas to forget Pearl and had been unable to do so.

All this was speculation. Rosco knew Pearl's first husband was old when she married him and he had taken forever to die. Rosco hated to think Mama Pearl had nursed Omer all those years, though she loved Wiley, and then, when Wiley left and Omer finally died, he (Rosco P. White) had come along and, after a time, courted Pearl and began to live with her—and the upshot of it was that she had never had a chance to be with the man she loved.

Wiley's death made Pearl seem remote and inaccessible. Her innermost feelings remained secret. How could Rosco ask her anything? Rosco knew his feelings about Wiley—part grief (but not for Wiley) and part anger (and not wholly at Wiley). It was as if, without trying, Wiley had beaten him for good. Being dead, Wiley was, and would al-ways be, the man Pearl loved and lost. Twice. Wiley would never have to prove the quality of his affection. His absence, first in Muleshoe, Texas, now in death, removed him from the necessity to do anything.

That hot summer afternoon, the family drove to Louisville. Mama Pearl sat rigid in the front seat next to Rosco. Lester had put on his suit, without anybody telling him to, and he did not once ask to drive. Augie and Audrey sat, uncom-monly quiet, in the back; Rosco thought they were writing notes to each other. Not once did they squabble or ask to stop for food or to go to the bathroom. Everybody was sneaking looks at Mama Pearl, for they had seen her cry once and they were afraid she might do it again.

Twice, without warning, Mama Pearl laid her hand on Rosco's. The first time she did it, he swerved the car a little and Pearl patted his hand before she withdrew hers. "All right," Rosco told himself, "Wiley has gone and killed himself and I am still here. Pearl did not have to make a choice, for Wiley did not give her the chance."

Another part of him said: "What if she had to make a choice?" Rosco cut his eyes toward Mama Pearl and wondered what she would have done.

By the time they got well out of Owen County, Lester began studying the map of Louisville. He had marked the way to get to Burns, Burns, and Bridges Funeral Home, and, miraculously, Rosco drove straight to it. They turned between the two bright yellow brick pillars they had been looking for. Mr. Grider, at the feed store, had told Lester what to look for, but he had not mentioned the mosaic crescent moons sitting atop the pillars. They followed a circular drive around a small lake; in the middle of the lake stood a concrete statue. They could hear music, and poorly hidden in the shrubbery were spotlights to shine on the statue. A half-dozen ducks floated on the water, and a seventh lay, neck stretched onto the bank, feet trailing into the water. The drive led to a longslung white and gray building.

A dark-haired woman wearing silver makeup met them just inside the door. Outside, they could hear "Sweet Hour of Prayer," but inside there was no music. The woman hardly moved her lips when she spoke, and her right arm rested on her left shoulder as if she were in perpetual alarm. When she saw uncle Rosco, her fingers rippled as if she were taking a tighter grip on herself.

Rosco told her they had come a long way to see Mr. Charles B. Frady. He said Mr. Frady had been good enough to call Mrs. White here, and tell her—well, he guessed she knew what Mr. Frady had called to tell Mrs. White and they had come just as quick as they could from Owen County and had found the place real easy and did she know one of the ducks out in the front yard was dead. The woman sighed as if she had known all along who they were. With the barest nod, she gestured loosely and, clasping her right shoulder with her left hand, swayed silently down a long corridor. They followed Indian fashion.

Every twenty or thirty feet, they would hear the sigh of different music coming from open doorways. Just inside each doorway stood a table with flowers, a book, and a pen on it. Brass plaques held cards with printed names. Rosco read the names, but he did not look inside the rooms.

Mr. Frady was standing behind the biggest desk Audrey and Augie had ever seen. His reflection shimmered in the desktop, and when they lined up in front of the desk, they could see their reflections too. Mr. Frady leaned forward ever so little and spoke to the woman who brought them in; she murmured and relaxed so far as to slide her left arm down her breast until it came to rest somewhere near her hip. She closed the door behind her, and an organ began to whisper "Sweet Hour of Prayer." Charles B. Frady offered his hand first to Mama Pearl and then to uncle Rosco. He gestured toward chairs, and then, as if he should have thought to do it even sooner, he offered to take them at once to see the deceased, but Mama Pearl said she did not guess there was any hurry.

Mr. Frady's eyebrows shot up to his hairline and stuck there. Mama Pearl explained that Wiley had never been the kind to make trouble and that she did not know what he had been thinking of this time. He must have caused Mr. Frady plenty of trouble already, and she thought they should first take care of their business and then go see Wiley.

Mr. Frady said he hoped all the arrangements would be satisfactory. He smirked a little when he said that and looked around the richly furnished room as if to imply that nothing done in such splendor could fail to satisfy.

"Under the unusual circumstances," he said, "we have made certain choices normally left to the family." The way he said "unusual" let everybody know he meant uncle Wiley's killing himself.

"Thank you," said Mama Pearl. "We did not expect Wiley to come home this way. I already had his bed made and a peach cobbler made—though this late in the year, I had to use canned peaches." Mr. Frady looked as if there were no possible answer to what he had just heard, and Mama Pearl sighed expressively. She was not about to talk to any stranger about what uncle Wiley had done, and she guessed peach pies were as good to talk about as anything else.

"Since the deceased left us written instructions," Mr. Frady began again, "we do not feel that we have exceeded our . . ."

"Wiley was never one to complain," Mama Pearl said reassuringly.

Mr. Frady looked as if he wished Certain People would

not interrupt him. "We have assumed you would wish to comply," he said.

"What does *comply* mean?" Augie wanted to know. "And does Mama Pearl have to do whatever it is?"

"It means agree, dummy," said Audrey and smirked at Mr. Frady.

"The letter," Mr. Frady said bravely. "The letter indicated that cost was no consideration and implied . . . a-ummmm, implied that the deceased was a man of some . . . ummmm affluence." He hit on that last word as if he had lately learned it and liked its sound. His eyebrows went, if possible, even higher. He looked to Mama Pearl for confirmation of Wiley's affluence. He clearly doubted Wiley's posthumous solvency.

"If you want a check, or something," said Mama Pearl.

"Goodness no, no—but I thought it might be well to say we have followed the deceased's implied instructions to the—ah—letter, as it were." He ran down for a minute, then struck up again. "The coffin, for instance, one of our roomier, more striking models—not a standard stock item."

"Yuk," said Audrey. "Roomy?" Augie giggled, and uncle Lester frowned fiercely at both of them.

"Wiley was not hard to please," Mama Pearl told the world at large. "He will be satisfied with whatever you have picked."

Mr. Frady laced his fingers together. Lester thought maybe he was counting to ten—more likely to fifty.

"You will see the casket soon," he told Mama Pearl. "I assume you will want to provide a vault?"

"A vault?" echoed Mama Pearl.

Addressing himself now to Rosco, Mr. Frady explained. "A vault assures that the casket remains dry, and though the expense increases—" he waved his hand to dismiss thoughts of money—"the family usually derives comfort from knowing the casket will remain dry and intact forever."

Rosco's neck began to tingle. He saw an awful picture: a casket locked in a huge cavern, a vault, and never changing regardless of what went on around it or outside. Casket and vault spun round and round, and the space around the casket constricted and the casket gleamed as if it were new.

"A vault then," said Mr. Frady touching one forefinger to the other as if making a note. "And who will open the grave?"

The family remained profoundly silent. The way Mr. Frady said it sounded as if Wiley's grave was waiting somewhere. It sounded as if Mr. Frady knew where every blessed one of their graves was and would be glad to send somebody out to open them all up. Augie began to whimper. He would not put it past Mr. Frady to start opening up their graves whether or not they were ready for them.

Rosco did not like the idea of anybody waiting around to open Wiley's grave, for that was something Rosco assumed it was his place to do. He sure Lord did not intend to let the likes of Charles B. Frady get the jump on him. Rosco looked hard at Mama Pearl and stood up sudden.

"Ace Bourne looks after the graveyard at home," he said. "He will pay Richard and a helper to dig Wiley's grave." As an afterthought, he added, "Wiley does not need a vault, for keeping dry is not what is on his mind now." He brushed his hands together as if preparing for a good hard job and clucked his cheek the way he sometimes did when he considered a subject closed.

"Well, Rosco," said Mama Pearl, "I do not know that anything is on Wiley's mind at the moment, but I think you are right. Nobody I know of at home has a vault. And you will tell Ace to see about getting the grave dug, if he has not thought of it already." Mr. Frady's hand flew to his chest; he gaped at Mama Pearl.

Lester and the children inched toward the door.

"We have held the body two days," Mr. Frady whispered. "Naturally, we assumed you would comply with . . ." He trailed off.

"Mama Pearl doesn't have to comply if she doesn't want to," Augie told him. Mr. Frady squinted murderously at Augie. Mama Pearl laid a hand on Augie's shoulder, and, thus sheltered, Augie dared more: "What did you hold him for?" he wanted to know. "You could have turned him loose and he wouldn't go anywhere."

Even Mama Pearl smiled, though, from force of habit, she said, "Now, Augie."

Emboldened, Rosco confided to Mr. Frady. "We got the plot already. Half the graveyard's full of our people, one way or another." Half the time Rosco forgot that neither he nor Mama Pearl was real kin to the Waters family and that his people were off down South. He used to say he wanted to be buried down there with his people, but lately he wasn't so sure they wanted him down there. Mama Pearl had tried to let them know Rosco was sick, but they didn't seem much concerned.

Mama Pearl put her hand on Rosco's arm and inclined her head to indicate she was ready to go when he was. Once Rosco got started talking, it was sometimes hard to stop him. "If Richard doesn't have a buddy to help him," Rosco said, "I'll give him a hand. It will not be the first grave I have dug."

"Yes, Rosco," Mama Pearl said. "You will take care of things, and I believe Wiley would like to know it was his own people helped dig his grave."

Turning to Mr. Frady, she said, "If Wiley is ready, we will see him a minute before we pick out a casket, and then we will go home." Mr. Frady's shoulders drooped. He later said that he would not have been surprised if "those people" had rented a U-Haul to take the body home for burial.

Wiley waited for them in a small room on a lower level of the building. His name was on the door, but there was no table or guest book. The casket filled one side of the room, flanked by gigantic baskets of flowers. The casket gleamed rich bronze.

Mr. Frady took Mama Pearl's arm companionably and steered her toward the casket. The rest of the family hung back. Over the casket hung a crucifix, and Mama Pearl wanted to tell Mr. Frady that, to her knowledge, Wiley was not a Catholic, but she decided that whoever put the crucifix there meant well so she said nothing. Mr. Frady opened the casket and Mama Pearl reached out to touch the flowers. She drew her hand back quickly and wiped it on her dress front. The flowers were fake.

She studied the crucifix for a minute and then looked briefly down at Wiley. He looked smaller than she recalled, more elegant. She could not tell if the flower in his buttonhole was real or fake, but she knew it did not belong there. The crucifix was one thing, but that pale waxy flower was another. It made her think of those flowers silly people put in their buttonholes and when you leant over to smell them, you got a squirt of water in the face.

"The flower," she said gravely to Mr. Frady. He leaned forward attentively.

"Oh, yes," he said, "the flower." With deft fingers, he took it from Wiley's lapel and offered it to Mama Pearl. She refused it outright.

"Thank you just the same," she said. "He favored black-eyed susans."

When she turned, Rosco stood just a few feet behind her. He was looking down at the carpeted floor. It had patterns of interlocked gold rings on a dark brown background. The rings were sculpted in the rug. Rosco felt a kind of responsibility to this man he had never seen alive, but he did not think that meant he had to look at him dead. If Pearl had loved Wiley, even if she still loved him, that was all right. Things change.

Rosco wanted it known he could dig a mansize grave, and he did, though he and Richard hit rock two feet down and had to hammer chisels through stone to get the grave deep enough. "All right, Wiley," Rosco thought, "you got your vault and it has already stood the test of time."

Lacing his shoes now in the chilly bathroom, Rosco thought how the events of the summer had drawn him closer to Pearl and the family. Wiley was part of it, and Augie going off by himself and worrying the soul out of everybody, and Erline getting herself picked up by the cops, and Lurline's coming home with a gospel singer she meant to marry. Part of it, Rosco knew, was that he was not taking anything for granted any more. Things change and we change with them, and Rosco knew that he was a part of the life of his country and his people and even his death would help make things different.

He thought about his own home, down in Georgia, and his family, but they had changed too. What he thought of was his mother, who had died even before he left home, and his father and young, pretty stepmother. And the slate stones in the family graveyard. Even they might, by now, be gone— replaced or eroded away with time. He had told Lester all the names and dates on those stones, and he thought maybe it didn't matter whether the stones were still there. How he remembered them was how they had been, and that was real for him.

The others—the ones he remembered as children or as people very nearly his age—would be middle-aged or old now, like him. No matter what Pearl said about how it was important for him to contact his family, Rosco could not decide it was right for him to go looking now for his brothers and sisters so they could be sorry when he died. They had doubtless suffered deaths of their own. He had not been in touch with them for twenty years and more, and he doubted they would draw closer to one another now just because he was sick.

Thinking this made Rosco realize that Wiley's death had done nothing more than make him accept what already was—and that included his loving Pearl and her loving him back. If they had not already loved each other, Wiley's death would have meant nothing but a break in the long summer's routine. The summer had let Rosco know, once and for all, his secure place in the family.

Who he was and what he meant to the family depended on him, not on somebody else. In Rosco's mind, Mama Pearl had always been head of the family, but he knew for sure who she counted on. That somebody was him, and he would represent Pearl and all the family when he went to the Thompson house.

In the kitchen, Rosco was surprised to find the stove burning briskly. Somebody had already dampered the stove down so it would make coals, and the oven was hovering around three hundred degrees. He filled the firebox with short, chunky rounds of maple. The kettle was full but not boiling; he set it on the hotplate so he could make a cup of instant coffee.

Outside the back door, he set his cup on a window ledge while he walked up the rise above the now-unused rootcellar to urinate. Over his shoulder, the morning star hesitated while he waited for the long stream of water. It steamed from the rocks and quickly disappeared between them. He stood a long minute, and the morning star disappeared behind the ridge. He zipped his trousers and returned to the house. He drained his now-cooled coffee cup and replaced it on the ledge.

He circled the house, looking upwards at its darkness, feeling secure that everyone but Lester was still in bed. Lester was sitting at the end of the front porch, just where Rosco expected to find him. The boy was staring toward the creek, his figure showing dark against the streaked sky. Rosco felt a rush of protectiveness. The boy looked slight and tense. Rosco wished he could find a way to make things easier for Lester, or maybe to make Lester take things easier, but something told him Lester did not expect things to be easy.

Rosco moved closer, and then waited for Lester to acknowledge his presence. Finally, Lester inclined his head toward the creek, which they could hear raging through the bottomland. He had not looked at Rosco, but the way he spoke sounded as if he was picking up where he had left off some other time, maybe the night before.

"There's something wrong," Lester said.

"I know." Rosco felt that he should somehow have foreseen what would happen, so he could have said something to get Lester ready. It was too late to say much of anything now, so the two of them stared at the nimbus of light indicating where, in the fog and mist, the Thompson house stood. "I'll go find out," Rosco said, not moving.

Then, he felt compelled to add: "You did not need to get up. It is for me to find out. These things are in the course of nature." He waited for Lester to say something. Finally, he added: "They happen." After a few seconds more, he said, "After a time, you come to expect them and then it is not so bad."

Lester, not moving, said, "You mean he's dead." It was not a question.

"Dead?" Rosco said vaguely. "Yes, dead or dying. It was the heart. He knew and took pills for it. He took them three times every day."

After a while, Rosco resumed. "Dead," he said in a conversational tone. "That's what the lights mean, and that's why the cars have been pulling in over there for the last little while." As if to confirm what he said, Sawdridge Creek Bridge rumbled, and a long minute later, Rosco and Lester saw a pair of headlights spooking through the fog. While they watched, the lights expired.

"Thanks for making the fire," Rosco said. His nod included Lester and the house and the whole hillside. He walked down the slope toward the creek, leaving Lester slumped in the swing. In a minute the boy rose and followed the darkening figure into the mist. Lester stopped under the walnut and stared after Rosco's disappearing shape, little more than a shadow merging with a tangle of other shadows.

Lester picked up a gnarled walnut and punctured its leathery casing with his thumbnail. He held it to his nose. He drew back to sail the walnut into the woods, but smelled it again instead and put it in his pocket. In the back yard, he took uncle Rosco's coffee cup off the window ledge. In the kitchen, he filled it for himself with Maxwell House instant coffee before he started breakfast preparations. Coffee was perking when Mama Pearl came downstairs. She sat with Lester while the sausage sputtered on the cookstove, and if she noticed Lester was drinking out of Rosco's cup, she did not say anything.

When Rosco left the room, Mama Pearl had not gone back to sleep. She listened for him to begin running water and then go downstairs. She knew that, after all his careful tiptoeing, he would forget and clump downstairs in his work shoes. Directly, she propped on her elbow to watch him go down the hill. She had one or two things to do she would as soon Rosco not know about. She saw Lester follow Rosco, and she saw him stop to pick something up. She waited until the boy came back toward the house before she switched on her bedside lamp.

Out of bed, she opened the door and listened for Lester to come back in the kitchen. She heard him open the stove and chunk in more wood. Then she closed the door and pulled a straightback chair over to the tall bureau. Standing on the chair, she was just barely able to reach her sewing basket. She had kept the basket there since the day she realized Audrey had gone through it and found Wiley's letters to her. She had burned the letters; they did not seem hers any more, now that someone else had read them.

On top of her clutter of threads and material scraps, needles and packets of pins, she had placed two china eggs, one brown and one white. Wiley had brought the china eggs to her from Cincinnati once; she had never shown them to anyone. She used them when she darned socks, but she had never said, "Here, these are the presents Wiley brought me once." She had never told anyone that Wiley would sit with her at night, after Omer was asleep, and that they sometimes talked as if the house and the farm were theirs and they were a couple. Then, Omer would call for her, and one, or both, of them would do for the old man, and when he was easy again, they would tiptoe to the kitchen and sit together until the kettle boiled. That was when they might have had a life together, and, finally, when nothing happened, Wiley left and Pearl remained with Omer until the old man was dead. It was already too late, even if Rosco had not come along. Pearl knew every word in the letters, and she was almost glad of an excuse to get rid of them. They were from the past. They reminded her of a time she and Wiley might have had a life together, and didn't.

When Pearl learned that Rosco had Hodgkin's disease, she did two things. First, she asked Lester to look it up and find out what they should expect; then, she began trying to figure out how to get in touch with Rosco's family. The results were not very heartening.

She put an ad in the weekly newspaper back where Rosco came from. The ad asked that any living kin of R. P. White write to her. Finally, she heard from a schoolteacher who said that she was eighty-four years old and remembered Rosco plain as day—but she, of course, called him R. P. The old lady said she remembered him because he loved to read, and was one of a precious few. She said R. P.'s family had mostly come to no good, but she had the addresses of two sisters and a brother who still lived in Walhalla, South Carolina, which was not much of a place now, though it had once been a thriving mill town.

Mama Pearl wrote the old lady to thank her, and the old lady wrote back to thank her for that letter and it seemed Mama Pearl would never get shut of her. For starters, Mama Pearl wrote to the brother. She got a postcard saying that R. P. had been off having himself a good time when the family needed him and if he was now down and out, that was just too bad. The handwriting looked like a woman's, and Mama Pearl wondered if Rosco's brother ever got a chance to see her letter.

"I did not say Rosco was 'down and out,'" she told herself for the umpteenth time. "I said that he is sick, and there is a world of difference between those two." She had lately written to one of the sisters and had received the following message typed on an index card:

Since we sold the shoreline on Lake Lanier (which is the biggest lake in the state of Georgia), everybody and his brother have tried to claim kin. What we got we worked for. Hope you can say the same.

Francine (White) Riggs

Mama Pearl did not know what she was doing wrong, but she was determined to try one more time. There was the last sister, Ernestine, but—somehow—Francine seemed a challenge to her. She wanted to let Francine know that Rosco had worked hard for what he had and that he had dug the grave, through solid rock, for a man he did not know and had every reason not to like. Most of all, she wanted to let Francine know that Rosco had a family which cared for him, even though they were no blood-kin.

She meant this very day to write Francine, and she hoped she would be able to get Rosco together with some of his people before it was all the way too late.

By six-thirty, Augie and Audrey and Lester had finished breakfast, and were ready to go to school. The children wore yellow slickers, and Lester wore a black one. Lester shepherded them toward the swinging bridge. He held open the gap and watched critically as Augie and Audrey walked the footlog across what they called The Dreaded Gulch. Yellow water swirled below the log.

At the swinging bridge, the children stood back while Lester climbed up and surveyed the span to make sure it was safe. The bridge stretched sixty feet across Sawdridge Creek; here and there, boards were missing from the walkway, but otherwise the bridge was fine. He signalled all-clear, and Augie pulled himself up the iron rails and onto the swaying bridge. Silently, he handed Lester his book satchel and, both hands sliding along the cables on either side, he crossed the bridge. He looked tiny in the middle of the bridge, framed by the parallel lines of the cables rising slightly to connect to the giant sycamore on the other side.

No sooner had Augie disappeared down the makeshift steps on the other side than Audrey pushed past Lester. Her books, hanging in a shoulder bag, made her lean slightly to one side as she crossed. You could tell she liked the feel of her books bumping against her side. In the middle of the bridge, she stopped and looked back at Lester. One hand was raised to hold the bookbag steady. Lester signalled her to go on, but she stood looking down into the water.

Lester knew she was playing out some drama she had begun during the walk. The bridge swayed and the sycamore creaked. That and the rushing water complemented her make-believe story. They had become functions of her imagination, hence harmless.

Something bobbed large in the water below. Lester leaned forward to see better. He took three steps forward onto the bridge. The something turned crazily, as if maybe snagged. Four rigid feet stuck upward. For seconds the water turned the dead cow's body; then, it broke loose. Lester saw the body turn, revealing the slack milk sack and the glassy staring eyes, before it washed downstream.

From the middle of the bridge, Audrey's face gleamed white at Lester. She leaned to the right, watching the carcass careen from rocks to fallen tree and then around the bend and out of sight. Without looking back at Lester, Audrey marched purposefully across the bridge. Lester followed quickly.

The bus would stop for them at the mailbox almost directly across from the Thompson house. Augie was fiddling with the flag on the mailbox, and Audrey was scraping mud from her boots. They could hear the low rumble of voices from a clump of men standing in the Thompson's yard.

Rosco detached himself from the clump and moved toward them. He and Lester exchanged stiff salutes, two fingers of one hand raised and quickly dropped. Audrey raced to uncle Rosco and threw herself upon him.

"It was AWFUL," she said. "To see CLEMentine floating down creek. Her poor FEET were stuck UP out of the WATER—and her poor FACE, just as sweet as COULD BE, but DEAD."

Rosco patted Audrey and looked over her head to Lester.

"Granny Hooke's heifer," Lester said. "Come by a minute ago, and Audrey seen her. Must of got caught and lost her balance."

"Granny Hooke's cow?" asked Augie. "Where?"

The school bus lights appeared on the bridge, and the bus rumbled across. "She wouldn't of seen it if she'd been doing what she should have," said Lester.

"That's all right," said Audrey, "I saw."

"I didn't," said Augie. "Show me, uncle Lester."

"There's no telling where Clementine is by now," said Rosco. "You leave Lester alone, hear, and—say—why don't you have some ice cream with lunch today?" Rosco shelled quarters into Augie and Audrey's hands, and then the bus was there. He held money out toward Lester, but the boy swung his face into Rosco's and demanded to know: "Is he?"

"At three-forty," Rosco said. "He called out around three, and by the time Mrs. Thompson got him easy and called the doctor it was too late."

"I saw him yesterday," Lester said dully. "At the feed store."

"She give him a pill," Rosco said. "Mrs. Thompson give him a pill, and that eased it some."

Lester's eyes were bright and dry. "You can't ease it," he said. "That pill maybe did *her* some good, but see where it got him."

Then, Lester was pulling onto the bus. Rosco rattled his handful of change. "I'll call Granny Hooke," he said. "She'll want to know what happened to her cow."

"That's right," Lester said from inside the bus. "She'll want to know. Tell her there wasn't anything I could do."

With the children out of the house and Erline (Thank the Lord) still asleep, Mama Pearl works slowly and methodically in the kitchen. The woodstove has steamed the windows, and Mama Pearl wipes all thirty-six panes in the big curved window so she can see outside while she shells crowder peas. The crowder peas are what are known as field peas. Before the first frost, she pulls up the pea vines and Rosco hangs them on strings in the smoke house. That way, the peas stay alive on the vine, and every day Mama Pearl shells five or six vines of them. She hangs the cherry tomatoes the same way, and they keep getting ripe, a few at a time, just as if they were still growing.

Today, Mama Pearl intends to cook a particularly large pot of peas so she can take some to the Thompsons. She has taken a ham hock from the freezer and it is simmering on the back of the stove. She has dropped a bay leaf in the water, and, later, she will pour the shelled peas in to cook. By that time, the ham will be off the bone, and, when the rich broth cools, she will skim off the congealed grease to season something else. On the counter near the stove, a large bowl of bread dough gently lifts the dishcloth she covered it with.

Rosco has already telephoned to say he has had breakfast

at the Thompsons' and will be home directly. Matter-of-factly, he has told her the funeral will be day after tomorrow at two o'clock and he will be a pall-bearer. She told Rosco that she is baking and will take fresh bread and a pot of ham and peas to the Thompsons for supper.

Mama Pearl shells the crowder peas directly into a colander. She splashes a dipper of springwater over them before pouring them into the pot. She punches the bread dough down and separates it into four nearly equal balls. These she presses into greased loaf pans which she lines up near the stove to rise again. She has saved a ball of dough to roll out for fried pies.

She cuts out two generous circles of dough. Now, she spoons cooked apples into a bowl. In another, smaller, bowl she blends hot apple juice, sugar, and corn starch. The mixture thickens as she stirs it, and she thins it slightly with lemon juice before she pours it over the apples. She stirs again, tastes, and adds brown sugar and cinnamon. In the middle of each circle of dough, she spreads apples. From the refrigerator, she takes a dollop of butter, cuts it in half and adds half to each pie. She folds the dough over and seals the edges with the tines of a fork. Finally, she punctures each pie with the fork.

Rosco will like the pies with mid-morning coffee. She waits to fry them, for she wants them to be hot. When they are done, she will roll them in a plate of confectioner's sugar.

She sits down at the kitchen table. She has already addressed an envelope, and on her writing pad she has written the date: October 14. The letter will not be easy to write, but she intends to finish it before Rosco comes back.

Upstairs, Erline is thinking about getting up. Her cigarettes are handy on the bedside table, but she has not lit one yet. She is suffering from cabin-fever, and wonders what errand she can think up to get her to Monterey, or maybe to Frankfort. Her car is parked on the far side of the creek. The sky outside is dark, but her clock-radio tells her it is after eight o'clock. Once she has made her bed, there will be nothing to do unless she can get across the creek. She smells coffee and sausage and the yeasty smell of bread.

Guilt attacks her. She is here to help Pearl, and what does she do but sleep half the day? She hangs one foot out of bed, pulls herself up, and then falls back into the pillows. She reaches for a Herbert Tareyton, and, thus fortified, tells herself she can maybe make it to the bathroom. She does not make anything of the lights at the Thompson place.

Downstairs, Mama Pearl hears Erline's footsteps and eyes the two apple pies waiting to be fried. Her letter is not finished, but she must either put the pies away or make another. Erline is sensitive, and will expect three pies. . . .

Mama Pearl studies her letter. Her last sentence began,

Hodgkin's disease is not something you 'catch'; you just have it, and it makes these little glands get bigger and bigger—

She stares at the page, and then, very deliberately, she adds: "until it kills you."

Upstairs the toilet flushed, water ran, and Erline padded back to her room. Mama Pearl still held her pen, wondering what she could say to take the edge off what she had already written. She began to write hurriedly; Erline would soon come downstairs and want to know what she was doing.

"What's up, Pearl?" Erline would ask, and come right over to look over her shoulder. "Who you writing, Pearl?" Mama Pearl shuddered slightly, and continued writing.

Treatment is possible and may do some good, but since the doctors do not really know what causes the swelling, all you can hope for is some relief. Rosco is supposed to start x-ray treatments this month, but he says he does not see the use of it. Lester (that is Erline and Lurline's brother) looked all this up for me, and he and I know what to expect, but it is like Rosco not to believe that anything is wrong.

Mama Pearl stood up a minute. She held the pen over the writing pad as if blessing it. Tears stood in her eyes, and she wiped them before starting to write again.

They say the pain is awful and that the x-ray ends up hurting almost as much as the disease. You finally have to rely on drugs, and that is just so that the patient (Rosco) will not wear himself out thrashing around and yelling. —I do not think I could stand it if Rosco was to yell, for he has never, to my knowledge, so much as raised his voice. . . .

When Erline appeared in the kitchen, dressed to go out, Mama Pearl was dipping Crisco into a deep skillet. On a plate nearby were three almost identical apple pies and a mound of confectioner's sugar.

"Your sausage and biscuits are in the warming oven," she told Erline. "The pan is hot for an egg if you want it, and I have just now poured your coffee." Erline dropped into her chair and took a sip of coffee, black and scalding. Idly, she reached across the table to lift a china egg from Mama Pearl's sewing basket.

"I do not see how you do it, Pearl," she said wearily. "Sewing on top of everything else."

That was Friday, and, off and on, the rain continued for the weekend. Saturday afternoon, the radio said the Ohio River had crested and the Kentucky River threatened to flood Frankfort. Sawdridge Creek crept daily closer to the barn. Everybody said it was a flood year; even Walter Cronkite said so, though, in Augie's opinion, Cronkite did not give the Kentucky River the prominence it deserved.

Sunday morning, uncle Lester put on his boots and slicker and went to the mailbox for the Louisville *Courier-Journal*. A picture on the front page showed residents of The Point, a low-lying section of Shippingport, wading away from their shanties. Their faces showed no surprise, no haste or regret; they were accustomed to being flooded out. Augie studied the picture and read the caption aloud several times.

"If Frankfort floods, uncle Rosco, do you think Monterey will flood too?"

The family was still in the kitchen after a leisurely breakfast—everybody, that is, but Erline, who was still in bed. Uncle Lester answered before Rosco had a chance. "If you looked out the school bus window Friday," he said, "you can answer that yourself. Monterey will likely flood no matter what Frankfort does."

Audrey looked up from the Arts and Leisure section of the paper. "Maybe," she breathed dramatically, "we will be marooned."

"Shoot," Augie shot back, "you can't be marooned where you already are: somebody's got to take you where you don't belong and leave you there. And besides," he added reasonably, "this house is on a ridge, and even if they're paddling boats between the bank and the grocery store in Monterey, we could walk to Owenton easy as anything." The way he said that last let it be known how sorry he was that there was no danger.

Audrey snorted something about how morons should not try and tell *her* how to use words, and Augie said a ten-year-old moron was a credit to the family, for a moron was somebody with the intellect of a twelve-year-old.

"Good Lord," Audrey groaned. "Shut up, both of you," said uncle Lester.

"Now, children," said Mama Pearl from her cloud of kitchen-sink steam where she was scalding milk jars. "I am sure you are both right, but I always thought maroon was a color."

The children whooped, and even uncle Lester grinned.

Mama Pearl began to strain milk from a bucket into a jar. "Live and Learn," she told them.

It cleared up in time for Mr. Thompson's funeral. Rosco and Mama Pearl and Erline set out right after lunch on Sunday, for they had to drive the abandoned road up the ridge and across to Monterey. Sawdridge Creek was impassable. Erline consented to ride in the pickup only on the condition that Rosco drive her back to where she had parked her own car. She wanted to drive it in the funeral procession, and Lester knew that meant she would think up some excuse to go off to Frankfort after the funeral. She still hoped she would one day run into Francis X. Lighter. She told everyone she intended to give him a piece of her mind, but, secretly, she hoped he was still in love with her.

Lester untangled himself from the porch swing where he had been waiting for Rosco and Pearl to return from the funeral. He watched the pickup sidewinding down the hill. Mama Pearl nodded to him as formally as she would to a stranger, for the funeral had made her feel solemn. When Rosco parked under the walnut tree, Lester strolled, elaborately indifferent, down the hill toward the barn.

When Rosco followed, he found Lester staring upwards at a slant of late-afternoon light. The barn was still, almost holy.

"It's what we been waiting for," said Lester. "You can hear the difference."

Together, they walked the length of the barn. A bird flew through, perhaps startled from its perch by their voices. Rosco fondled a leaf of burley. They could hear nothing but the roar of the creek rushing toward the Kentucky River.

"The weather says 'cool and clearing,'" Lester reported. "We can start stripping tomorrow if you want."

"We?" said Rosco.

"Yeah, all of us—even Erline."

"Let's tell Pearl and the children," Rosco said.

They stamped uncommonly hard on the back porch to get the mud off their feet. Audrey and Augie were playing Rummy at the kitchen table, and Mama Pearl was dipping chicken in seasoned flour.

"No school tomorrow," Rosco told the children.

They cheered. "Is it going to flood?" Augie wanted to know.

"The tobacco's come in case," Lester told them. "And uncle Rosco needs all our help."

Mama Pearl saw that the skillet was beginning to smoke and pushed it back on the stove. She looked hard at Rosco, who dropped his head and began searching his pants pocket.

"What we were talking about yesterday," Mama Pearl began. Rosco held a scrap of paper out to her.

"It's Francine's and Ernestine's telephone numbers," he told her. "Long-distance information give them to me. You can call them and say we will be in Walhalla for Thanksgiving and we'd like them to come here Christmas if they can."

"After you get done calling Will Living and whoever else you aim to have help us strip the tobacco, I'll call them," Mama Pearl said. "The rates go down after nine."

It was the miracle the year had waited for, and, in thanks, she began dropping chicken into the bubbling fat.